9987

/37

9987

Nik Jones

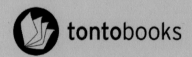

www.tontobooks.com

Published in 2009 by Tonto Books Limited

ISBN-13:
9780955632662

British Library Cataloguing in Publication Data:
A catalogue record for this book is available
from the British Library

Printed & bound in Great Britain by CPI Antony Rowe,
Wiltshire, SN14 6LH

Tonto Books Ltd
Blaydon-on-Tyne
United Kingdom

www.tontobooks.com

For Caroline, for spotting this one in a very large pile, and for everything since. And that is quite a lot to thank you for. I am forever grateful.

For Sarah, who supported me, edited for me, read my pages and put up with me, even after I stopped deserving it.

I

The Queen's face is splattered with blood. This is strange for a Wednesday. The heavier clots around the eyes still smear as he hands over the note. He doesn't look at me as I pass him the change, but few people do when they're renting porn.

I slip the bloodstained note into the till; he drops the film into a bag and leaves. His heavy boots stamp mud into my carpet as he goes. My bloodstained thumb curls around my coffee mug. I sigh, open the storeroom cupboard, and take out the Hoover.

Later, while the drunk kids undress each other in the front porchway, I find myself staring at the note. A lady, more squeamish than me perhaps, refused the note and took coins instead. So I sit, alone again, in the quiet shop with the note in my hands and my thumbprint in blood smeared across Her Majesty's frown. I'm not sure if I really care but I know I don't have the energy to worry about this. Outside, it rains; in living rooms all over Elmfield Park the soaps have finished and the shop is getting busy.

I search through the float bag until I find a clean note. Crisp and fresh and with the Queen's clean face scowling back at me. I throw the bag in the safe and forget about it. I watch the rain splattering against the window, heavy spittle-like globs slithering down the pane. The shop begins to fill.

In Alphabetical DVD a giant blonde wig bobs up and down in time to some unknown beat. A mammoth body-builder–doorman–boxer in drag. The wig slides sideways across the bald head underneath. I watch, not quite bored, as his pink lips purse in frustration. Pig eyes, wrapped in dusty green eyeshadow, narrow and an un-shaven chin tightens. In the Disney section by the door a family have camped, cowering from the rain. Two films, two boys arguing, one mother mediating. Their father stands, hands in pockets, stomach bulging from a tight waistband. He stares at the big screen behind me.

'Get them both,' he says. 'It'll keep them out of our way for a few hours.'

The shop fills. The windows mist. My work starts again and so I recommend and advise against, I change over films, I smile my special stupid-customer smile and I forget, almost entirely, about the bloodstained note.

II

Next day, Algarry, Neville, membership number 7451, comes back in to return the film and I place it on the pile behind me. Porn and Disney, blockbuster and indie, all in neat little stacks on the bench against the back wall. I barely look up from my coffee.

He's back again later in the day, this time with a friend, ducking inside from the sunlit street, still wearing sunglasses. They giggle like school kids around the corner where the Adult films lurk behind loose curtains. A sign reads 'Adults Only', and the curtain hangs open a little, the films just out of reach, just visible enough to tempt. Like Pacino said in that film: Look, but don't touch.

He arrives at the counter. He's more confident this time: new notes, new clothes, everything fresh and clean. He smiles, a grin with gum between his teeth, *Lesbian Nurses* in one hand, fiver in the other, friend with a Threshers bag full of bottles. Everything is clean. Scrubbed fingernails and the smell of soap and deodorant. He has shaved today. He wears a tie. I hand over the film and some dirty coins, another smile, and he goes, stomping heavy wet bloodstains into the carpet and out into the sun on to Moorland Road.

For a long time I just stare at the blood on my carpet. I

blink and it remains. I close my eyes and turn back to my tepid coffee. The blood seeps silently into the fresh, spongy pile. My head tilts slightly to one side; I feel my brow furrow and most likely look deep in thought. I'm not. For a long time I watch people walk through it, watch the blood creep slowly around the shop, sinking, insidious, into the already dirty carpet.

Soon, I'm crouched in a busy shop investigating, dipping my fingers in blood, sticky and dark against the ruby carpet. No one else seems to notice and people dance around me: up and down the aisles, arms full of empty film cases, dead stars staring out. By now the bloody footprints lead you round the shop in circles; countless pairs of injured feet meander forward and back while I squat in the centre aisle. Heavy Doc Martens and fragile-looking heels and behind them all a faint trail of blood, the lightest touch of rusting red against the dark-ruby carpet. Outside a puddle is tainted pink.

I move to the Adult section but there is no shame in this, no guilty pleasure: I work here, so it's OK. A tough job, but it needs doing. I smile at an old man in a worn brown mac; the pockets stained a greasy yellow, the cuffs stained black. A child bumps into my leg and I push him out and away, aiming him at the Disney section by the door.

I sigh and dream of coffee.

Behind the curtain it's darker; one spotlight angled at each of the three walls, the floor in shadow. For a moment it goes quiet. All around me are women staring, women stripping, women with tits bursting out for the whole world to see, glistening behind shiny covers. Pinks and reds and skin like peaches, like caramel, like melted butter. One of the cases juts out, ruining the display, and so I reach out toward a wall of nipples and tongues, the spotlight slithering across my sweaty limb, until, with one outstretched finger, I touch the cover.

The silence breaks and the crowd's background chatter rolls through the curtains, yelling and laughing, and a small girl pleads, 'But please, Mummy. I love this one.' Quickly I examine the floor, it's sticky in here too, but I don't touch it, just feel the squelch beneath my feet. I leave the upset case and return to the desk.

The shop is busy and the queue at the counter obscures my view so the bloody prints are hidden behind impatient faces. I smile and reach out for the next film, the sound grows and the light dims. I smile and reach out for the next membership card, the street lights flicker into life outside. I smile and reach out for the next crumpled note, the next filthy coin. My limbs work in easy rhythm, fingers typing, one arm stretching. My heart pumps the blood that powers my legs, which run up and down the four steps leading to the storeroom.

Something clicks into gear and I work, monotonous and peaceful, for the next hour. I know the script and my lips form the words and I retreat somewhere dark and quiet while the world goes on around me, while questions buzz past me and all the while my body knows the plan, my tongue forms the answers. I retreat somewhere dark and quiet and ponder and think of bloody footsteps and where they lead.

III

Home is little more than a bedsit behind a small industrial estate and I trudge there through the threat of rain, a handful of new releases held tight under my armpit. The stars are hidden behind pregnant rainclouds and I'm in darkness. The quickest way back from the shop leads me around the back of a long-abandoned brickworks and the track is littered with shopping trolleys and beer cans and crisp packets and cigarette butts and condoms speared on to the high fence at regular intervals. On the side wall of the works some-one has spray painted a giant vagina; the legs spread out wide, each thigh my height. The clitoris is swollen and ridiculously red and covering the surface around it other backstreet artists, less talented with a spray can, have stamped penis after penis after penis, hairy, erect, blue tipped and wet.

I stop between the monstrous thighs to read the text sprayed above the pubic hair. 'Abandon hope', it reads, 'all ye who enter her.' I look up past the crotch and to the looming sky. Above me the old brickworks' chimneys are silhouettes, erect against the orange-stained night, and penetrate the heavy black clouds that straddle the city. I slip a little on the muddy pathway and, head down, struggle onward.

I rent two rooms, three floors up. The building is stone-fronted, red-brick backed, and is a slightly damp town-house toward the top end of Elmfield Park. On a bright day I can see right across the city and watch families stroll through Elizabeth Park. Tonight, the lights of the Lower Bristle Road are smeared across my sweaty window, splashing thick and dribbling downward as the rain hits the glass. In the tiny kitchenette that completes my open-plan living space I fill the kettle and move through my bedroom and into the toilet.

Later, I sit in my chair and sip my coffee and watch while Bruce Campbell shuffles his Zimmer frame down a Texas corridor. Outside the rain lashes against my greasy windows, a soft, soothing staccato. I keep the TV down low so I can listen to the rain. I close my eyes. Above me I can hear my upstairs neighbours talking and laughing, muffled by their carpet and my ceiling, so all I get is a baseline, the percussion version of their lives drifting down through my cracked ceiling tiles. From below comes another TV.

On the hob I hear my pan begin to wiggle, a harsh metallic clatter against the soft pattering of the rain, so I settle down at the little table with a bowl of soup and a toasted ham sandwich. On my tiny TV screen Bruce is battling an oversized and poorly made rubber scarab beetle, but I find myself staring out the window. I watch the rain trickle down the filthy pane; watch it run off the edge of the sill. There is a flash of lightning and I raise my eyes to the street, to the winding roads that meander up the hill. Whatever it is I expect to see there isn't. I turn back to the TV.

From above soft music grumbles down through the floorboards. Barry White is underwater, distorted by my ceiling, drowning somewhere above me. I stare at the water that dribbles down my dirty panes, at the bulging brown damp that swells beneath the window. The ceiling starts to creak, slowly, rhythmically, wooden beams groaning as my upstairs neighbours circle their flat, dancing. My stomach rumbles and I shift my lazy gaze to the empty soup bowl, to the crumbs on the plate. Twelve slices of bread remain, six days until payday, two slices per toastie. I lick my finger and carefully circle the plate, collecting tiny crumbs with my sticky spit. My stomach still rumbles.

When the phone rings I glance at the clock above the fridge and find it's half one in the morning. I've been asleep, but for no more than half an hour. My spine aches as I get up from the chair and the final credits roll silently on my tiny television screen. The phone still rings. The rain still falls. The drops are gummy and stick to the window in huge phlegmy globs, distorting the street lights beyond. From somewhere over the city comes a rumble, which rolls casually up my hillside. Blue lights flicker by outside and a siren is squeezed into the night as it reaches a junction. The phone still rings.

The line is full of static, just white noise, which echoes as the storm rumbles again outside.

'Hello?' I say, but get nothing in reply. 'Hello? Is anyone there?' I try and the static slowly clears until I hear a woman. She says something that I can't catch, her voice warped by the static on the line. There's another flash of lightning and the lights in my open-plan living space flicker, a deep grumble sounds and the building shivers.

My head hurts, a heavy sort of pain like a pressure all round me, in the air, forcing me down. Another flash of electric white outside and I swear I see a figure at the bottom of the street. A girl, a woman, wet and cold, dark hair hanging over a white dress, but I blink and she is gone, just a plastic bag swirling down the street. The static breaks again and the woman on the phone is back and this time I hear her, this time she's screaming. The pain I hear makes me close my eyes, I hear a sob and a sigh and then she's muffled like she's biting her lip and with another distant flash the storm is over.

The rain stops, the lightning is gone and the woman at the other end of the line giggles, breathing deep and satisfied. I hang up. I put the kettle on, take out my coffee jar. Above me a bed starts moving, banging softly against a wall, and someone else bites their lip. I turn off the TV and flick off the lights and sit quiet in my seat. I sip my coffee and listen to the couple above as they moan.

IV

Lesbian Nurses is late; he didn't bring it back yesterday. I wasn't here, but the list in front of me tells me everything: membership number, name, phone number, film number, film name, days overdue. The list is multicoloured. Yellow for one day, pink for two, green for three or more, left white if they're not coming back. Someone has had a Chart title for eighty-seven days and we have lost all hope, next to his name is written: thieving wanker.

I phone him out of habit through an echoing phone line.

'Mr Johnson,' I say. 'It's Total Rental here, you thieving bastard.'

'Fuck off,' he replies and the phone goes dead.

The name next to *Lesbian Nurses* reads Algarry, Neville, membership number 7451. The phone number is a mobile. I ring but get no answer. One by one I go down the list calling each number, pestering each member, threatening fines and legal action. So far only Mr Johnson knows the truth. We only pretend; we can't really be bothered. We're all talk.

7451, Algarry, Neville arrives, not quite so clean today, same clothes, not so new, battered and rumpled already after only two days.

'It's late,' I tell him, and he nods and hands over the fine. He smiles a little and is gone, free from fines and legal action; the carpet is safe, his boots are clean. The bins are full and so I head out the back.

Between me and the outside world lie two doors. One solid wooden door and beyond that is a space about a metre square, then a heavy steel-plated door with a heavy iron gate, all of which have to be opened before I can put the bins out.

Later I return the films. Down in the back room I suffer the rotting damp smell and avoid the shelves I still haven't remounted. They lie in a heap by the sink, surrounded by tools I have no intention of ever using: unloved screwdrivers; an uncharged drill; an impotent hammer. I kick the hammer into a dark corner and feel better: I can't work if I don't have the tools. I swap over the cases. Ours are a dull earthy brown, each emblazoned with 'Total Rental' in fading, tarnished red. I take the Technicolor originals back out on to the shop floor.

I stroll through the aisles admiring the shelves, adjusting the cases, laying flat the Hollywood grins, letting their impossibly white teeth catch the light. In one hand a pile of faces and names, anonymous in their fame, detached and interchangeable and so very comforting. In the other hand a cloth, fresh out the bag, with which I wipe the dirt from Tom's smile, polish Russell's chin, trace Nicole's body. The shop is empty, just me and the stars and the big screen behind the counter with Brad staring wistfully into the middle distance. I stand in the middle of the quiet shop, a stupid smile still hovering around my lips, holding the final case. *Lesbian Nurses.*

Headlights sweep the shop sending shadows fleeing toward the counter, across the shop, over the shelves. The light catches on pearl-white grins and slips under air-brushed bodies, it creeps behind the curtain and into the always-dim Adult section. My hand is shaking. On the big screen by the counter Brad runs in armour toward a beach while I spread out my fingers across the case. Brad hits the enemy in a blaze of sunlight and shining steel and I stare at the case, a huge bloody palm print across the front, sticky red fingers entwined in mine.

V

The police aren't interested.

'Bloodstains, you say?' comes a bored voice over the phone. 'Could be anything, besides don't you think a murderer would be a little more careful than to leave a trail of blood?'

I ask anyway. 'Could you at least pick it up and have a look? Please.'

There is a sigh, then, 'Yeah, OK, could take a while though. What's the film called, anyway?'

'*Lesbian Nurses*,' I say. There is a pause.

'We'll be there in five minutes.'

They arrive in three, two of them, grinning in padded body armour. It is night now, autumn is well entrenched and the street lights come on at five o'clock. Past the posters in the window I can see the fluorescents of the police car glowing under the street light and two young boys are wasting no time spraying swastikas along the driver's side door. I point and the policemen are off again, sprinting and swearing into the orange haze of the street lights.

I'm on the shop floor when they come back, my arms full of DVD cases. They look tired, out of breath. Someone has slashed their tyres but I don't think they know that yet. I'm placing the cases back alphabetically along the side wall while one of the policeman, who I know rents a lot of emotional dramas, is talking to me, slowly and patiently, like I'm some sort of idiot. Behind him the younger one, who isn't a member, is scribbling notes.

'Well, he's been a member for years,' I say while the police boy scribbles, 'since May 2001, I think.' Scribble scribble, his tongue is slowly forcing its way out the side of his mouth. He squints as he writes, his head cocked slightly to one side. It strikes me that maybe the policeman is talking slowly for his benefit, not mine, that maybe the scribbler's the idiot. 'But I can check that,' I add, and pause, waiting for the backward police child to catch up.

In stops and starts I tell them everything I know about member 7451, Algarry, Neville and his rental habits and the people he comes in with and the mess he leaves on my carpet and the sticky red handprint on the case of *Lesbian Nurses*.

'Can we see the case?' asks the older policeman, whose shoulder reads 8814 but who I think is actually called 1765, Bradshaw, Mark.

He follows me behind the counter, which he's not meant to do as it's Staff Only, and I hand him the case. I cough and nod at the sign on the door which reads Staff Only. No one pays me much attention. 1765, Bradshaw, Mark leans against the drinks fridge and brings the case up close to his hairy red nose. I stand because he's stolen my space. I'm not sure where to lean so I try resting my hand against the counter but it feels unnatural so I slump instead against the workbench next to the CCTV equipment. The younger policeman, with the spotty chin and runny nose who isn't a member but I think comes in to buy ex-rentals from time to time, sniffs loudly and leans against the door frame, which leads out on to the shop floor, notebook in hand.

PC Bradshaw shows the case to his partner, the foetus, and looks at me. His tongue runs along the front of his teeth but behind his lips so it looks like Bugs Bunny moving around underground, just a lump on the surface moving back and forth. He looks tired.

'There's nothing there,' he says gesturing to the case. 'It's just dirt.'

'No,' I say, 'it's dried blood. Take it. Test it. You'll see.' I smile slightly, with just the corners of my mouth, like I do with difficult customers or the ones who don't know the difference the Coens and the Farrellys. PC Bradshaw flicks his tongue against the top of his teeth while he thinks about this, strokes his jaw, stretches his jowls. He wipes sweat away from his eyes and massages the bags beneath them. He doesn't look convinced. The younger officer behind him leans forward and whispers something into his ear. They both smile.

'OK, look,' he says, 'we'll take it away for testing, but we'll need to take the DVD too ... to check for fingerprints ... and stuff.' He shrugs vaguely and turns slightly to examine the case again. Behind him the young officer turns gently red and I can't help wondering if his mother knows he's out this late. 'So can we take the film please?' PC Bradshaw stands up, expectant.

I shrug back and ask, 'Do you have your membership card with you?'

VI

My Mam's house is huge, perched on a hilltop outside the city, but this is not home. I sit in the living room, freshly painted red over last month's pale blue, watching my father drink himself to death in front of the football.

'Aww. Haway man,' he cries, splashing beer across the chocolate-leather sofa.

From the kitchen my Mam puts on mock concern. 'Not going well, dear?' she asks.

He growls, because it's her fault. I know this because he told me: it's her fault he is here, down south, rather than there, at St James', getting drunk with his friends instead of sulking with his son. I don't remember much about it up there, just my bedroom and the tatty Peter Beardsley poster my father had insisted on. I watch him spit beer and fling his arms into the air as someone I don't know misses an open goal I don't care about. I'd happily cope were he not here, I think, were he far away, were he fighting for breath in a gutter somewhere.

Finally she finishes fussing and comes in to join us. A tray with teacups and a pot and stacked high with biscuits is placed on the coffee table and she pours out a cup.

'You still off the sugar, darling?' she asks and I nod because I'm trying to lose weight. 'You don't need to lose weight, dear, in fact I'm worried you've lost too much already,' she says and smiles at me, pats my belly. 'There's plenty out there who would love you to have a little meat on your bones.'

From his corner my father mutters something but I choose to ignore him. My Mam settles back into the couch, crosses her legs, cup held on a saucer on her lap. She sips and stares at me for a moment while I perch, back straight, on the edge of the couch. I sip my tea and stare at the television. The away fans wear red and the cameraman sweeps across the stand as they bounce, a turbulent wave of reds and blacks and in the middle a boy painted red raises one scarlet finger into the air. I worry that I am overreacting, that it's only dirt on the case.

'Mam ...' I begin, wondering how best to phrase this. 'I have this customer ...' My father mutters something that sounds like 'rent boy' and so I agree. 'At the rental shop, yes,' I say. 'I think that maybe ...' My Mam smiles at me, encourages me. 'I just wonder if he's ...' She gently rests a hand on my knee, nods a little, eyes on mine. I can't finish. It sounds stupid. I shrug and shake my head; the police will sort it out. 'Never mind.'

Mam smiles and leans forward.

'Your cousin Susan's wedding is coming up soon.' She smiles again and raises an eyebrow. 'Do you think you might want to bring anyone? Anyone on the horizon?'

I shake my head and brush hair from my eyes, tuck it behind my ear and tell her: 'No, I'm too busy, I don't even know if I'm going to make it myself.'

'Oh, no, darling, no, you must come, please.' She puts the saucer and cup on the table and grabs my hand. 'You deserve a break and you're the manager, surely you can tell someone to cover for you. Please, darling, it wouldn't be right without you.' She strokes my hand gently; her eyes wide and pleading and from my father in his pit by the fire comes: 'Aww hey! F' fuck's sake, man.'

My Mam shudders a little and selects a biscuit. She dips carefully. She wraps her slender fingers around the thin cup and meets my eyes for a moment before glancing sadly at my father.

Twice a week over dinner my Mam asks me how my life is going and twice a week over dinner my father grunts laughter toward me in short sharp slaps. Tonight is no different. We sit around a new distressed-pine table sipping wine and playing with our food, no one particularly comfortable.

Mam pats my hand. 'How's the script going?'

I lie, shamelessly, to her face. 'Fine,' I say, 'I've started taking it in a new direction ...' I shrug and finish lamely: 'I'm quite excited about it.'

She smiles, satisfied, not quite proud I don't think but perhaps relieved that at least it's something. At least I'm not wasting my life somewhere. At least I'm aiming higher than to run my own rental store in the backend of the city. I smile back, and play with my gravy.

Of course, there is no script. I think my father knows this, I hope my Mam does not. Five years ago, two months after I'd returned home early from university, I started work at Total and told her I took it because it gave me access to resources, to films, to the movie-going public.

Sometime after ten I say goodnight and hug my Mam and feel her hands squeeze tight behind my back, feel her head on my shoulder. For a second when she raises her head I think she's crying but she's gone before I can ask. My father gives me a drunken pat across the cheek and grins before slamming the door. It rains while I walk through the trees to the bus stop.

VII

The next few days are dull. I sit and I stare and from time to time I alphabetise, from time to time I organise the Chart, from time to time I make an impression that no one chooses to see. I work and I sleep.

I must be in trouble because the Area Manager turns up one day to complain I have lost *Lesbian Nurses*.

'It's one of our best renters,' she says. 'It doesn't stay on the shelf for any more than two minutes, and it's deleted now, so what are you doing giving it to the police? We'll never get it back.'

I worry for our Area Manager. She's so small and frail and pale and being around her means I can't shake the feeling I'm in a cheap zombie film. I can't help thinking that just out of shot is a trail of half-eaten corpses, a bloody smear between me and her car, her ripping the flesh off of anyone who stumbles too close. She's not just pale but sort of grey, almost transparent under the fluorescent lighting. Her body died a long time ago, struck down in her prime by some wasting disease. She stares at me with foggy grey eyes, her pupils wide and black, and maybe it's her willpower that keeps her going, a stubbornness that stops her body dropping to the floor and rotting on my carpet.

She changes tack, smiling at me with blue lips painted

red, overcast eyes on mine.

'I understand you were trying to do the right thing, but come on,' she says swaying slightly, rippling like a charmed snake, and I'm looking toward the man in Alphabetical DVDs because he has a turban and maybe a flute.

'Come on,' she says, 'a murderer leaving bloodstains wherever he goes?' She shakes her head and adds, 'That's ridiculous and you know it.' Regardless of my own thoughts I feel that I should probably agree so I nod. She's making me dizzy and I want her to leave.

'I'll sort it out,' I say. She smiles but only with her mouth, her eyes stay the same, still staring at me, too shiny, too round to be real. The skin wrinkles at the corners of her mouth.

'Look,' she says leaning toward me. 'The shop is in trouble enough anyway, you've been turning away customers. This isn't a club, it's a business.' She pauses for effect. I watch her counting. On three she continues. 'So no matter what their feelings or their knowledge of films, you let them join and you let them rent.' She straightens up and flops an arm on the counter, resting against it uneasily, pretending to shift her weight against it but instead sort of hovering between standing and leaning like a puppet acting casual. I look up for the strings and her expression drops. She stares at me with dead eyes, her face a mask, a plaster cast.

'You're on the edge, the shop is failing,' she says, and turns to go. 'Sort it out,' she calls, and she's gone. I wait for screams from the street. For panicked shoppers running. For a riot. Anything. I wait patiently for the innocent to flee the oncoming Dead but nothing happens.

On the phone to the local police station I swear I can hear a woman. 'Oooh, you look hot,' she says. 'I'd better use my special thermometer.' But the guy on the other end of the line is telling me, 'No, sorry, it's still being tested, we'll let you know.' The line goes dead.

Out of habit I call Mr Johnson.

'It's Total Rental here,' I say. 'How are you this evening, you thieving wanker?' His wife tells me where to shove it and hangs up.

One by one I go down the list. I drink my coffee and watch the kids on the front porchway again, same two as last time, fumbling around in the hazy red light of freshly lit street lamps.

VIII

Behind The Grapes is a square, St Michael's Place. It is here that I spend my days off. Nestled into a corner, surrounded on three sides by the hulking, empty shell of the Still-Unfinished Spa, is the Little Theatre. It is usually quiet during the day so I can watch in peace, undisturbed, and with my long legs hooked over the back of the seat in front. They don't do buttered popcorn here but that is probably for the best as my jeans no longer fit quite right.

Today's film is a Spanish one and normally I wouldn't bother but as I turned the corner and headed down the alley, shuffling between a pet shop and The Grapes toward the Little Theatre, I found myself walking behind a couple. They strolled ahead of me, arms wrapped around each other, hair tangled in knots, bound together like Velcro. The breeze carried words toward me, bouncing off the walls of the alleyway as we ambled toward the Little Theatre.

'Come on,' he said, letting the wind steal the words from his lips. 'We can't go home, can we? Not with him staying,' she giggled and muttered something like, 'No. No, we can't, what if someone sees?' but it was clear even to me that they could. She laughed, like she was embarrassed, but she'd already decided and he settled the matter saying, 'Come on, no one goes to see these foreign films, let's just do it.'

He grabbed her hand and pulled her toward the entrance to the Little Theatre. I walked past. The square was deserted, my feet slapped against cobbles and the noise bounced around the square, rebounded off stone walls, was lost in glass panels. I strolled to the far end of the square, stared up at the Still-Unfinished Spa. It was no taller than the other buildings that backed on to the square, but it seemed bigger. All new sandstone and chrome and glass panelling and shadowy, mysterious corners. Only the Little Theatre was smaller, was dwarfed, cowered in a dark corner.

I strolled around the empty square with one hand in my pocket and the other swinging in time with my step. Acting all casual, pretending like I had a rolled umbrella and possibly a bowler hat. But then I changed my mind and turned up my collar, thrust my hands deep into my jacket pockets because I decided this was important business. Secret business.

For a while I stared at my reflection in the glass walls of the Still-Unfinished Spa, saw my face floating in the cool dark beyond the windows. I tucked my hair back behind my ears and turned to the entrance of the Little Theatre. Quietly I crept inside, found a seat in one dark corner and settled down.

I munch slowly on my salted popcorn, being careful to be quiet and watch the trailers, watch the couple away to my right kiss nervously, then passionately. This is the first time in a long time I've had company at the cinema, no one goes here usually, and it will be nice to share the film with someone.

On screen the language is Spanish but in here it's all giggles and me slowly chewing popcorn. The music starts from speakers all around us, her jacket comes off and the voiceover kicks in, a dry and sultry Hispanic woman, she sounds sad, the music mourns and his hand slips under her skirt. She giggles, while on screen a dark-skinned woman is crying, soot-stained tears running down her dirty, swollen face.

From my right there is a gasp and I watch while she lowers herself down on to him. On screen the shot widens, pans out across the Spanish interior, all browns and golds and olive greens and the Mediterranean sky blazing above it all. A low groan from the couple to my right and the gentle squeak and strain of the softly bouncing seat.

A village comes into view. White stone and red tile and the creeping, glittering blue of a river crawling beneath an ancient bridge. To my right she is rocking on top of him, her mouth forms muscular Os and she sweeps her hair from side to side and then she bites his lip. Her skirt is up around her waist, his hands clutching her ass and I can see his fingers, pale against the flushing pink of her flesh. On the screen a child runs down the dusty track toward the camera, a woman runs behind him, a white dress streaming and flicking in the wind.

Another groan from my right, she arches her back and his face disappears into her chest, she groans again, louder this time and from somewhere inside of her he grunts and reaches his lips up to her neck.

She turns her head.

On the screen the silence ends in an explosion of red and the woman to my right looks right at me as I finger popcorn into my dry mouth. She screams and on the screen the woman in white falls to the ground, a look of shock and surprise and agony on her face until suddenly the screen is alive with blood and gunshots.

To my right the woman continues to scream and scrambles off her partner, she pauses only to find her knickers and runs toward the door, hair streaming behind her, slipping on her heels. He stands slowly, watching me all the time. He buttons up his jeans, slaps his belt tight, collects his coat and walks along the aisle. He stops opposite me. I stare up at him, feed myself popcorn, and he glares at me. The screen behind him is on fire, women cry and he leans toward me.

'Pervert,' he growls, and slaps my popcorn to the floor. I wait for a good ten minutes to make sure he's really gone then head out to the foyer, money in hand, for more popcorn.

IX

It is almost a week until 7451, Algarry, Neville comes back. I'm tense when I see him, unsure how I'm meant to act. The shop is heaving, people cram into every space and move through the crowd like currents of water, or better yet like food through the body, forcing their way between muscles that contract and release to squeeze people further and further into the bowels of the shop, a vacuum forming behind, which sucks in the next customer and the next.

7451, Algarry, Neville looks undercooked, a beard, tatty and incomplete, like the ones grown by boys in schools when puberty hits. Patches haven't grown properly and hair crawls down his neck where the jaw meets the ear. His clothes are dirty, all muddy and crumpled, except for his T-shirt, which looks new and is a bright clean white. I decide to play it cool.

A girl appears after him; she is released from the crowd with a pop as the vacuum gives her up. She's pale and quiet and like my Area Manager is a creature trapped somewhere between life and death, only attitude or caffeine determining the extent of reanimation. Like everyone else she looks tired. Like no one else she looks beautiful; fragile and fleeting, and her pale skin glows under the fluorescents with dark hair hanging loose to her shoulders and eyes like a tropical sea. 7451, Algarry, Neville is smiling, he's the only one who looks active these days, and I tell him *Lesbian Nurses* is out and won't be back for some time. His smile fades a little, tightens around his jaw. I grin and glance at his girlfriend. Maybe she isn't listening or maybe she doesn't care because she is rummaging in a small red bag.

He passes me a comedy, a new one from the Chart, which I dutifully change over. The Queen's face is crisp and new and he looks right at me as he hands it over. His eyes are like mine.

'Thanks,' he says, holding my gaze, letting his smile dissolve. Headlights scurry across the heads of the customers, whip across his face and his eyes glow a little. I shuffle backward and he turns to go, the girl shakes her head and follows behind.

She is wearing a crumpled blue blouse, which the blood seeps through, heavy and dark, in long straight lines running diagonally down her back. She spots a gap in the crowd and is carried away, not a single customer pays her any attention. The shop vomits the two of them out and they go, ambling away past the windows and into the night while I sit in the rectum and stare at the customer in front of me. The blood from the girl has rubbed off on to his shirt, second-hand stains printed diagonally across his stomach. I point and he shrugs.

I call the police again but this time bring up the records for 1765, Bradshaw, Mark and call him at home. In the background I'm convinced I can I hear a woman with a bad American accent saying, 'My chest hurts, nurse, could you rub on some cream?' But PC Bradshaw is too

34

loud, saying, 'I'll come in next time I'm on duty, but don't ever ring me at home again.'

Later, I drink my coffee and watch the drunk kids on the front porch. She has one leg lifted to his waist, coiled around his thigh, her back pressed up against the wall. It's almost closing time and the shop has died, has emptied its bowels, there's just cancerous old me sipping hot black caffeine.

Outside the girl has fake blonde hair and fake red nails and she turns her head and stares right at me while the boy kisses her neck. Through the posters on the window I can see his hand under her skirt. He is kissing her neck but his eyes are open, brow furrowed, and he is obviously struggling to put things where they ought to be. She stares right at me. Heavy green eyeshadow and mascara running down her cheeks. It's raining but I think she's crying.

The phone rings and I pick up, still staring at her staring at me, while the boy finally seems to figure it out and turns his lips to hers.

I say 'Hello,' her green shaded eyes still on mine.

At first there is no answer but then, very faintly, I hear a woman with a laughable Swedish accent saying, 'I give you a mud bath now, ja? Maybe we can wrestle ...' and then the line goes dead. I drink my coffee and watch the kids on the porchway, she lowers her leg, pushes him back and thrusts her hand in his trousers. He grins.

The phone rings again and this time it's the Area Manager and I hope that when I die I can use the phone as often as she does.

'Have you sorted the film out yet? Is it back on the shelves?'

'No,' I say, 'it's still away for testing. I'll call them again on Monday.'

'Get those takings up,' she warns me. 'I'm warning you,' and she hangs up. Phone in hand and looking anywhere but the front porchway I phone my Mam. I'm not supposed to make personal calls from this line but I won't be long. It rings and rings and eventually picks up. 'Hi,' I say, 'it's me.' My father grunts, growls something like 'I'll just get her,' and hangs up the phone. I sip my tepid coffee.

X

It is the weekend and the shop is busy, people fill every aisle chatting and laughing. Over by the Chart wall an argument breaks out over which Tarantino film is best and whether it is true that Michael Madsen is a prize-winning poet. I know the answer to both of these but know they will never ask. In the Alphabetical DVD section a little girl in a fairy costume is clutching a copy of *Barbie Does Swan Lake* and following her mother up and down the aisles, tugging at her skirt, her voice a whine, 'Please Mummy, please.'

Meanwhile member 231, Mitchell, Jack, is clutching *Debbie Does Dallas* and waiting for the girls at the counter to move away. The girls, one of whom is member 4889, Davies, Daisy, pile popcorn and Ben & Jerry's on the counter and are renting horror. I smile and tell them to sleep with the light on. No one laughs until they leave the shop and I hear a squeaky impersonation of my voice singing 'Leave the light on' down the street.

Returning from the storeroom with *Debbie Does Dallas* for 231, Mitchell, Jack, I find a young boy sitting in front of the freezer eating ice cream with dirty fingers. I tell him to stand outside and he moans, 'But it's raining.' His nose is snotty and he has dried-up gunk on his upper lip, wet ice cream dribbling down his chin.

'I don't care,' I say, pushing him toward the door. 'You're not to come back in here without a parent holding your hand.'

The shop is loud and bright with the Adult section the only place I know that will be quiet and cool. I gaze out over the heads of the customers, staring at the wet orange glow of the street lights. Through the posters on the window I see the snot-nosed kid holding the hand of a middle-aged man, who leads him into a car. In the Chart section the argument over Tarantino and Michael Madsen continues, a long-haired guy in a leather jacket joins in, mentioning Tarantino's foot fetish. The little girl in the fairy costume is chewing the corner of *Barbie Does Swan Lake* while her mother dithers over Richard Gere or Robert Redford. From the Adult section comes a moan, because *Lesbian Nurses* is not on display. Behind me, above me, towering over all of us, the big screen blasts out music. Dennis Quaid wants to save the world but no one is listening.

It starts to rain again, hard and fast, and in no time at all the front porchway becomes a mess of puddles and floating crisp packets. There is a flash and somewhere over the city a low rumble rolls across the slippery rooftops and down toward the shop. I come out from behind the counter to close the door, keep us all warm in this sweaty little womb, but as my hand touches the latch holding the beaten red door open there is another flash and a crash right above us and even the windows shake a little. Everyone stops to look outside, and through the darkness and the sudden silence a women in a sodden and see-through dress sprints barefoot across the street. Dark hair plastered against her face, small breasts bouncing through the rain, dark nipples hard under the wet white dress, eyes as blue as a summer sky.

XI

Next day and the shop is rotting where it stands. Dirty water has seeped in under the door during the storm and the ruby carpet is now a deep polished mahogany. The whole place is slippery underfoot.

I move carefully through the debris, the bottom shelves were hit hard and bodies are strewn across the aisles. Desperate and twisted, Vince and Jennifer die in each other's arms; Meryl is buried beneath mud and crisp mulch. It's cold but the sun is shining.

Behind the counter the darkness is thicker, tangible, moisture swirling slowly, falling toward the back of the shop. Passing through the door marked 'Staff Only' I notice the stench of damp is stronger, fouler, somehow wrong. I stare down toward the storeroom, my feet perched on the edge of the top step, the smell making me nauseous, the darkness liquid, rippling slightly in the faint breeze coming from the basement storeroom. I press the light switch. Nothing happens. I've seen this film before, I know what's coming, but I also know my role. I hold my breath and sink into the darkness.

What little light creeps through the front window doesn't reach down here; down here is only the faintest, greyest whisper of sunlight. Corners and edges pulsing, pale and dull. The smell is worse, is heavier, is meatier. The floor is out of sight but I feel the wet, slippery filth beneath and my shoes scrape against the concrete as I shuffle between the stacks.

Slowly my eyes adjust to the gloom, the shapeless dark between the stacks forms up into neat ranks, film cases stretching out toward distant corners, cobwebbed by the ceiling, warped with damp by the floor.

I shuffle back toward the sink, fumble on the bench and flick the switch on the kettle. A tiny red glow begins, emanating warmth from the slowly boiling kettle. I watch, hands against the bench, as the light grows, melting away the darkness in front of me. I breathe in the steam, breathe in the warmth. I blink and the glowing red light surrounds me, I see my mug, my coffee, the covers on the stack opposite me glitter, the text almost legible. I look down at the filthy floor: wet leaves, clumps of sodden dust made dirt, shoelaces. A shoe. A leg.

From nowhere, a face in the gloom, twisted in the hot red light. A smile, the skin pulled too tight over the cheeks, jagged teeth parted and strung with spit. I see the strings, the arms jerk out sideways and the whole body convulses upward. My Area Manager dangles before me, suspended on her strings. I blink and the lights come on. She thrusts a mug at me, the high tide mark clearly visible.

'First, coffee.' Her lips move out of sync, bad dubbing, she must be foreign. 'Then we get this place cleaned up.'

I open up the front door to air out the smell of death and damp carpet, which is gag thick in this decaying little womb. It's lunchtime and thin crowds shuffle along the paths either side of the road, hands in pockets, noses red and blue, while I huddle in the porchway sipping my coffee.

I turn on the big screen and let Jim Carrey convince me it's better to have loved and lost than never to have loved at all. I can't really comment and so I wait for the shop to fill up, watching mid-afternoon porn renters wriggle in past the door like sperm to an egg, and by three o'clock the Adult section is full, a stream of dirty footprints leading to the heavy curtain.

My Area Manager shuffles awkwardly in the pale light outside and I relax into the day. The Disney section fills up with parents desperate to keep the kids quiet for a few hours after school and the older kids shuffle around the ice cream freezer and sneak peeks into the crowded Adult section, challenging each other to go in. From time to time they glance at me while I sip more coffee and from time to time I raise my eyebrow at them, daring them to enter.

The evening drags on, the light fades and the street lights flicker into being, diffusing into the early evening, heavy orange teabags staining the night. I stand behind the counter and sip my coffee. Above me, above everyone, everywhere, Ron Perlman is red and smashes through a sewer, the white noise of the shop rolls up against the counter and I smile, polite, and answer stupid questions.

Then, as Ron holds back the gates of Hell, she walks in. The girl. The phantom. The friend of 7451, Algarry, Neville, and, I pray, not his girlfriend. She's dry this time, her dress too short for the chill autumn night and too thin for this wind. Her hair is wet but it's not raining and her eyes glitter blue but pale today, the sea rough. She smiles at me, alive, with red in her cheeks, and goose bumps.

The shop floor drifts out of focus as she approaches the counter, one hand rummaging in a heavy pink sports bag hanging off one shoulder. Everything slows down, she rushes close while the shop drops back, a Hitchcock moment as I zoom in and the camera pulls back. The world ends. There is just her, bouncing lightly through the crowded shop, her hair swinging left to right with every step, the hem riding slowly up her thighs, her breasts bobbing softly underneath the thin dress. Everything delicate and fresh and so very enticing. She lays herself bare on the counter before me, her chest heaving under the light cotton. Phone bill, gas bill, bank statement, a passport that says she's twenty-four and born in Carlisle. We connect instantly. Within seconds I know she shops at the Asda out on the ring road and donates to Mind. Once a month she buys flowers from Interflora and every week deposits one hundred and eighteen pounds and seventy four pence into an ISA under someone else's name. I know she has recently been to Mexico and stays up all night making long-distance calls.

'Can I use these to join?' she asks and I nod and smile and stammer out, 'Yes, yes, of course you can,' and just like that she does. A member now, no more secrets.

Our newest member, number 9987, Santino, Scarlett, smiles at me again, takes her laminated membership card and sweeps across to Alphabetical DVDs. Only then do I remember about her back, but it looks better already, only pale white skin above the dress, shoulder blades like tiny wings nestled softly into the lucent skin. I try not to stare at her as she moves slowly through the aisles, try not to sigh as she leans down to a lower shelf and I see, for a second, the curve of one small but perfect tit and the dark brown hint of nipple. I try not to kiss her as she bites her lip, torn between two films. I try to look busy when she catches my eye.

She swings her hips as she comes over, a case in each hand. She lays them both flat on the counter and leans her elbows on the edge.

'Which do you think?' she asks, and as I glance down to the covers she pushes her elbows together and squeezes her tits into one succulent peach and I smile because I know it's for me.

'Well,' I say, acting all cool and calm and pretending like I haven't noticed, 'I'd say this one,' and pick up *Secretary*. 'It's well directed, superbly acted and ...' I lean in closer so I can see all the way down her dress, so I can smell her hair and almost taste her lips. 'And it's got a certain ... sexuality about the whole thing, like ... like you know it's wrong to watch it but you can't help it.'

She frowns a little and leans back, picks up the case. 'I don't ...' she looks around nervously. 'I don't want porn,' she says, lowering her voice like she's embarrassed to say it.

'Oh, no, it's not porn,' I say, 'it's ... it's just very sensuous.'

She doesn't look too convinced but shrugs and says, 'Ah, what the hell, but if I don't like it I'm coming back for you.'

XII

It's raining but an umbrella would be too conspicuous. 9987, Santino, Scarlett lives in an old town house now converted into flats overlooking the city in the valley below. Somewhere behind me on the opposite hillside, past the steaming rooftops and flickering street lights of the squatting city, is my own tiny flat and above it my neighbours, most likely damaging floorboards. 9987, Santino, Scarlett's flat is number 3C and I'm not sure what side of the building it is on but it's drier here than anywhere else so I'm not moving until I know for certain.

It was a little after midnight when I got here and it's almost two in the morning now. I haven't seen any lights on the third floor yet. Her phone bill says she starts making long-distance phone calls between two and three so I'm assuming she's either not home or napping. I shuffle my feet in the mud and rub my hands to keep warm. I brought a little camping stool with me but the ground is too soft, the legs keep sinking, so I have to stand.

The back of 9987, Santino, Scarlett's converted town house faces a school and lucky for me on this side of the hill people are still fairly confident in their safety so the fences surrounding it weren't too high and weren't too sharp. I trudged around the edge of the playing fields toward the trees at the far end of the grounds, camping stool in one hand, my digital camcorder in the other, and found myself somewhere reasonably dry under the thick foliage, staring at what I hope are 9987 Santino, Scarlett's back windows.

There's not much happened since I got here. One by one the lights on the lower floors went out, someone on the ground floor threw a cat out the back door and I watched it shrink into itself for a moment, protesting against the rain, before it leapt on to the back wall and over into next door's garden. From here the house is far less grand than it appeared from the front, all the houses are. Their well-maintained frontages and neat gardens and shiny new cars all become so much fiction on this side of the row. From here I can make out rotten wooden fencing and flaking paint on windowsills. Ugly concrete extensions with corrugated roofs and pebbledash loom up into the darkness, hidden from the sandstone facades.

Most of the windows have curtains drawn or have lowered blinds, except the ones of the flat on the third floor, and it is those windows I have watched intently for the last two hours, staring into dark rooms and watching the wet street lamps reflecting off the cool glass.

It is now two-thirty, so 9987, Santino, Scarlett is late and not for the first time I consider moving around to the front of the house so I can watch her approach, maybe bump into her.

'Oh, I'm terribly sorry,' I'll say and she'll smile as she recognises me. 'Oh, hello, what are you doing here? You look frozen. Come on up for a coffee.' But at some point she'd ask me what I was doing on her street and it would sound a little desperate telling her I was waiting in the hope of seeing her so I crouch down in the mud and wrap my arms around my shins to keep warm and wait.

The top floor, the one above 9987, Santino, Scarlett is an attic room and from the dust and dirt on the windows it looks empty. A yellowed net curtain hangs crooked from the only window, tattered and filthy. The wind picks up and shakes the trees above me so the rain is shaken loose and I suffer my own personal rainstorm under the dark green canopy.

Three o'clock rolls around and I'm numb all over, I can feel water between my toes and the feathery breeze that slips under the tree line from time to time feels like knife wounds sinking deep into bone. I hate to admit it but I'm close to giving up: in six hours' time I have to open the shop, have to start my day all over again. I sneeze and stand up, ready to go, listening to my knees crack and stretching out my limbs for the first time in a long wet hour.

Up on the third floor a light comes on, then another, and I can see into the flat at last and it glows like a beacon. She appears at the window in a blue dress, moving from room to room. The bigger window on the left, on the corner, is a living room painted terracotta red and I can make out the tops of plants and framed pictures on the wall and she moves from this window to a smaller window toward the middle of the building. The room is smaller, the light has no trouble finding the corners and the lilac glows softly. I guess it's a bedroom: there is a wardrobe in the corner. She glances quickly out of the window and I smile, give a clumsy little wave and raise the camera, flicking the power button as I go. Her expression doesn't change but she turns her back to the window and unzips the dress. I lower the camera while, back to the window, she removes her bra and tights and pulls on a pair of loose tracksuit trousers and a big baggy jumper. Once dressed I raise the camera again and sit for another half hour while she paces the big window, on the phone, laughing and frowning and biting her lips and grinning and giggling.

By the time I get home it's just gone half four and I sit naked in my chair wrapped in my quilt watching the footage again and again until the sun creeps across my carpet and reaches my toes.

XIII

Wednesday night I call the police station again and a WPC answers the phone asking me what I can see when she bends over and whether her uniform is too tight, then the line goes dead. The list before me tells all. Both 7451, Algarry, Neville and 9987, Santino, Scarlett have late films.

I smile. That's my Scarlett, so absent minded. I see her rushing into the shop, breathless, her hair tied up, her long porcelain neck exposed. She smiles, her cheeks red. 'I'm so sorry.' She says, 'I enjoyed it so much, I had to watch it again and again. It was brilliant.' I smile back and shrug, not wanting to be too cocky but I'd obviously known all along. 'I'm here to help' I say and she beams at me. 'You're wonderful' she says. 'What shall I rent this time?' I smile back. 'Well, what do you fancy?' I ask and she says 'You,' and stops, shocked and embarrassed. 'I mean ...' she says, flushing red, 'I mean would you like to watch one with me?' I smile back, place my hand over hers, brush my hair away from my forehead. 'Of course I will,' I say.

I pick up the phone and call 7451, Algarry, Neville first. The list says *Texas Chainsaw Massacre* is a week late. The phone rings. And rings. And rings. And answers.

'Good evening Mr Algarry,' I say, still cheerful. 'It's Total Rental here ...' I say, and then stop. I swear I can hear crying on the other end of the line.

It's a woman sobbing, I'm sure of it. Through the posters outside the kids are back, sipping at two-litre bottles of cheap white cider; one is waving a Stanley knife and laughing and on the other end of the line is a woman in tears. On the shop floor a young couple edge closer and closer to the Adult section grinning at each other and waiting for the other customers to turn away; in the Disney section by the door a mother is trying to distract her children from the language used by the kids outside and drifting in through the open door. From the other end of the line comes the sound of a sharp, hard slap and a cry of pain and muffled sobs.

'Hello?' I say, but the call ends and a heavy tone fills the line like a heart flatlining. I hang up the phone.

Outside the kids are smoking, oversized cigarettes held tight between childish lips, while inside a child is crying. In the Adult section the young couple argue and behind the counter is me, staring at the phone, and somewhere on the other end of a disconnected line a woman cries as someone slaps her.

Through the smoke outside the kid with the knife has drawn blood, one of the girls has a hand pressed hard against her cheek but it does no good. Her white tracksuit top slowly turns red as the blood squeezes between her fingers and drips, heavy, into the night. She cries black tears, mascara dribbling down her face, before she turns and runs. The kid with the Stanley knife looks almost as shocked as her but then he grins; he laughs and calls and echoing through the darkness comes, 'It was an accident!'

I call the police but some woman is saying, 'The doctor prescribed an orgasm, can you help me?'

And I say, 'No, there's no time, you don't understand: one of my customers is being murdered. She's crying.'

'Just stay calm and we will send someone round to see her then,' comes the voice down the phone.

'Thank you,' I say but the line is already dead. I try the number for 7451, Algarry, Neville again but for ages no one answers, then a robot picks up and says I'm through to an answer phone but would I like a sponge bath? I try the number for 9987, Santino, Scarlett but I get her answer machine too and she giggles at me and says she's probably up to no good but please leave a message. The bleep sounds and I stammer and suddenly I'm not sure what to say but I know it should be clever and witty. Behind the phone a tape whirls away recording my awkward silence and nervous breath and eventually I manage an 'I ... It's ...' when the tape ends.

XIV

The rain hasn't helped down here under the trees but this time I'm prepared: a thick plywood slab, torn off one of the brickworks' broken windows, makes an ideal little platform on which I can rest my camping stool. Tonight I have an umbrella, black beneath the dark canopy, and my Digicam safe in a waterproof plastic case. I've brought coffee with me.

Up on the third floor the lights are off, street lights making the wet glass sparkle and shimmer. Down here, at my level, the cat is sharpening its claws on the rotting fence and I watch it for a while, crouched beneath the bushes, slinking from shadow to shadow before disappearing into the darkness. I sip from my flask and watch the shadows for signs of the cat but it's already gone. A bathroom window flares into life on the second floor and through the frosted glass I watch a dark-haired man scratch his stomach while he pisses. In the same flat someone is watching TV, its flashing blue–grey light spilling out into the night. The third floor remains empty and still.

It's just gone two in the morning and I set up the Digicam's tripod on the plywood floor. The tripod has a sort of compass at the top, a ring of little numbers. The living room is zero, the bedroom is one point three and I practise swinging the camera from one position to the other in smooth easy motions, following her from room to room.

I sit and stare at the empty window of the attic room and the tatty net curtains, watching the rain dribble off the edge of my umbrella. Somewhere behind me the wind brushes through the trees, flicking the grass in hesitant little waves toward my platform. I turn slightly on my stool, suddenly uneasy with the movement behind me.

I stare, carefully moving from shrub to tree to weed to the rippling grass, staring past the green and into the bruised purple behind. Ten feet or so off to my left I meet yellow slivers and stare into slitted feline eyes. The body is hidden but the soul stares right at me, hunkered low to the ground, and something behind it weaves slowly from side to side.

'What do you want, you little bastard?' I whisper, but I can hear the catch in my voice, me stumbling over the words. The cat relaxes one eye from a moment, like a raised eyebrow, like a snigger, maybe, and it edges forward a little into the light, wriggling silently toward my platform. With about six feet to go it stops, eyes like scalpel wounds, two slightly curved slits of yellow.

It's bigger than I thought, but still only a cat, I tell myself, and find myself lowering the umbrella. Its tail still swings gently from side to side, languid and calm, while I release the catch and the umbrella folds down into my hands. The tail stops and arches over its hunched back, like a scorpion, and the cat scuttles forward another half foot. I can see its back legs tensed, its hunter's flanks glow slightly in the second-hand street lights, rain slithering over rich fur and ready muscles. I stay on my stool.

My hair, heavy with the rain, hangs low over my face and down my neck. I lick the sweaty drops from my lips and gripping the umbrella with both hands I draw it back over my shoulder while the cat stretches out its claws into the long grass. We stare at each other now. A stalemate, both ready, both armed.

The light changes, the flickering blue is gone and I suddenly realise how much my eyes had adjusted to that borrowed light and I flash a glance over to a darkened window in the second-floor flat. There is movement inside, a lamp comes on, then a hallway light, then a muffled yell and a definite scream. Suddenly the cat relaxes, stretches out its long back legs and pads softly across the grass toward me. I stare up at the pale window while the cat rubs its muscular flanks against my leg, and my hand drops to my side. I feel the cold wet fur, wrap my fingers inside its coat. I look down. The cat smiles at me, winks once and slinks away into the night.

I look up to the window where the hallway light briefly illuminates a woman who stems a bloody nose and a swollen eye. She is staring up into the dirty, oily night sky, cheeks wet with tears, when the light goes off behind her and the rain sparkles against her window.

I am cold and wet and I pack away my things and slip off into the wet night, leaving muddy footprints on my platform.

XV

My father is drunk again, eyes glazing over in front of the television. I sit, straight backed, perched on the edge of the sofa, while Mam clatters around in the kitchen. There's a film on, an old war movie, and John Wayne is crouched behind a crumbling wall, cigar in mouth, calmly ordering his men to their deaths. My father is loving this. He laughs with every death, heavy explosive bursts of belly-rumbling guffaws. In the kitchen Mam is chatting away, possibly to me, possibly to my father, but he isn't listening and I can't hear.

Eventually she arrives and looks at me with eyebrows raised and so I guess she was talking to me. She passes me some tea and I refuse a biscuit. She gets settled into the sofa and raises her eyebrows again.

'Well?' She asks.

I sip at my tea, watch my father slurp his beer, meet my Mam's eyes and ask, 'What? Sorry, I didn't hear you.'

She pretends like she's annoyed, a little tut and shake of the head, but about her lips plays a smile. 'I suppose it was the television was it?' She looks over at my father and we watch him splutter out a laugh as a marine gets gunned down, watch him grinning with unfocused red-rimmed eyes and spraying stale beer from his wet lips.

Mam turns back to me and it is only when she grins that I realise how miserable she looked before, how drawn, how tired. She smiles at me with everything but her eyes,

'I was asking if you're going to make it to the wedding. Can you get the time off?'

I pretend like I'm stressed, like I've been desperately searching for someone to cover me, like it's the single most important thing in my life, like I actually care, and I say something like, 'I've tried, Mam, I really have, but I've got staff off sick and the Area Manager breathing down my neck to get the sales up and I just don't know how I ...' I trail off, shake my head, generally do my best to look distraught, and it works. My Mam's hand squeezes my knee, squeezes my thigh, and I meet her eyes.

My father growls, 'Divven't cry about it, man. I thought y'were meant t' be the managah? Just fuckin' tell em to de y'shift.' He shifts his glassy gaze on to me, on to Mam, on to her hand on my leg, and she pulls it away quickly. My father growls again and turns back to John Wayne, cigar in mouth, strafing Nazis.

Later I help Mam in the kitchen: two cups, two saucers, one plate covered with biscuit crumbs and seven crumpled cans of Caffrey's. I can still hear the television, hear my father's bursts of laughter, and try to ignore it. Mam talks about my cousin Susan but I'm not really listening. I nod from time to time and know when to laugh. Mam is wearing an apron and drags a dirty-looking cloth slowly across the plates, dipping them in soapy water again and again. I stand by the draining board watching her: dip and wipe and dip and wipe. I hold a dry tea towel, waiting for the dishes, but Mam isn't handing them to me, instead she wipes and dips and rinses and drops them into the sink again.

I sense she wants to talk. She wipes the same plates again and again, gently lowering them into the now tepid water and raising them again for another slow wipe. In the living room the atmosphere is different, the music has changed. Tense, suspicious, the music creeps through corridors and I assume John has reached the bunker which has claimed so many of his men.

'Mam,' I start and lean as casually as I can against the workbench so she can see me better. She turns to face me. A long sliver of dark hair has unravelled itself from the tight knot tied at the top of her neck. It hangs against her cheek, uncertain how far to fall, unused to any freedoms. She looks old, tired. I can see crow's feet at the corners of her eyes and notice the lines that gather around her mouth, smile lines she can't get rid of despite the sadness I see in her eyes.

'I ...' But I don't know. She's holding another plate, the cloth slowly circles the fading pattern, her fingers wrinkled from the once hot water. I meet her eyes and they glitter and I think that maybe she wants to cry but I can't think of what to say so instead I raise my hand toward her face, trace her cheek with the back of my fingers. She sighs as I brush the stray hair from her face.

'Mam,' I start, almost as if I know what I'm doing, wondering if now might be the time to tell her about my Scarlett, but from the living room music hits a crescendo. There is a smattering of machine gun fire and a shadow in the doorway takes the light from her eyes. My father stinks of sweat and beer, his hand is heavy on my shoulder. He squeezes and I drop the towel, twisting toward him, watch him adjust his belt with his free hand. I realise my fists have closed and I feel my nails in my palms but my father is marching me toward the front door.

'Same time next week then?' is all he says as the front door closes behind me. I stand in the rain and stare at the door handle. A distant street lamp helps it glow a faint dusty gold. Shadows hide the chipped corners; devour the cracks around the door frame. My head drops and I shove my hands deep into my trouser pockets and shuffle out the garden toward the bus stop at the end of the street. I stop at the gate and turn back to the window. My father's chair sits empty, flashing blue and green light and shadow in time to the TV screen. A pool of light from the open kitchen door falls heavily against Mam's china cabinet. Rain dribbles slow and thick down the window pane, a hesitant wave, a clumsy fade to change the subject. Something dark swings across the polished china and I think I hear a scream. The shadow sweeps across the china again and I do hear a scream, but from behind me now, so I turn to see a wall of water leap up to meet me, the crest dazzling like broken glass in the car's sweeping headlights.

My trousers are soaked, heavy with water. I watch the car drive away into the darkness. A child hangs out the passenger window waving a bottle at me, waving two fingers at me. Brakes screech and the car is gone.

Mam's windows are suddenly dark, just tiny pinpricks of orange from the distant street light shimmering on the surface. Head down, I walk through the rain to the bus stop.

XVI

At work I need distracting. For once the sun shines and so I have to suffer alone in the shadows while families, desperate to cling on to the fading memories of the past summer, march past the window holding footballs and Frisbees, girls walk past showing off goose-pimpled flesh, men follow close behind. For a while I watch a group of kids on BMXs, probably not yet in their teens, ride round and round in circles, cigarettes squeezed tight between fat pink lips, until the beaten bottle of 'coke' they are sharing is exhausted and they leave in search of more. More cigarettes, more alcohol, more vulnerable old. *More coffee*, I think, and take a break from my window watching.

No one is interested today; even the midday porn crowd must have better things to do today. Earlier I saw one, 341, de Beck, Charles, strolling down Moorland Road with his family, all shorts and polo shirts and flip-flops. I stepped outside to say hello, my coffee cradled against my chest, he saw me, I smiled, and he hurriedly dragged his family into the Spar next door, promising ice cream. I stepped back inside and closed the door.

I daydream.

My Scarlett steps out from Alphabetical DVD, her long dark hair dropping in curls to her shoulders. She wears her short cotton dress, her skin glowing. 'We could go to Elizabeth Park,' she says, 'have a picnic ...' I smile at her, shake my head, because she can be so silly sometimes. 'I'm sorry, sweetheart,' I say, 'but I can't close the shop, can I?' She smiles back at me, realising how silly she's been. 'You're so dedicated,' she says, and twirls her hair around her fingers. She sighs, her chest heaves. 'Oh ... OK then,' I say, and she beams at me, throws her arms around my neck.

Above the sky is blue, cloudless, the sun burning bright; beneath the grass is a lush green, cool, and swaying in the breeze. We lie on a chequered rug, the basket at our feet. She has her head on my chest and snoozes gently. I wrap my strong arms around her; feel her breath against my neck. She stirs, tips back her head, raises her lips to mine.

I decide to organise.

On the phone to Head Office I hear a woman cry, 'Oh my, I've just spilt water all down my top ... I'll have to take it off.'

'Fine, no problem,' I say, 'but when you're done can I get a new top forty please?' and hang up the phone. For a moment I wonder whether or not I should ring back, whether she was really listening to me, but it's not long before the fax machine blinks into life and rolls out a new top forty for me.

Some rental shops don't use charts anymore, they put everything together alphabetically. My Area Zombie wants me to do the same; she claims that we would rent more of the older films if they were right next to the Chart title people wanted. She may well be right, but I don't want to spend my days endlessly trudging around the filthy squelching carpet pointing out which films are new releases. The top forty is depressing reading, there's very little there to get excited about. Blockbuster after disappointing epic after overrated box-office smash after depressingly obvious horror/thriller/action/romance. To cheer myself up I turn on the big screen and hunt down an old, almost worn out copy of *Battle Royale* and set to work.

It's already nearly October, another Halloween approaches, so I start setting up a special Halloween night section. The secret to rental displays is to make them exciting, unexpected and as educational as possible. I start with the blockbusters and the Hollywood franchises, otherwise Area Zombie will get upset. Next to these films, these Frankenstein's monsters of the movie world, I grade my own recommendations. I make a sign. 'Are you retarded? Do you enjoy *Resident Evil* films? Then why not give these a try?'

I manage half of one wall before I'm defeated. I'm on my knees, Takeshi Kitano is gleefully reading out a list of fatalities, and two snotty little kids walk in. Inevitably they are in tracksuits, incredibly they are sober. One of them, the smaller one, is bleached blonde and chews at me, sneering with every ridiculously wet chomp. They get excited by the half-finished section: 'Mint!' slurps the smaller one, '*Resident Evil*!'

I order them out, pointing to the door, but they just stare at me, chewing malignantly with curling upper lips.

'I said out!' I yell and jab my finger toward the door. The smaller one strolls over, he looks right at me, blue eyes and blonde hair, and leans in close.

'See ya,' he says. His chin hangs low and his mouth hangs open. I can see his tongue as he tilts his head backward, spits 'mate' at me and leaves. The taller one looks me up and down, thrusts his hand deep into his tracksuit pockets and grins at me. As he leaves I watch him smear his gum across the door frame. I stare at the door frame, glance to the window. I hold my hands up to my face and realise I am shaking. I leave the film cases where they are in neat, ordered piles on the floor and go put the kettle on.

With a coffee between my shaking hands I feel more relaxed and I sit for a while behind the high counter scanning the late list. 7451, Algarry, Neville still has *Texas Chainsaw Massacre*; he's had it for ten days now. It's not even the good version, just another remake. I take a last slurp of my coffee and pick up the phone. Even before I reach the second ring a voice cuts in, a woman, breathless and excited. 'A sponge bath, nurse? Well if you insist …' she says and then a beep for me to leave my message.

'Mr Algarry,' I say, 'it's Total Rental here. I'm calling to remind you, yet again, that *Texas Chainsaw Massacre* is late. Very late. We need it back as soon as possible or we have to involve our solicitors.' I drum my fingers across the desk, exhale through my cheeks. I'm bored. Out of habit rather than hope I dial Mr Johnson's number but I hang up before he answers, too bored even for that. I'm looking at 9987, Santino, Scarlett's name on the late list. She still has *Secretary*, her only rental so far, and it is now eight days late. Again I drum my fingers across the counter. Again I pick up the phone. Again I put it down before anyone answers. I head down the back to change over some returns.

The afternoon drags on. I stare out the window, watching. A young couple, late teens maybe, stumbles past, clinging so tight to each other they can hardly stand let alone walk. I grin and wave as they pass the window but they don't see me. An old man on a bike powers past, docking his flat cap to passers-by. The shop is empty still and the sun has long since passed midday and started dropping down behind the shop. I sit in twilight while the dry cleaners opposite sparkles in the last hour of sun. The chewing gum is still sticky on the door frame. My horror section lies only half done. There's no hurry. No one will be here for a while yet.

On the phone to the police station I'm sure I can hear a woman in pain, long howls and fast heavy panting like she's crying. Someone on the other end of the line says something about *Lesbian Nurses* being sent to the regional headquarters for further testing, but it's hard to make out because the woman is getting louder and louder, her breathless moans faster and faster until finally, just as the line goes dead, I hear a great 'Ahh' of relief. I don't know how long I listen to the dial tone but when I look up the shop is full.

A group of students is gathered by the doorway clutching piles of paper, letters and bills and anything else they can find with their address on. In the kid's section, by Disney, a small boy is picking up cases one by one and examining the front covers while he scratches his bum through long shorts. In Alphabetical DVD a couple argue quietly between comedy romance and action comedy. She is calm and controlled, tight blonde hair fastened back into a ponytail, while he turns constantly, spinning around to face her, to face action, to face comedy, he swings his arms as he speaks and rolls his eyes as she replies.

The students by the door shuffle forward, staying close together in their tight huddle. In the kid's section the small itchy boy has moved towards the door and is now pulling covers off the shelf and on to the floor. His choices seem random but he is methodical, he pauses over each one before reaching a decision on tipping it to the floor or leaving it on the shelf. In Alphabetical DVD the guy's shoulders droop. He stands still, hands in pockets, staring absently forward. The students shuffle in formation, passing papers toward the front of the scuttling gaggle. The boy with an itchy arse is playing Guess Who, I realise. The covers that remain standing are those filled predominantly with faces, the ones without are scattered on the floor. The child stands, hand on hips, examining the covers one by one. The students shuffle on.

The sun is almost set now, only the chimneys opposite still glow warmly in real light. I can see red flashes to the left of the shop where the shadows fall darker and the street light is flickering slowly into being. The students are almost at the desk when I notice someone else enter the shop. She skips past the itchy-bummed boy by the door and glides over to the Chart wall. I smile and 9987, Santino, Scarlett meanders slowly up and down the Chart wall wearing old jeans and a black T-shirt, which makes her pale skin leap out as a harsh, almost-glowing white. Her hair hangs in a loose ponytail, a thick strand falling playfully across one eye.

The students have stopped at the desk, blocking my view. I turn to the leader, the skinny sort-of-bearded one with greasy blonde hair that is clutching the papers. I stare at them and they stare back at me.

'Yes?' I ask and the students ripple from the outside in, nudges from the back of the group to the front.

'Um,' the leader starts, his voice plummy, his indecision well bred, a Hugh Grant without the looks. 'Can we use any of these to join?' He spreads the pile of letters across the counter. I try to see past them, try to catch the eye of 9987, Santino, Scarlett, try to raise my eyebrows and share a joke but they are hemming me in, filling all the space in front of the counter. I flick through the pile. I shake my head.

'The addresses,' I say and look up. The students stare back at me. 'They aren't local addresses. If you're any further than two miles out you can't join.' As one the students deflate, falling into each other. The greasy sort-of-bearded leader suddenly seems even more sallow-faced, as if his head operates purely as a peg on which to hang skin and hair. I shrug.

'But we're students,' he frowns, as if that might fix things.

'I know,' I reply. We stare at each other.

Whispers from the back of the group bubble to the surface, the sort-of-bearded leader leans back to meet the message from below. His eyes never leave mine but the weight of greasy hair seems to stretch the flapping skin above his eyes so his hairline recedes by a good inch. He shrugs.

'Fine,' he says. 'Maybe Blockbuster will be more accommodating.'

'Maybe,' I say, and smile. As one, the students shuffle backwards and out on to the shaded side of the street.

9987, Santino, Scarlett crosses the shop and I catch her eye as she does so. I smile and wave, she smiles back and disappears quickly into Alphabetical DVDs. I pick up the phone.

'Hello? Blockbuster?' I say.

From the other end I hear a muffled and distracted, 'Yeah?'

I wait a moment for the 'How may I help you?' but it doesn't arrive so I press on. 'It's Total Rental here,' I say. 'I've just had some students in wanting to join.'

From the other end of the line I hear chewing and a bored 'Uh huh, and ...?'

'And,' I say, 'a couple of them already have memberships they've used to rent out new titles they've not returned.'

From Blockbuster comes chewing, the sound of a page being turned and a 'So?'

I sigh, Blockbuster chews.

'So they owe us three hundred and twenty seven pounds and counting. Just thought you'd like to know.'

From Blockbuster: silence. Then: 'Oh, shit, thanks mate. I'll keep a lookout then.'

I smile and put down the phone. From next door to the right I hear shutters rolling down; from the left comes laughter and swearing as the day crowd goes home and the evening trade comes out. 9987, Santino, Scarlett has left, the shop is empty again. Darker. Alone again I sip at my coffee and wait for the teenagers to have sex in the porchway.

XVII

I t is finally past payday and I have no more bread for toasties so I sit on the bus as we speed up the ring road. Normally I don't shop out at the Asda, I try to stay local, help out my community, but I miss 9987, Santino, Scarlett. I sit about halfway down, three or four seats separating me from the kids at the back. One of them must be around twelve with long black hair and clumsy ruby lips. She smokes and grins at the driver through the rear-view mirror and rests a packet of cigarettes on her pregnant stomach. Toward the front is an old couple, all greens and browns and waterproof coats despite the sun outside. Their hands: claws. Grappled together, rigid and pale and shaking, liver spots like pennies.

It's hot, far too hot for the start of October, and I want to press my cheek to the window, which I know will be cool, but the pane is smeared with oily grime. I angle myself so the light hits the window just right and fingerprints criss-cross the glass: penises, breasts and smiling faces, fuck yous, and down in the corner in a neat little square the words: I love bum.

The supermarket is air-conditioned but heaving and I am buffeted and shunted from all angles as I make my way to the baskets. Ahead of me shoppers force trolleys down narrow aisles and I stand by the entrance waiting for a gap in the traffic. I feel lightweight with my basket, vulnerable to the trolley-wielding housewives, and as I head down the fruit and vegetable aisle a small child sits on top of a trolley, perched like a turret gunner, with one fat finger up its nose. As I pass I feel something slimy in my hair and hear it giggle. I hurry on.

Tinned food is calmer and I have time to consider my purchases properly. My budget is tight but my requirements simple so I fill my basket with buy-one-get-one-free own-brand curries, stewed steak and bolognaise, all tinned. Further down the aisle is 1187, Stewart, Charles, fan of soft porn and Steven Seagal. He passes me but does not smile. Tinned food gives way to convenience food and I drop instant noodles and easy-cook rice into my basket.

For a while I loiter in frozen meats. A woman with copper-coloured hair and blonde eyebrows is poking at a frozen turkey with inch-long nails. A man waddles past carrying his stomach on the trolley handles, his trolley almost empty except for a bag of celery sticks and an industrial-size tub of peanut butter. I am staring at the frozen lamb. It's dinner with Mam again tomorrow and she's promised me lamb. She always promises lamb. I'm tempted, for a moment, to buy some myself, to ring the doorbell tomorrow with lamb chops in one hand and a bottle of wine in the other. I do the sums in my head and come up short. Lamb and wine or cheese and ham for toasties. The lamb will have to wait. Besides, I'm not willing to spend money on my father, even if he'd only benefit by association.

The lines are long, too long, a tailback of red faces and screaming children. Besides, I haven't seen 9987, Santino, Scarlett, I don't want her to think I stood her up. I spy the turret gunner a little way off, blowing bubbles of spittle. The lines smell of sweat, of fake tan and cheap deodorant, so strong it is almost visible, and I decide not to queue. Instead I stroll toward the entertainment area at the rear of the store. My camera is as good as I can afford so I ignore the digital cameras and stereos and head for the DVDs.

I'm immediately jealous of the setup in here. Midway along the back wall is a screen, like those in cinemas, only smaller, on to which they project a loop of forthcoming trailers. This Halloween, the screen says, could well be your last: a knife slashes down the screen, which fades to red. From this central point the aisles quite literally fan out, like spokes on a wheel, across a generous arc, meaning whichever direction you enter from you walk towards the big screen. It's clever. It's clever and I want one. 'Get the sales up' chants my undead Area Zombie, 'Get the sales up, and I'll see what I can do.' I browse for a while.

I surface some time later when the store is quieter. It seems darker somehow, with fewer people, as if someone had kindly dimmed the lights to simulate the evening outside. The aisles are bigger now, the air conditioning soothing, and I stroll aimlessly through frozen foods toward biscuits and cereals.

The ginger nuts are own brand and I'm disappointed by the gaps where McVitie's should be. I ponder. On the up side they are only thirty-one pence so even if they are awful I'm not wasting too much money. On the other hand I've come a long way, the bus fare there and back is almost an hour's pay, and I think it only fair that I be able to get what I want. If I can't get it here I could always head down the corner shop tomorrow and risk their biscuits. I glance up and down the aisle. I'm alone. From another aisle I can hear an electronic sweeper thing swishing toward the freezer section, two disgruntled employees are moaning about the coffee in the staff room. I'm alone in the aisle and I open the packet of own-brand biscuits.

The colour seems fine, a delicate rusty orange, not too brown, not too yellow, the weight too feels about right. I snap the biscuit in two and am satisfied with the break, nice and solid without too many crumbs. I open my mouth. There is movement at the end of the aisle and I turn to meet the gaze of a small, dirty-faced child of indeterminable sex. It looks at me, tilts its head, and I think of the scene from *Jurassic Park* with the guy in the jeep whose name I never remember, the one where the venom-spitting dinosaurs get him. Much like in the film it pads a little closer, tilts its head to the other side and squeaks a little. I am standing in the aisle still clutching own-brand ginger nuts and on my tongue is half a stolen biscuit. The dirty child looks at me, narrows its eyes a little and edges closer. I'm nervous, worried it'll start spitting venom. It squeaks again, quiet and desperate, its hands are held up toward its chest, fingers drooping down, and its eyes move to the other half of the stolen biscuit. I close my dry mouth and suck hard on the half ginger nut; I hold out my hand to the child, offering it the other half. For a moment we look at each other and look at the half of a stolen biscuit in my hand. I raise my arm out and attempt a smile, but my mouth is full of ginger nut, which makes things difficult. The child crinkles its mud-smeared nose. I shrug and withdraw the biscuit. I'm about to turn when the child leaps forward and in one movement the biscuit is gone and so is the child, up and away into another aisle. I smell TCP and sweat and listen to quick little footsteps disappear into the bakery section. I no longer feel like biscuits but drop them into the basket for later. I take my basket and head for the tills.

As I round Crisps and Crackers I spot 9987, Santino, Scarlett.

She pushes a trolley casually through the central aisle, her head tilted upward to read the signs above as if deciding whether or not to venture any further. She wears jeans, tight at the waist and flaring out past her calves, with a pink T-shirt and a denim jacket. Her hair is tied up again and again stray locks dangle down across her cheeks and ears. She pauses at toiletries, glances down at a list in her hand and turns in. My breathing is surprisingly quick; I can feel my heart, see it through my jumper, beating loud and violent. My hands are clammy, my basket slipping through my fingers. I breathe deep, trying to slow my heart, and follow her.

In comparison I feel dank, dingy, my end of the aisle dark. 9987, Santino, Scarlett is bathed in light, her end of the aisle bright, as if the sun were rising directly behind her. Her hair burns against white cheeks. Ahead of me, stood closer to the light, an old lady, pink bobbled and stooped, dithers between denture glues. A young woman holds the hand of a small boy; he twists and turns, desperate to break free of his mother's grasp. He runs until his mother's arm is outstretched. Annoyed, she snaps her arm back to her side and he tumbles, slides, squeaks across the floor. 9987, Santino, Scarlett floats in female hygiene, her trolley almost empty: peppers, carrots, a bottle of white wine, tub of Ben & Jerry's. She leans over, her jeans clinging tight. I drop my basket. It clatters against the plastic floor. I hear my ginger nuts shatter and look up into the sparkling blue eyes of 9987, Santino, Scarlett.

Breathing hard, I smile, scoop up my basket and shuffle quickly to her. She smiles at me, head slightly cocked, eyes flicking over my face. She recognises me.

'You work in the Spar, right?' I shake my head, still smiling, content to play her game.

'Guess again,' I say, tucking hair behind my ear. Her smile tangles itself across her lips, her eyes narrow a little.

'Um ... OK ...' She says this slowly, lifting a box from the shelves as she does so. 'I've got to go now,' she says, and turns, dropping the box as she spins. It hits the floor with a light slap, a rustle, and I reach down to get it for her, suddenly needing an excuse to keep her here. I am muttering something as I pick it up, I say something like 'Let me get that for you ...' and I look forward to the gratitude in her face, the moment when she realises gentlemen still exist. I stretch out my arm to her, box in hand and read the words 'Heavy Flow'. Suddenly I'm sweating again.

Her smile is gone now. She whips the box from my hand and I stand motionless in the aisle, stooped, arm dangling before me, the handles of my basket digging into my palm. I say something like 'I ... I ...' but she isn't looking at me, she is glancing at the bobbled old women, she watches the child drop to the ground, defeated, hand still held tight, shoulder raised from the floor by his mother's insistent grip.

'Did you enjoy the film?' I ask and I hear my voice come out high pitched and whining.

'Yes, thank you,' she says, and without smiling, without looking at me, she turns into the light. I blink once, twice, squint into her aura and she dissolves into the glow and is gone.

In the aisle is the bobbled woman, still dithering, is the child who is dragged, limp, to the opposite set of shelves and is me, red faced and sweating. My breath short, sharp, trembling. I stare down at my shattered ginger nuts, drop my basket and slink away into the darkness.

XVIII

I've never been to a police station before so this is all very new and exciting. I get off the bus at the main station and cross Manvers Street. I decide on a casual-style stroll up to the police station. The car park out the front of the station is crammed full of police cars, which I shouldn't find surprising, but two of them are up on bricks and a third is parked up on the kerb of the pavement, its headlights on, the back door open and the engine is still grumbling away. I look around but no one else seems interested so I practise my casual stroll again and head up the ramp to the front doors.

From the outside the station is dull and concrete and so very nineteen-sixties with sandstone breeze blocks to ensure it fits in seamlessly with the rest of Georgian facades. Inside the building is cramped and dirty and so very local government grey. A high desk and a half a dozen metal chairs make up the reception area. I stare at the chairs, most no longer with their original padding: one has a gaffer-taped leg; another has a yellow stain smeared across the backrest. Old posters of forgotten schemes are splattered across the walls, notice boards are piled high with leaflets and adverts and warnings and posters. One solitary thank you card is placed carefully in the centre. It reads: *Dear Sirs, thank you all so much for your hard work. If he were still here I know my Sidney would appreciate it. All the best to your families and I wish you all the happiness you deserve. Yours, Mrs H. Wetherton. P.S. Give the bastard a few good slaps from me and my Sidney!* I close the card, the front of which is one of those patched-up grey bear things holding a flower and a badly spelt 'Fank Yoo' sign.

It is a cramped space and rather full. Three men, a woman and a foul-smelling homeless person with long leaf-filled hair and vomit stains are in a queue at the high desk. I don't want to stand behind the homeless person. I can hear him burping and coughing and get a sudden whiff of whisky and bile. I sit down on the only chair still reasonably intact.

Yesterday, at work, whilst filling in for Anna who was off sick, again, for the third time this week, my Area Zombie turned up, dragging her corpse along with her.

'Where is *Lesbian Nurses*?' she asked and I couldn't but wonder why she cared so much. The shop was failing, yes, but *Lesbian Nurses* is only one of a reasonable selection of Adult films we have available.

'It's still with the police,' I replied. 'Still away for testing.' She wasn't happy with that. I rang the station but couldn't really hear what was said, someone in the background was moaning and panting and asking: 'Why, Officer, what are you going to do with those handcuffs?'

'I'll just come down there then,' I told the phone, and hung up.

My Area Zombie nodded and pulled the string on her back that makes her corpse go: 'The shop is failing, get the takings up.' And she left.

Today I sit on an uncomfortable and slightly damp seat in a litter-filled police station trying not to smell the homeless person at the back of the queue. On the floor, next to a McDonald's wrapper and a small brown stain, is a copy of yesterday's *Chronicle*. Carefully I pick it up and check the underside for more dirt. The sports page is also brown, but dry, so that's not too bad, and holding the paper away from me with finger and thumb I read the front page. Missing Child, it says, and underneath is a blurry photo of a small boy in shorts clutching an ice cream. He grins and dribbles ice cream down his front so his T-shirt is a sticky green mess, like snot or phlegm. I'm not in the least concerned and any parent who shows that photo off to the public can't be too concerned about him either.

I flick through the paper, careful not to let the brown stain on the sports pages come into contact with my trousers, which are newly cleaned and ironed. An advert says the leisure centre has an offer on new gym memberships and I glance down at my stomach, which still bulges ever so slightly from my waistband. I haven't the time, I decide, and turn the page. In the personals a fifty-year-old woman, fourteen stone, cuddly, five-foot-five, gsoh, wants to meet man, twenty-five to thirty, for fun and frolics, no strings attached. Another woman, eighteen, slim and big breasted, wants a man, fifty-five plus, as sugar Daddy. I close the paper.

The homeless person is now at the front of the queue and is gabbling and slurring his way through some story about a cat and a badger and someone's mother who sells cigarettes to kids. The officer behind the desk is shaking his head and squinting against the smell of alcohol and vomit and, more recently, I realise, a hot, sharp smell of urine. I look at the floor, which is now wet, and the damp footprints that lead to the desk. The officer is trying to be attentive and professional but is obviously struggling. He is a fairly young policeman, about my age, but taller and slimmer. The homeless person stops and lowers his head to his chest, breathing deeply.

The officer braves the stench and leans forward. 'Are you OK?' he asks and the homeless person nods and raises his head again. He grins at the officer and sprays the desk with vomit, retching again and again as wave after wave splatters against the desk, the floor, the policeman receptionist. I stand up to leave as the officer begins to shout into his radio. As I leave two policemen appear in the doorway, carrying truncheons. They nod a greeting to me and push past into the reception area. I decide not to wait and to try calling them again later.

XIX

I can't shake the image of the vomiting drunk. All afternoon I sit at work and am terrified every time someone approaches the front desk. I have a bucket next to my stool just in case. Luckily for me it's quiet; the weather is bored, grey, overcast and dull. I sit and stare and drink my coffee and wonder whether or not to change the posters in the front window.

Behind me, above me, everywhere, Uma Thurman is slicing off body parts and through the front door comes 17, Jones, Andrew and his new girlfriend. He smiles and waves, his new girlfriend does not. She knows that I know that she is sleeping with his brother, 26, Jones, Brian, and rents porn. 17, Jones, Andrew heads straight for my new Asian Cinema section while his new girlfriend sulks near Alphabetical DVDs.

I pick up the phone and look at the late list. The list is multicoloured and tells me everything. Once again 7451, Algarry, Neville is late, this time with *Blue Velvet*, which annoys me because it's one of my favourites. Down the line comes ringing but no answer. I leave a message, polite and to the point. Purely through boredom I call Mr Johnson and a small voice answers and tells me her Dad isn't home.

'Can you pass on a message?' I ask and she says she

can. 'Can you tell him he's a thieving wanker? Thank you very much. No, that's the whole message, OK then? Thanks again, bye.' Mr Johnson is ninety-nine days late and we have lost all hope.

9987, Santino, Scarlett has been in to return her late film and is no longer on my list. I check her records and discover she returned it to Anna on one of the rare shifts she turned up for. Anna neglected to charge her. I sip my coffee and stare at the screen and sigh because now I have to be the bad guy and charge her the late fee. Combine this with yesterday's disaster in Asda and our relationship looks to be going through a bit of a rough patch. For a moment my fingers hover over the keyboard and I debate just deleting the fine but my Area Zombie screams in my head 'Get the takings up!' and it echoes through my skull. I sip my coffee because my head hurts and I search the office in vain for a ginger nut. 17, Jones, Andrew arrives at the desk with *Ichi the Killer* and I am forced to admire his taste in film if not in women. I smile hello and change over the film. I wave goodbye and fill up the kettle. It's getting dark outside and the kids are out in luminous tracksuits. Two are on bikes and swoop through the darkening night like glow-in-the-dark bats.

Through the whooping nightlife outside comes 3211, Winstone, Christopher and family. He waves a hello and pushes his children toward the Disney section and drags his wife through the heavy velvet curtain and into the Adult section.

One child, a boy I think, with long hair and scabby knees, calls out: 'But why, Dad? We want a Jackie Chan film!'

3211, Winstone, Christopher pokes his head out from

the curtain and insists on Disney. 'Disney or nothing,' he says. 'And you're going straight to your room to watch it.'

I frown and shake my head a little. There is something very wrong about a man who forces Disney on his children. A cry goes up outside and a child emerges from the Spar next door with a two-litre bottle of cider. He grins and places a cigarette between two thick lips. The kids outside clamour to his aid, all brandishing lighters, and I sit hoping that one of the nylon-coated bastards goes up in flames. I am disappointed and they fade away into the night sky, glowing slightly under the street lights. A Winstone child is wandering too close to the curtain and I leave the desk to push it back toward Disney.

The kids are back. The cider is gone and each one holds a cigarette tightly between lips. I watch for a while as the two on bikes ride in circles on the road, luminous tracksuits still glowing in the buzzing orange street light. The kids that come at night are on the porchway, they hold hands, he makes a joke and she laughs. It's the first time I've seen her smile.

The kettle boils and I make coffee and start sorting out the new releases ready for tomorrow. I check my watch: it's almost ten, so Percy should be here soon. I hide my coffee. The kids outside get louder, the ones on bikes are now racing up and down the street, the rest cheering and swearing and throwing empty pop cans at the cyclists. In front of the dry cleaners, parked opposite the shop, sits a blue and purple bruised, beaten-looking car. Its windows are cautiously open, two red eyes flare in time and inside shadows suck on light.

The shop is empty so I head down the stairs and into

the back to sort out the equipment needed for the new releases. There is an old computer down here which I flick on as I go past and it whirs and crackles to life, flickering and spluttering and beeping. I hear the door go on the shop floor, the little buzzer that brings us to attention, and from further away, from outside, a screech of brakes, a horn and laughter from the kids outside. I hear a squeaking cheer from the road, a cry of 'Hey, hey, you got any more that stuff you had last week?' I look up the stairs toward the high desk and there, wrapped in smoke and clad in cords, is Percy.

He grins, which is a mistake, because his teeth are yellow, his lips cracked and smoke still drifts from the corners of his mouth.

'Alright mate?' he says, still grinning, always grinning. 'Been busy then, or what?' Percy is southern and his accent largely dull, a sort of nondescript amalgamation of the Home Counties, which he tries to twist to suit his fictional working-class roots. His grin fills the area behind the desk so I remain where I am, safe and sheltered in the flickering computer screen light. 'Any coffee mate?' he asks, smoke trailing from his lips, weeping from his jacket and he heads down the stairs.

'No, sorry,' I say. 'We've run out again.'

'Oh,' he says and frowns, and raises his nose as he smells my fresh coffee. He grins again and his teeth aren't just yellow but blackening at the roots. 'Hang on,' he says and reaches one long arm into a drawer and behind a pile of paper work. He emerges with my hidden coffee.

He grins. 'I'll just put the kettle on shall I?'

I hate Percy.

I have on the desk in front of me three boxes and in each box is twenty DVDs. Before I leave here tonight and leave the place to Percy I need to unpack each box, enter each film on the system, assign each film a number, put the disks into our dirty brown cases, put the correct number on each film and file away each of the dirty brown cases in the right place down here so they can be found easily later. I also need to check the smoke alarms.

'So what's happening tonight that means you want off early? It's not like you,' Percy is calling down from the front desk. I see smoke creeping across the ceiling, collecting in pockets on the uneven surface.

'I'm busy,' I reply. 'Got somewhere I need to be.'

'Hot date is it?' Percy calls and I can feel him grinning. I blush but luckily he can't see me.

'It's none of your business,' I tell him, and work faster.

I tell Percy I've entered the films on the system and remind him to clear a space on the New Releases wall so I can put them out in the morning. As I leave he calls out down the street 'Make sure you give her one! God knows you need it!' I stop and shudder and hear the kids outside start to laugh. I see smoke drift past me and I follow it quickly up the hill.

XX

It takes me the best part of an hour and a half before I arrive at 9987, Santino, Scarlett's flat. The night is cool, a soft wet breeze creeps under the trees from time to time and I shiver and decide it's time to buy a heavier coat. It's been a while since we had a night in together but tonight looks hopeful: the lights are on, although no one's home. I try to remember her electric bill and vaguely recall it being fairly low. She's not the type to leave her lights on if she's gone out for the night.

Last night she never showed, I sat cold and wet and sipping tepid coffee from my cheap Thermos. The cat came back but there was no sign of her. I wonder if perhaps she's gone away for a short break, although I don't remember her packing. I remember a Newcastle number that appeared fairly often on her phone bill, maybe she has a friend up there she went to visit. I decide no, she's not gone far, not without turning off the lights. Not without letting me know.

I adjust the camera, a little more central, a touch higher, and zoom in toward her bedroom window. The lilac is glowing softly, light seeping gently into the room from the open door. The wardrobe is pine I think, a little wooden arch on the top for decoration, and behind the arch is a box. I zoom in further. The box is new I think, I don't remember it being there before, although I could be wrong. It looks like a shoe box, held shut with string or a band of some kind. On one corner is a small pink heart.

On the ground floor a door opens and for a second or two I can hear screams and violins and a woman in the doorway half turns and yells: 'Turn that fucking thing down!' Then the door slams shut and echoes through the trees, across the yard, and I hear it clap again, far off against the school walls behind me. The cat must be out. I reach into my jacket and take out the Whiskas treats I bought at the Spar.

Somewhere above the trees the moon is up, the row of townhouses glistens a wet, shimmering silver; above them the night glows orange and yellow and red. The street lights blaze on upwards and obscure the stars. I sit on my sodden chipboard platform with cold toes and warm coffee and my hands smell of cat treat. A shape leaps through the trees to my right, a blur flitting from shadow to shadow to shadow, and then cautiously it approaches the platform. I throw a treat to it and it backs off, arches up and stares. Yellow eyes. It nods and chews thoughtfully on the treat. From a window on the first floor flickers the blue and white of late-night television. A bathroom lights up, a kitchen darkens, a bedroom is badly lit and glowing red. I hear moaning. The cat rubs against my leg and purrs.

On the third floor a figure appears at the window. I jump, surprised, and flick the camera to record. The cat leaps into my lap. She's wearing that blue dress again and stares past me, up the hill. She runs her hand through her hair, fingers a necklace. I zoom in but she moves away and into the bedroom. The lilac shines a little brighter, the door is left open, and 9987, Santino, Scarlett floats past the window and out of sight. The cat pads around in a circle on my lap before lying down. It rests its head against my thigh. She reappears in pyjamas and hangs the blue dress on the wardrobe door.

Back in the living room and she is going through her large pink sports bag. She throws a book and a small make-up bag to one side and takes out two plastic cases. They are dirty brown and I swear and hate Percy even more because I know he has met her now and probably had a longer conversation with her too. Smoke twirls gracefully toward her ceiling, curling serenely from the DVD cases. She reads the labels, obviously deciding between the two, then sits. The light goes off and she disappears.

The cat stretches out its paws, digs in its claws and I feel its lithe little frame tense. On the wall opposite the living room window I can see her, projected on to the big screen behind the sofa. The light is bright white. Is blue. Is red. Is a soft peaceful green and I watch her shadow against the wall as she watches the film.

The cat has gone and I wake up shivering. My bones ache and my feet are numb. My palms hurt and I unfold my tightly gripped fists to find nail marks and blood. Above me, around me, the trees are grey and the light is strange and new and pale. I check my watch and it's almost six in the morning.

On the first floor a window opens and I can smell burnt toast. Somewhere behind me I hear birds and a car that won't start. On the third floor a figure stands in the window, her hands wrapped around a large pink mug.

She stares out up the hill, she breathes deeply. She drinks and closes her eyes. I see her shoulders relax and she opens her eyes.

She gazes again toward the top of the hill. I turn and try to remember what is up that way but the trees block my vision and I'm too cold, too tired and can't think. I turn back and she's looking down to the trees. I feel my breath get sucked into my bowels.

I'm up and moving and throwing my little stool behind me before I realise I'm still in shadow. I stand and she stares and I wave but she can't see. Quickly, quietly I gather my things and weave back through the trees. I keep deep in the undergrowth, avoiding the open yard, avoiding the school playing area. I carry my camera in its little bag and the tripod in my back pack, with the stool.

I reach the wall as a car pulls into the school car park and I scramble quickly over and on to the street. A couple, sagging and wrinkled, step backwards. Their dog barks and her hands clutch his arm. I nod a good morning and head for home.

XXI

The flat smells of damp and feet and I discover my bread is sitting in a puddle on the worktop. Above, an ugly mould-green stain is growing. I watch a sweaty bead of moisture drip on to my loaf. I am no longer hungry.

Luckily the damp hasn't spread to the electrics and I snuggle up in my chair in front of the heater. I stretch out my fingers, which ache still from last night, and I feel the scabs on my palm crack open. Blood oozes down my wrists and stains my jumper. I watch the blood seeping into the material, too tired and too sore to move.

I wake up in front of the heater, my face hot, my legs burning. I turn off the heater and try to stand. The stool is not suitable for sleeping on, nor is my chair, and I can hardly stand my back is so sore. I press my hands against the wall and try to invert my spine, pressing my stomach into the wall and my head back. It hurts but feels good, feels beneficial. I keep the position as long as I can and count the dead insects in the light fitting above me.

The clock says I've been asleep for a little over two hours. It's almost nine in the morning and I stare at the phone. Anna is due to open. Slowly I drop my head to my chest, trying hard to feel each vertebrate as I move. I drop my shoulders toward the wall and stretch my shoulder blades until they are almost touching. Quickly I push myself upright and move to the toilet-slash-shower-room just beyond the living-room-cum-kitchen and next to the bedroom-dash-study.

My urine smells of caffeine. I turn the kettle on. Two bloody palm prints adorn the woodchip wallpaper. I sigh and sip my coffee and settle into my chair. Nine comes and goes and the phone doesn't ring so Anna must have managed to get off her death bed for one last stab at working life. I finish my coffee and put the kettle on.

Whilst the kettle boils I open up the camera case and plug the camera into the television. I rewind to her watching the film and press play. I sip my coffee and at last am warm and comfortable. I sit and watch her watching a film on her chair in my chair wrapped in blankets and sipping coffee. About an hour into the film her shadow jumps, startled, and the lights on the screen stop flickering as she pauses the film. She stands up and I see her face, red and puffy. I think she's crying; her cheeks sparkle in the light from the television.

She moves out of shot. I watch her flat, stare at the walls, frozen blue. Something, a bat maybe, flutters past the camera. I swear at myself, annoyed for falling asleep and neglecting her like this. What was she doing? I fast forward and at last she returns to the window. She looks happier, still red but smiling. She laughs and as she turns I see her holding a mobile phone. She laughs again and speaks. I watch her lips move. She is far away but close enough, I can see her eyes crease as she laughs, can see a dimple to the right of her mouth as she smiles. I watch her lips move. She flicks her hair. She fingers the necklace. I watch her lips move. She smiles and laughs.

She finishes the call. She sits down and I watch her shadow watch the film. Later, with the film over, she stands and stretches and I see her belly button when she arches her back, her arms above her head, and her breasts point upwards, point outwards. She leaves the window. Scene ends. I fast forward until I recognise the scene. She stands in the window cradling a large pink cup, sipping thoughtfully. She fingers the necklace and stares toward the top of the hill.

I stare out my window but my flat faces the wrong way, faces downhill and over the city. Somewhere in here I have an A to Z. Somewhere. In my bedroom a bookcase is squeezed in next to my wardrobe and I search the shelves. Magazines, old newspapers, some Philip K Dick short stories and some old DVDs, but no map. The living space is empty. Hotplate, toastie maker, kettle, TV, chair, blood-stained walls. I sit back down. Maybe she's just staring, staring and thinking, staring and daydreaming. I stare and just stare and sip my coffee and stare at the TV screen without really seeing.

I like her blue dress, I decide. I look at the clock and discover it's now almost eleven. I rewind the tape to watch her in her dress. My coffee is cold. I boil the kettle.

The dress is a light shade of blue with white-trimmed collars and sleeves and ill fitting. It looks vaguely familiar, like something I've seen before. I stare hard at something on her breast. A stain maybe? A pattern? I'm tired and my eyes hurt. I can't think. The coffee is failing me. I turn off the TV and close my eyes. I'm tired. Behind the caffeine I feel drained, an empty shell. I stand up. I feel dizzy. How long since I had a proper sleep?

I find myself in bed. I'm warm and safe and I sleep. I sleep. I dream of cats with blue, and red hands holding cold coffee. I sleep and I dream of trees at night and bats. I sleep and I dream of her and I smile.

The phone rings but I don't answer. I lie in my bed, fully clothed. I am wet. The phone rings and slowly I unravel the twisted bedclothes. I am wet and sticky. The phone rings and I answer and I hear my Mam asking if am I bringing a friend tonight or just myself. I murmur something I don't make out and stare, wide eyed, at the cold sticky mess on my crotch.

XXII

Mam's garden smells of honeysuckle. For once, the night is warm. Behind me the sun is setting pink and purple, the clouds licked beneath with yellow. The air is sweet. Under my arm is a plastic bag with my ruined trousers. My reflection in the front door's frosted glass stares miserably back at me. I move some hair away from my face and tuck it behind my ears. I tuck in my shirt and press the doorbell.

My father is smiling when he opens the door. He looks genuinely happy, eyes sparkling, teeth showing. He is wearing a tie. I smile back.

'Oh,' he says, and his smile fades. He puts his teeth away, extinguishes his eyes. 'It's you.' He leans past me and into the street, looking left and right. I'm still smiling, but only with my mouth now, a fixed grin and heavy eyelids. My father steps back into the doorway, gives me another look and closes the door.

Behind me the sunset is streaked with navy blue, the air smells of honeysuckle, the plastic bag under my arm rustles as I put my hands in my pockets. From inside I hear yelling, someone stamps up the stairs. Through the frosted glass I make out vague shapes: a larger one, my father, comes heavily down the stairs, fussing about his waist as he does so. Even from here I can hear his heavy angry footsteps. He moves past and down the long hall I know leads to the kitchen.

A long time passes. I consider pressing the bell again.

At the top of the stairs my Mam appears. She moves slowly and unsteadily, resting heavily against the banister as she negotiates the stairs. At last she makes it to the door.

When the door opens my Mam is standing upright, elegant in a floral print dress, shoulders back, chin raised, feet together. I slouch in my cream denim jacket and glance at the dirt around the cuffs. I smile. She smiles, her whole body seems to swell with the effort and she falls forward toward me, her arms wrapped tight around my shoulders. I touch her back, stroke the fabric. She stands, her eyes wet, and leads me inside.

Outside the sunset starts to turn a light shade of purple and the smell of honeysuckle clings to my clothes; inside is roasted pork, apples and gravy. The dining room flickers, shadows bouncing off the walls in candlelight.

'I thought I'd go all out tonight,' Mam says. 'It's nice to treat yourself once in a while.' She smiles that wet, weak smile again. I take the bag from my armpit.

'Sorry,' I say. 'Mine's broken again.' She smiles and nods and slips into oven mitts. I move away to the utility room and to the washing machine.

From the living room comes laughter which sounds almost fake, the sounds too well pronounced, the pauses too long, but then a gunshot rings through the house and I hear that awful machine gun patter and know that the television screen will now be wet. A can crumples and a voice calls out 'Where's my Caffrey's?' I can hear the spit between syllables, the whole sentence dripping wet with phlegm.

Over dinner my father is unusually quiet. I was expecting abuse and had rehearsed accordingly: the takings are up, talk of big things at Head Office, the screenplay is taking exciting new directions. If pushed I even had: and I've met a girl, it's still early days, but I think there is something there. My father is still wearing a tie and is carefully scooping up gravy with a soup spoon. No abuse yet. No attention at all, in fact. I am unwilling to waste my prepared lines if they are not needed and so stay quiet and watch my father gingerly slurp his gravy.

Mam is fussing. 'Gravy?'

I shake my head. 'I'm fine, thank you,' I say.

'More crackling?'

'No, thank you.' She smiles and I smile back. My father is still quiet. It's not just the tie, I realise, but the shirt too is clean and pressed. I watch him from behind my forkful of stuffing. Less red, his eyes almost focused. He has shaved and an odd smell lingers under the pork and apple and gravy: he is wearing aftershave.

My father dabs his freshly shaven chin with a napkin. I've never seen him do this. It looks strange, his fingers delicately pressing the napkin to his big red lips. He sniffs and raises the napkin to blow his nose. This is better, more familiar. He throws the napkin into the gravy boat just as I change my mind and am about to pour some on to my vegetables.

'You've got to get shot of that shite in the spare room,' he says. He sniffs and his hand moves to his empty can. I see his eyes dart to the doorway, to the fridge, and his swollen fish lips part. I watch his jaw clench, his fingers squeeze the can a little too hard, and I frown, confused.

'The shite. In the spare room,' he says, eyes on me again, and focused for once. 'All that crap you left when you moved out. I want it gone.' I nod. He sniffs.

'Your Dad wants to turn it into a gym,' Mam says, and I can't meet my father's eyes. I'm grinning. He stands.

'It's my fuckin' house! I'll do what the fuck I want with it!'

He leaves and I hear the television come on next door. An explosion and sirens. I look at my Mam, who is staring sadly at his empty seat.

The spare room was once my room and I sit on my old bed and stare at the wall. It is mauve. Mam chose it. There is not a lot left: some boxes, some old clothes in the wardrobe, a roll of posters I don't remember ever hanging. In my hand I have bin liners and so I set to work. I don't even open the boxes. I've no idea what's in them, but I can't imagine it's anything I would still want.

One bin liner is full when I hear a soft knock at the door and Mam calls out: 'Can I come in?' I open the door; she smiles that sad, damp little smile I keep seeing. 'Need a hand?' she asks. She takes my hand and wraps hers around it. She holds tight.

I don't need help but I nod and smile and say, 'Thanks, Mam, that would be great.'

Mam is disappointed to learn that the boxes have remained unopened.

'What about your memories?' she asks.

'There're just things, Mam,' I shrug.

She shakes her head and opens one of the remaining

boxes. Photographs. She taps the edge of the bed next to her and I sit.

'Oh, you must remember this. This was our holiday to Weymouth, do you remember?' She is holding a photograph of a small child. Its hair is long and fair, its face hidden by thick strands and shadows. It wears nothing but red swimming trunks and stands sulkily, arms by its side. Mam hands it to me.

'I loved your hair like that,' she says. 'You did too. You cried when your Dad took you to the barbers.' I nod. 'Do you remember,' she says, 'we were staying in a bed and breakfast on the seafront and every morning we used to get up early to watch the boats coming in?' I nod. I don't remember getting up early. I don't remember the boats. I do remember the afternoon my father came home from the pub, already drunk despite the early hour. I remember him grabbing me and Mam crying and him dragging me down the seafront. I remember not wearing any shoes and cutting my feet on broken glass. I remember being thrown into a chair at the barbers and my father demanding my head be shaved. I remember him muttering 'Last time my son gets called a fuckin' puff.'

I smile and nod. 'OK Mam,' I say. 'I'll keep this box.' She smiles and passes it to me. We both see the envelope at the same time and I flush red as we reach for it. Mam gets it first and I cringe, my back starts sweating. The envelope reads 'Jo'. Mam opens it.

The envelope is brown and old and sellotaped together. The name is written in red and sits cradled in a huge pink heart. Mam smiles as she withdraws the photographs.

'I don't remember any Jo,' she says, smiling at me.

'You kept this quiet'. She flicks through the photographs.

The photographs are old, older than the rest in the box, the corners rounded. Mam frowns as she flicks through them one at a time. Each is of a girl, perhaps sixteen. Her hair is short, dark, her mouth large and always painted red or pink. She wears eyeliner and occasionally earrings. In one she poses in a short skirt next to an old Morris Minor. In another she is on holiday, the photographer has caught her unawares and she skips across a beach in a bikini and flopping straw hat. Mam holds up another. The girl is in a long purple dress. Her hair is longer now but tied up above her head, revealing a long slender neck. She wears a pendant, which plunges into cleavage the dress does little to conceal. Mam fingers the chain around her neck.

'Where did you get these?' she asks. I look at her for the first time since the envelope appeared. Her hair is tied up and I trace the line of her neck to her shoulders. I look at her painted red lips and the smudges beneath her eyes where eyeliner was once. I'm red and sweating.

'Why do you have these labelled Jo?' she has turned over the picture of the girl in the dress. On the back is written 'Me and Jo get ready to go out.'

I wipe away the hair in my eyes, tuck it back behind my ear where it sits heavy and greasy. I look at Mam.

'It was college,' I say. I can't look at Mam but she doesn't take her eyes off me. My face is hot, my back sweats. My shoulders droop.

'It was college,' I say again. 'I, I liked this girl, Jane.' I look up and Mam meets my sodden gaze. She nods. 'Look, I … College was awful, Mam,' I say and she takes me hand. 'Everyone had boyfriends or girlfriends and always wandered around in pairs or fours or sixes and I ...' Mam strokes my hand gently, squeezes my fingers a little. 'I was lonely, Mam. No one talked to me, no one would even sit next to me in class. I was single and they all thought that was really sad. Even the ugly girls had boyfriends. Even the weird ones who wore black make-up and those fishnet thingies weren't interested in me.' Mam has both hands cradling mine. She isn't smiling but holds tight.

'Anyway,' I continue, my face still hot and red. 'Anyway, one day I'm at Gran's and I find all these photographs, which she says I can have if I want, so I put them in my bag and forget about them.' I look up and Mam is still looking at me, still not smiling. I take a deep breath. 'So,' I say, 'next day at college and I'm working in the study area and I've left my bag open and this guy, Steven I think his name was, walks past and grabs them. "Wow," he says to me, really loud so everyone can hear, "Wow, she's really hot. Who is she?"' I pause and look at Mam, she smiles a little and strokes back a strand of hair that has escaped my ear. Her fingers brushing my cheek.

'Just then,' I say, 'this girl, Jane, who I really liked, she comes up and says, "Hey, she's pretty. She looks Greek, am I right?" she asked. It was the first time she'd ever spoken to me and I didn't know what to do. She asked if she was my girlfriend and I ...' I pause to look at Mam, she has a sympathetic look, her mouth smiling from only one side, her eyes wide and sad. 'I said yes,' I tell her. 'I said I met her on holiday and I said the first name that popped into my head, Jo, like Gran. Suddenly people talk to me so I find new photographs at Gran's and make up stories and ...' Mam is crying softly now and I look at the damp patches on my knees and realise I am too. Mam lets go of my hands and opens her arms.

I cry and am held tight and safe and warm against her breast. I cry and she strokes my hair and she rocks me slowly, slowly, slowly. I cry and she holds me and I cling tightly as she rocks me.

'It's OK,' I tell her, my voice whispering from somewhere deep within her chest. I can hear her heart beating. 'It's OK,' I say again. 'I've been holding back a little Mam, didn't want to jinx it and stuff.' She pulls my head away, brushes wet hair from my eyes, strokes the hair on the back of my neck. 'I've met someone,' I tell her. 'It's early days, but I really think there is something there.' Mam smiles, sniffs back her tears. She pulls me closer and wraps her arms around my back, puts her head on my shoulder and I feel her lips against my neck, brushing softly against my skin as she says something like, 'Oh, darling. That's wonderful news.'

I put one arm around her shoulder; stoke her hair with my free hand. I close my eyes and feel my Mam's breath curl gently across my throat. She slides her hand from behind my back and rests it on my thigh. It sits, warm and comfortable.

'Yes,' I say. 'She's wonderful.'

XXIII

The Grapes is full as I pass. Through steamed windows and sweating curtains heads bounce between pint glasses. The locals cheer at the TV screen. A man in a Stetson with a huge handlebar moustache is holding a bottle of Budweiser and frowns at the screen, as confused by the sport as I am. Behind the bar a woman with huge breasts and a tight white tank top is ignored completely and stares out the window as I pass, her face emotionless, thoughtless, pointless without attention.

I pause outside the Little Theatre, alone in the square. Behind me the dark and unfinished Spa looms, the sunlight sucked through the huge dark windows and lost in the gloom. I check my watch. She is late.

Mam wouldn't let it lie. It's been a long time since I saw her that happy. I may have gotten carried away. Too many questions, and as well as 9987, Santino, Scarlett and I know each other there were some embarrassing gaps.

'What does she do?' Mam had asked.

'We don't talk about work, Mam. We talk about real things. Important things.'

'Oh?' she'd asked. 'Like what?'

'Like films.'

I look at my watch again. I look at my reflection in the deep black of the Spa's windows. My hair hangs past my cheeks, my jacket hangs open, my shirt hangs over the too-tight belt. I brush away my hair, tuck it behind my ears. I tuck in my shirt and pull back my shoulders. I stare past my pale, puffy face and behind me comes my Scarlett.

She puts her arms around my waist, rests her head on my shoulder and we look at each other through the reflection in the window. The window is made up of sections of glass, small panes, each handmade, and so our faces are distorted, sliced through by fillers, separated by the joins in the glass. She kisses my neck.

Inside we sit side by side, my arm across her shoulder, her hand on my knee. The theatre is empty except for us and we sit in the middle, an ocean of empty seats surround us. We share popcorn, salted and buttered, and we argue playfully during the trailers, friendly bickering over which films look good and which don't. When the film starts neither of us speak.

On the screen, in soft focus, a women stands against a boat railing. She stares out to sea, wistful, sad. The music is slow, orchestral; my Scarlett crunches her popcorn in my ear, and we sit, bound together and adrift in the theatre. Up on the screen the woman turns, her long hair gently flowing on the sea breeze, and the shot backs away to reveal a man. He stands on the deck in uniform, his peaked cap under his arm, his hair tucked behind his ears, white jacket buttoned tight over a muscular frame. The music climbs, violins soar and the woman smiles, relieved. She runs to him, the violins swoop and my Scarlett whispers, 'Oh, it's so romantic darling.' She squeezes my arm tight, moves her hand back to my knee. I smile and chew on my popcorn.

The man on screen is speaking, his face intense, serious, furrowed brow, tight jaw, he holds the woman by the shoulders while she looks on, her mouth opening and closing, her eyes fill with tears. He tells her he is leaving, a mission of vital import. He promises they'll meet again. 'I don't know where,' he says. 'I don't know when. But I'll find you again.' He kisses her, forces his lips against hers, and she beats at his chest, squirming to get free before finally succumbing to him. She puts her arms around him, the violins return, swooping overhead. A close up of the man, his long hair blowing in the wind. He winks, throws his hat in the air, and dives from the boat. My Scarlett gasps, her hand jumping from my knee to my thigh and she stares wide-eyed at the screen. I hold her closer, feel her head nuzzle into my neck.

Above me, above us, everywhere, the woman cries and my Scarlett gently presses her lips to my neck. The orchestra stirs back into life and the camera sweeps across the choppy seas as the man in uniform swims toward a submarine. The woman rushes to the railing, cries out to him, and my Scarlett runs her hand up my thigh, gently bites my earlobe. He reaches the submarine and clambers aboard. She waves and calls out again. 'I love you, Johnny!' she yells and my Scarlett quietly reaches for my belt. He blows her a kiss, calls back, 'We'll meet again soon, I promise!' and my Scarlett loosens my trousers.

I check my watch, pretending like I'm waiting for someone. The Spa blocks out the sun and I stand in shadow, waiting. From The Grapes comes a cheer, a roar, and two men fall out into the alley. One laughs and raises his glass to his lips. The other is bearded, smaller. He stumbles and falls, splashes into a puddle by the wall. The first man laughs again, raises his glass in a silent toast to his partner. From the puddle comes a laugh, joyless and angry, and a fist connects with a crotch. The drinker drops, drowns in the puddle and is kicked. I hear a snap of ribs and the bearded victor returns to the pub.

I turn to the theatre, I check my watch and I slip silently away past the Spa toward the bus station.

XXIV

The sun is out and I have Percy washing the front windows. I smile and wave and he seethes grey smoke into the air. I sip my coffee and watch the world go by through clean, vomit-free windows. The sky is bright and so the big screen is useless today, instead the radio mumbles forth the day's news. The Spa still isn't finished, the rugby club has signed some oversized Samoan, congestion increases, small child still missing (police suspect foul play). I sip my coffee and watch Percy scowl through the last dirty pane.

I feel lighter today, easier. I sip my coffee and watch the world go by. A gaggle of elderly ladies shuffles forward in time, a day trip to the post office and back, maybe a scone if there is time. Kids in light jackets with water pistols are running from parents, laughing and screaming and spraying water over everything. One catches his father, a splash of water cuts right across his face. The child stops. The whole family stops. I stop. He laughs, the father laughs and leans over his son, arms wide and growls and smiles and the boy screams and runs and sprays water again. Two teenage boys, designer jackets, expensive shoes and throbbing spots, lean against the dry cleaner's windows. They chew and spit and laugh. They watch two girls walk past. The girls wiggle as they pass, short skirts flicking high in the cool breeze. The girls hold hands. The boys follow. A battered blue car ambles past the window, its windows opened hopefully. Two red eyes wink at Percy but he doesn't see. The bruised curb crawler releases tentacles of exhaust fume, which curl around Percy's ankles, creep up the inside of his legs. I smile at Percy as the tentacles circle his chest, circle his throat and for a moment he stops, wrapped in smoke, and he nervously glances at the passing crowds.

Percy has finished. I check my watch. Twelve.

'Right then, I'm off,' he says and dumps the bucket down the back. 'You want anything before I go?' I shake my head and sip my coffee. I watch the world go by, I watch Percy go by. He strides across to the dry cleaners and I watch him chat to the child behind the counter. Percy fumbles in his pocket, shakes the child's hand and returns his hand to his pocket. Smoke creeps from his jacket and I fear for the dry cleaning but he turns, grins at me and strides away through the sunlight, smoke trailing behind him, an exhaust that powers his gangly form.

Later I sweep the front porchway: plastic bottles, takeaway boxes and one used condom. I sweep it all on to the street and it ceases to be my problem. Inside I alphabetise. I organise. I sit at the high counter and go through the books. I check the accounts. The takings are down.

A young man comes in, torn jeans, designer T-shirt, all very studenty, and asks 'Do you have any of the *Scary Movie* films?' I smile sweetly and tell him to leave. I sip my coffee.

I am busy preparing the orders for next week and have decided to move away from the hollow Hollywood block-busters and am searching through the distributor's catalogue for more interesting films. My Asian Cinema section is growing and, so far, is reasonably popular. Over in New Releases is a man in leather: leather jacket, leather trousers, leather shoes, string vest. He approaches the counter with a new Clint Eastwood release and nods politely. I'm suspicious of the string vest but the man turns out to be 4409, Archer-Rathborne, Lionel so I oblige.

A litter of still-pubescing girls giggle up to the counter, all baby boobs, high socks and ponytails. One of them, the one with make-up and high heels, has one hand on her hip, the other flicking her ponytail, and asks: 'Do you have the new Lindsay Lohan film?'

I nod and say, 'Yes, it's in the Children's section.' She scowls at me, cocks her hip and points, limp wristed with all the attitude of a thirteen year old.

'It's not a children's film,' she says. 'It's for more so-phisticated teenagers. Like us.' She sneers and nods as if she's won. I smile.

'Well,' I say, all polite. 'I'm so very sorry, how stupid of me. If I remember rightly,' I say, 'the film has a very sophisticated 12A rating, so if one of you ladies' (I inject the word with bile and roll my eyes, I think I may even have a hand on my hip) 'would like to show me some proof of age I'll get the film for you.'

They stare at me blankly. The leader, the one in heels, deflates, the hip drops, and hands come together at her face and she nibbles on her pink sparkling nails. The litter congregates for a moment and reinflates, all attitude and hot air. The one in heels has her both hands on hips now.

'My mother is in here all the time and knows your boss. I don't think she'd be too pleased to hear about how you ruined our weekend.' Her free hand sweeps slowly across her friends, she cocks her head and smiles, smug. She flicks her ponytail off her shoulder. I laugh and lean forward.

'Why don't you,' I say, very reasonably and polite, 'why don't you just fuck right off and come back when you are old enough to think for yourself. This is serious business I run here,' I say. 'For serious connoisseurs of film. Not', I continue, 'for silly little girls.' I smile sweetly. 'So,' I say again, 'just fuck right off.'

I search in vain for signs of tears on the carpet because I'm sure I heard sobbing as they left, but I could be wrong. I'm crouched by the counter, hand on carpet, feeling for moisture, and a figure stands in the doorway. I look up. It's bright outside and the figure stands, silhouetted, the light pours past it and renders its limbs almost stick thin. It shuffles forward, awkward, unbalanced movements. My undead Area Manager has grey hands on wasted hips. She leans down toward me and I hear bones snapping and groaning as she does so.

'Am I right in thinking ...' she hisses, her breath fetid and heavy, and I wonder if it is the smell of human flesh caught between back teeth. I wonder if maybe I should find her a toothpick. 'Am I right in thinking that I have just seen a group of young girls leaving here in tears?'

I'm thinking, *Yes, success*, but I'm saying, 'Oh, oh no, I hope not. They were here, certainly, but unfortunately we were unable to meet their needs.' I smile weakly and stand up. I'm taller than her now and quickly look for the strings for this strange zombie puppet. No luck, however. It speaks again, hands on hips, but she's not resting them there exactly, rather holding them very close to her hips, unable to get closer lest she tangle her strings.

'What did they want? Is it something you think we should have?' I shake my head and tell her they wanted the new Lindsay Lohan film. 'We have that,' she says, 'it's over there,' and twists one arm behind her back and toward the Disney section. The position looks painful, she is cringing, but I suspect at me rather than any pain. I wonder whether the dead feel pain.

I say, 'Yes, but she was after a *sophisticated* Lindsay Lohan film and ...'

She raises her arms and almost screams. Instead the sound that squeezes past her blue lips is a sort of constipated groan.

'How many times do I have to say this?' She steps forward. I step back. 'This is not, I repeat, NOT, your own personal film appreciation club.' She steps forward again and I retreat until my back is up against the counter. 'This is a BUSINESS!' She steps forward again and I lean back as far as I can. Her eyes are on mine, staring up at me from somewhere near my chest, and I suddenly get an image of her crawling up my legs, over my stomach, dragging herself up from the grave to meet me face to face.

'This is a business that is failing,' she says quietly. 'And right now, it's failing because of you.' She steps back and looks at me, her eyes wide and grey and clouded over. She slumps and I realise how small she really is. I try to say I'm sorry but she waves it off, and says: 'Put that kettle on and show me the sales figures.' She heads down the back.

I feel itchy now, restless. Down the back the zombie goes through my sales figures and I get ready to answer for the inadequacy of film knowledge in Elmfield Park. I wonder if this is what Renfield felt like.

I hear a cup clattering into the sink so I call down: 'Like another?'

There is a pause, then: 'Yes, yes I think I will. Thank you.' I put the kettle on again. Zombie curses from the darkness, she has found the pile of unhung shelves.

'I've not got a hammer,' I call, but there is only silence.

The kettle wheezes to a climax and I sit and drum my fingers against the counter, coffee ready spooned into two mugs. The zombie takes milk but no sugar and this has been accounted for. I think the milk may be a little off but she's dead, it can't make any difference. Outside the sky starts to darken, heavy clouds blow across the valley and an exploratory breeze curls into the shop. People still pass in heavy-looking jackets but they scurry now, less laughter, less play. The teenage boys return and glow in the last rays of sunshine. They grin and laugh and one of them strokes a long wound across his cheek which glitters and weeps. They pass and head off toward the Chinese.

In the shop is a man in a suit and polished shoes. Under his arm he has a thin leather briefcase and he flicks a mobile phone open and closed as he browses. Over by the Disney section a small girl sits reading the back of a Barbie movie. Her parents amble through Alphabetical DVDs, ignore my new Asian Cinema section and go

108

straight to the new release blockbusters. From outside I hear a rumbling and the breeze takes on an icy chill. In the doorway is 7451, Algarry, Neville in a crumpled denim jacket and tracksuit bottoms. He is clean shaven, his hair cut close to his scalp. He wears flip-flops, which trail dust on to my carpet.

He looks calm, no sign of tension, and I stare closely at his flip-flops. No sign of blood. His head is shaved but he is still very much recognisable so if he's on the run he's not doing very well. I watch carefully as he browses, watch his sleeves recede as he reaches out, watch for signs of struggle. Nothing.

From the back comes 'Can I see your order list for next week?' and I gather my paperwork and take it down into the crypt.

When I re-emerge behind the counter 7451, Algarry, Neville has gone. The child is still there, as are her parents, and the man with the briefcase. All as it should be bar some dusty footprints and a case or two in the wrong place. I am about to go and organise when 7451, Algarry, Neville appears at the counter. He spreads his palms wide as the desk and I notice old scars on his knuckles.

'Where' he whispers, glancing at the small girl who now dances in circles in horror and thrillers, 'is *Lesbian Nurses*?' I stammer, thrown sideways still from the shock.

I say something like: 'It's unavailable at the moment.' He leans over the counter, which he's not meant to do, and I don't like him being this close to me. His jacket is crumpled and dirty, I realise, greasy, and his T-shirt has sweaty stains around the stomach.

'I've been waiting for it to come back for the best part of a week now. It's a big favourite of mine and I'm getting annoyed that it never seems to be here.'

I say something along the lines of 'Erm, well, I ...'

He curls his fingers across the edge of the counter, they brush the panic button, slip across the reminders and job lists which dangle before me. The scars on his knuckles are white, his fingernails yellowed with a dark scarlet red beneath the tips. He stands back and says, 'Well, might I reserve it for another night? For this Friday, perhaps?'

He is suddenly very polite and I'm almost genuine when I say, 'I'm very sorry, Sir, but I'm not sure when we will have it back. It's gone for ...' I glance at his wrists, which are pale and unbloodied, his hands are clean and harbour only older crimes. I do some quick maths. Almost three weeks since he handed me a bloodstained disk, knuckles can heal in three weeks.

I say, 'It's gone for ...' and I pause here for effect, 'cleaning.' His eyes are meant to widen, I expect his pulse to quicken as he realises that I know, because now I do know. The scabs from a beating he administered, the blood he couldn't clean off, the flesh he hides beneath the nails. I know he's up to no good. I'm nervous and wait for a response and hear the footsteps of the Dead behind me. A witness. *I'm safe*, I think, and my heart beats fast. 7451, Algarry, Neville shrugs.

Beside me Death says, 'Is there a problem, Sir?' and smiles sweetly with blue lips painted red.

7451, Algarry, Neville shakes his head and says, 'No, no, just a little disappointed that's all. I'm after a film that's been sent off for cleaning.' He smiles at my Area Manager and finishes with, 'It's not a problem though, I'll try again at the weekend.'

He is about to leave when my Area Manager asks, 'Away for cleaning? We don't send films away for cleaning, it's done in store.'

She looks at me with a raised eyebrow and I say, '*Lesbian Nurses.*'

'Oh, I see,' she says and 7451, Algarry, Neville turns red, his eyes widen and I think, *Yes, got you. I knew it.*

'Right,' says the zombie. 'I've had enough of this,' and she turns to me. 'Ring the station, right now, and get it returned. No excuses, this gentleman deserves to be able to rent whatever film he wants.'

She turns back to 7451, Algarry, Neville and smiles. He mutters something like: 'That's really not necessary.' But Death has handed me the phone and I dial reluctantly.

'Hello?' I say.

I hear a women reply saying 'Manvers Street Police Station, how may I help you?' and I tell her I need my film returning but I don't think she's listening. I can hear her say 'Oooh, oooooh, I like that ...' and I say 'No, please, I need to speak to someone about my film, it's away for ...' I glance at 7451, Algarry, Neville, suddenly aware that he knows now that I know and I can't help thinking I'm in trouble. 'Cleaning,' I say. The woman isn't listening though, she is saying 'Ooooooh ... Here, here use my night stick ... yeah, ahhhhhh.'

7451, Algarry, Neville and my undead Area Manager are both watching me and from the phone line comes: 'Ahhhh, ohhhh, hmmmm.'

I say something like, 'So it's in the post already then is it?'

The woman replies 'Yes, yes, oh YES ...'

I say 'Great, thank you very much.' I hang up.

'Right then,' says the zombie Area Manger next to me, 'we should have your film ready and waiting on Friday, Mr ...'

'Algarry,' I say. 7451, Algarry, Neville looks at me, surprised, as if we don't know each other.

'Mr Algarry,' Death says. 'We look forward to seeing you' she finishes and 7451, Algarry, Neville rushes out the shop past the little girl, who is doing headstands against Romance.

XXV

I can't help thinking that it was a mistake confronting 7451, Algarry, Neville. He knows that I know that he is up to no good. I might have pushed him into doing something stupid. He knows that I've sent the film off somewhere and probably suspects the worst. I can't help thinking I've made a mistake. I've done something really stupid. So now here I am, wet and cold at half one in the morning, on guard. I've been lazy, I should have done something a long time ago.

There's no sign of 9987, Santino, Scarlett yet and this worries me. I worry that something has happened to her. Under the trees the world seems small, just me on my platform, the slowly decaying townhouses in front, and to my left I see the cat prowling through the darkness. As always my toes are cold, as always I sip tepid coffee and wish I'd bought a better Thermos. On the ground floor a kitchen light spills light into the night but there is no movement within. On the first floor a window is open, a radio plays softly, catching on shrubs and discarded cider bottles. The top floor is dead, net curtains still hang crooked, dust on the windows. 9987, Santino, Scarlett is still not home and I worry. I worry he has taken her, or hurt her. I worry that she is wrapped up in all this, unable to escape. I worry that I've put her in danger.

On the third floor the lights are out, the windows reflect the lights that creep slowly up the hill behind me. I see flashing blue, bouncing down the hill, off the window, under the trees, and a siren mourns faintly in the night. I stare at the reflections in the tatty rear windows of the apparently well-appointed town houses and follow the winding road up the hill, toward Odd Down.

From the undergrowth creeps the cat, belly to the ground, yellow eyes wide and bright and staring at me. Tonight I have Felix and I pray for a little less pain. I throw a chewy strip of whatever it is Felix thinks cats like. It sniffs it, circles it. It pounces. On the first floor the radio stops and a moment later a light appears behind frosted glass. A fat man leans back, arms above his head in a stretch. A flush, water down the drainpipes and the light goes off. The cat rubs against my legs. The radio starts up again. I sip my tepid coffee.

My watch says it's now two thirty-seven and I tell myself I'm overreacting. I've never yet seen 7451, Algarry, Neville here and there is very little reason to expect him here tonight. Perhaps he didn't know about the bloody handprints, I doubt he'd have handed the film back in like that if he did. Perhaps he has no idea. Maybe he thinks he's gotten away with it. I sip my cold coffee and shudder. It tastes slimy and bitter and I empty my Thermos. The cat lies curled in my lap, Felix treats all gone. It has one yellow eye open, a slither that watches the third floor as eagerly as I do.

The papers have made no mention of any deaths. Nothing about a mutilated victim or a trail of bloody prints leading from an abandoned body. I wonder what it is he did. The cat stretches out its claws, tenses its hunter's body and I feel it tear into the flesh on my thighs. I stroke the cat's velvet head, tickle behind its ears and the claws disappear. I stroke the cat and I watch the flat and I wonder what it is that 7451, Algarry, Neville is getting away with.

A little after three I feel a sharp pain in my thigh and wake up to see a light in the flat. I stroke the cat and flick on my camera. The living room glows warm and inviting and I sigh. 9987, Santino, Scarlett stands for a moment inside the doorway, throws her keys on to what I assume is a side table by the door. She is wearing that blue dress again. I stroke the cat and the camera zooms in toward her breast where the mysterious pattern rests but she moves out of shot too quickly. A minute goes by. Then another. Then one more and then she stands at the window, pink cup cradled close, and the camera traces the line of her right breast. Her breast says: Scarlett Santino. And underneath is written: R.U.H. I smile and she stares upward toward the top of the hill. Toward the hospital. Royal University Hospital.

9987, Santino, Scarlett is a nurse. I make a note to include occupation on the membership forms. She moves away from the window and the lilac bedroom is illuminated for me and my camera to peruse. She looks tired, my camera close enough to make out bags under her eyes, to see the grey haunt to her white skin. She needs a rest, I think, she needs a break. The cup sits on the windowsill and from the wardrobe she has pulled her tracksuit bottoms and a thick jumper. She takes off the dress.

I am about to turn off the camera when she turns to

face me. The dress drops to the floor and she stands, an angel in the night, a warm and inviting glow in the darkness. She wears a pink bra and white pants. She runs her fingers through her hair. The cat moves, uneasy now, and stretches out claws again. She turns slightly, her arms behind her back to release the clasp of her bra which slides down her arms and to the floor. Her nipples stand out a delicious mocha against her pale skin and the cat shuffles again, disturbed and uncomfortable.

She stretches upwards, pulls the jumper above her head and I stare at her, stood there in pants, her arms stretched high over her head, her back arched backward and her perfect body pouts outward just for me and my camera. I am warm and sweating. I can hear myself breathing and my legs are twisted together, tight and tense, and I can feel the cat's claws deep in my thigh.

My trousers are suddenly tight around my crotch. The cat is standing now, straddling my aching thighs, its claws deep. 9987, Santino, Scarlett pulls the jumper down and I realise with horror what is happening as a shudder passes up my legs and I explode into my trousers.

I feel sick.

I feel dirty and perverted looking at her while I'm like this. I try to stand but the cat won't move. I push it hard and feel claws in my forearm, feel them cut downward toward my wrist. I stand, the cat drops to the ground and bounds away beneath the trees.

I turn off the camera and collect my things. It is only as I shuffle down the hill and home that I notice the street lights are dribbling, moving, no longer stationary, and I feel tears run down my cheeks.

XXVI

I am wearing a jumper despite the sun and already regret coming into the city proper. My arm still hurts, the rough jumper rubs painfully against the scratches, which run in neat parallel lines from elbow to palm of my left arm. I have no choice but to wear last night's trousers, my other pair is still at Mam's, and everyone I pass seems to stare at my crotch.

I feel dirty.

From the main bus stop I head through the shopping centre and up Stall Street. At night from time to time, but mainly at dusk, I love to stroll these streets. Today I look up at the Georgian facades, at the faux Roman pillars and try to feel the cobbles and the paving stones beneath my feet. Stall Street is busy and the pedestrian throng intensifies as I move uphill on to Union Street. I pass the stalls and ignore the banter. Whenever I can I look up, not out. Whenever I can I ignore the gaudy shop fronts, I try not to notice the huge sale posters in the windows and the ultra-hip mannequins. I do my best to shut out the ringing of mobile phones and the off-key plucking of the buskers and instead I look up. The high street is beautiful in the mornings, when the streets are quiet and you can stroll for hours with your thoughts and the cool breeze and the memories the buildings exude. At sunrise the city is beautiful, but by sun up: a whore.

I am jostled by a troupe of children spluttering French and infecting the Abbey, clogging up the Pump Room, and I shuffle through. One child, level with my waist, points and laughs and sprays forth something I don't understand but points again and I move my hands to my sullied crotch and move on faster.

I stand and enjoy the archway to the Central Arcade and try to collect my thoughts. The coloured glass, caressed between twisting iron branches, shatters the light as it passes and jagged colours lie against the pavement past the archway but no one seems to notice. Instead a woman passes and glances at my crotch stifling a smile. I breathe deep and smell burgers and fried onions. A clipboard has accosted me; it is attached to a person who asks me to donate to a soil awareness charity. I make the mistake of not leaving, of not instantly turning my back and running as fast as my stained trousers will allow. By the time I leave the clipboard has a signature and a promise of a standing order. As I pass my bank I remind myself to cancel the standing order as soon as possible. I see a shop with a sign reading 'Huge Reductions Inside' and so in I go.

The shop is surprisingly dark and hot and already I wish I'd held out a little longer for somewhere else. Everything looks brown or grey or faded green. Music is playing, a heavy bass beat that makes the sweaty air pulse. I push through the students, push past the tourists and in my wake I hear laughter. The shop is enormous and I press deeper and deeper into the bowels looking for jeans to replace my old soiled pair. The heart of the store is all grease-stained denim and tight T-shirts and I am acutely aware of my stomach pinching tight against my belt beneath my jumper. I am dripping. I wipe my forehead and leave a dirty smear across my sleeve. My armpits are sodden and I feel perspiration dribbling down my back.

From the darkness and the denim a woman appears, her teeth sparkling white against in the half light, she blinds me with a smile and says: 'Hi, my name is Jenni, with an "i", and I'm here to help you.'

I frown. 'Jenni with an "i"?' I say. 'Not a "y"?'

She shakes her head, still smiling,

'No,' she says. 'An "i". What can I help you with today?' Jenni with an 'i' continues to smile and I have to look away, worried for my retinas.

'I need new jeans' I say. 'These are … old.' Jenni with an 'i' nods, her beam briefly illuminates the crotch of my jeans and I flinch away. She turns, and is gone.

This far in the shop is now ridiculously dark. I flail around feeling the sweat in my boxer shorts, my hair plastered to my cheeks, heavy and wet. I pass clothes hanging on racks, which steam gently in the hot air. Jenni with an 'i' has gone, lost in the clothes and mannequins and noise and students and tourists. I am struggling to breathe and turn to search for an exit.

From behind a display of ties I can see a faint haze which could be sunlight and wade toward it, my breath dribbling down my chin. I reach the ties and I stop, suddenly caught in a spotlight.

'There you are, silly!' says a voice and I turn to see Jenni with an 'i' beaming at me, two pairs of jeans draped over her arm. 'You're thirty waist, about thirty leg, right?' She turns off her smile for a minute to scowl at another salesgirl hovering nearby. She growls, flexes her claws. The interloper leaves, quickly, disappearing into the bowels of this high-street hellhole. The light is on because Jenni with an 'i' is grinning again. She moves closer.

'Which is the cheapest?' I say and gesture toward the jeans on her arm. She holds the bottom pair out to me and I see movement behind her eyes. Before she starts to speak I take the jeans. 'Thank you for your help' I say and I head fast toward daylight hoping there is a till by the door.

Paid for and bagged, the jeans and I are about to leave, but I turn in time to see a young man, tall and bearded with a slightly comical nose, stop short in the aisle. He stares ahead, eyes wide, caught in the head-lights as Jenni with an 'i' approaches. He sees her and turns, but it is too late. Behind him I spot the interloper, she glides through the clothing racks, her progress marked by a slight parting in the undergrowth. She appears at his side. I hear a whispered 'Clever girl' and he is gone, dragged down into the casual wear. I slip quietly out the front door and on to the high street.

Quickly I head on to Bridge Street and around to the Newmarket. On my left is my bus stop, on my right a pub. I look again at my soiled trousers and head into the pub. Inside is cool and quiet with a comfy-looking settee by the window and booths along the wall. I follow the signs to the toilets, which take me downstairs. The toilets are white and bright, my reflection pale and dirty, sweaty marks under my arms and down my back. I enter the single cubicle. Someone, presumably drunk, has sprayed urine in a wide arch from wall to wall and the floor is wet and sticky. I'm obviously not the first to change here; in one corner is a carefully folded blue shirt, a tie and a pair of black shoes, highly polished and placed neatly on top of the shirt.

I pull off my soiled jeans and change into the stiff new ones, pulling of labels and stickers as I go. There is no where to put my old jeans so I fold them and add them tidily to the pile in the corner, carefully placing them underneath the shoes already there. I look down. Jenni with an 'i' is clearly an imbecile. My jeans hang loose around my waist, my belt folding the stiff denim into my waist. The legs are too short. A good three inches too short. I look sadly at my socks, which show beneath the cuffs. On the floor my soiled jeans calmly soak up a puddle of drunken piss. Desperate I pull up my socks to try and hide my pale ankles and I head back upstairs where, not wanting to be rude, I order a lemonade and sit on the comfy settee awaiting the bus. I cross my legs and reveal my shins.

The bus is late and I sit and suffer a cackle of middle-aged women who find my trousers hilarious. At last, though, an orange double-length bus arrives and I step outside. I wait for traffic to file past, patient as the bus queue is a long one, and I watch the passengers stand and file off. A romp of students fight each other for space, laughing and pushing; a wholly modern family, mother and children, cling tightly for support, and at the end of the queue, quiet and still, is 7451, Algarry, Neville.

Very calm, very cool, he steps off the bus and heads across the end of the bridge toward the Podium. I stand for a moment and watch him go. I glance toward the bus, I think about home, about food and shelter, but I know I

121

have a duty and so I follow. I cross the street and fall in behind him. I follow and I tell her I'm doing it for love, because I'm sorry, because I've let her down.

We pass quickly through the Podium and my stomach pangs as the Chinese buffet smell invades my nostrils, but I must go on, and so I follow. 7451, Algarry, Neville moves confidently on long graceful legs while I waddle after him, through the main doors, past the flower stalls and right on to the loop road. Loop is quiet, the streets around me bustle, bursting with shoppers, with a drift of pensioners queuing outside the Post Office. I hold back until he reaches the exit to the Podium car park before following.

I am excited. I admit it. This may be for love but it's also for me and I run through scenes in my head, practise Eastwood quips, train De Niro-like senses on the terrain, tense and ready. 7451, Algarry, Neville is strolling casually through what the signposts call the Artisan Quarter, up toward Saracen Street. I follow and raise my hood so as to look inconspicuous, and press my finger to my ear, listening for intel from other agents. None arrives and 7451, Algarry, Neville steps off the main street and heads right, toward the river.

At the corner I pause, my bag against a shop window, and peer carefully down the street. The road is cobbled, the buildings tall, stone-built like the rest, Georgian elegance as always, idyllic almost but for the blacked-out windows and neon red sign of Sven's Adult Toy Store. 7451, Algarry, Neville gives a quick look up the street. I hold my hand to my ear as if on the phone, I stare at the pavement, I move my lips. I look casual. 7451, Algarry, Neville, steps inside.

I've never been in a place like this before but I can't help thinking it's vaguely familiar. The neon outside is just the beginning, inside it is everywhere. Across the walls the neon runs in vertical strips every metre or so and in between the neon strips are huge display cases, wall mounted and protected by black wire meshing. The shop floor is all dirty films. I enter in the 'Classics' section. In front I can see 'Amateur' and beyond that is 'Celeb Sex Tapes'. 7451, Algarry, Neville is browsing one of the wall displays by the counter. I move toward the back of the store, past 'Girl on Girl' and 'Anal' until I reach the back wall. Behind me is a display case full of leather. It all looks painful, strange devices with straps and I can't work out what body part they would fit on to. A mannequin head wears a hideous-looking black leather mask, two tiny eye holes and a zipped-up mouth. Another head sports a headband, a huge red penis attached to the front. The mannequin head is smiling.

7451, Algarry, Neville calls the clerk over and points out some items. The neon makes it difficult to see what is in the display case. The clerk moves between me and 7451, Algarry, Neville and opens the case. I can't see, the clerk is between me and him, and the clerk is too wide to see around. 7451, Algarry, Neville nods and laughs and accompanies the clerk to the desk. He pays and turns to go. I turn around and crouch down a little to disguise my height. I make out something on the lower shelves has caught my interest and bend over so he cannot see me. I hear the bell on the door ring and the door closes.

From the counter I hear: 'Hey! You better not be playing with yourself over there!' I stand up and flush red. My

123

hood is still up and I push it back so I can cool off.

The clerk calls again: 'You found something you like you buy it and take it home. I've got no private booths, mate.' I look at the shelves in front of me. I look into the eyes of a man who stares out from the cover, his hair is slicked back, his body tanned and muscular and he stands naked beneath the words *Vicars and Bishops*. The man's waist is obscured by another man, equally muscular, kneeling at his feet and holding his penis. The second man wears a mitre. I stumble backward and come face to face with two men bent over a table and the words *Chef's Special Meat Balls* on the cover. I look up at the sign above the shelves: 'Man-on-Man Action', it reads.

I shuffle quickly to the display case 7451, Algarry, Neville was looking at. Handcuffs, leather straps, things that could be gags – one of those ball gags from Pulp Fiction. Restraints.

'Excuse me,' I call to the clerk. 'Excuse me, but the gentlemen who just left ...' The clerk makes a noise that could be 'yes' and I ask: 'What did he buy?' The clerk looks up from his magazine. He is short, tubby. Long blonde hair hangs down over his face. He leans against the counter and sips his coffee.

'Do you have a membership card?' he asks. I shake my head. He leans forward and smiles. I smile back. 'Then fuck right off,' he says, and goes back to his magazine. I look again at the handcuffs, look again at the ball gag, I glance back toward the strange mask and the frightening head gear against the back wall and I leave.

Outside is bright and I blink at the light, stumbling across the cobbles. I walk into a brood of mothers, each pushing a pram, leaving a house opposite. Each of them looks at me. Each of them curls her lips. Each of them dismisses me and strolls away. I worry about the handcuffs and wonder how much time she has left. I watch the mothers go and, once safely out of sight, I skulk away in my ridiculous trousers.

XXVII

The shop is ridiculously busy and I am finding it hard to concentrate. In the Disney section a nest of sweating children squabble over Pixar releases and *Barbie and Ken's Cracked Nuts*. In Alphabetical DVD a middle-aged couple wander around picking up titles seemingly at random and then replacing them further round the aisles. A drunken man in a sailor's hat and floral shorts tries to chat up a woman with huge breasts and sagging jowls. Meanwhile in my new Asian Cinema section five boys examine the Anime titles for suggestions of nudity. Behind the velvet curtain is a stag party and whoops and jeers are farted forth at irregular intervals. By the door, by New Releases, are eight couples. Sixteen pairs of hands grabbing and depositing films in a quest to find one to bind them all, one to rule them all, and they are making a mess as they go. It is almost lunchtime and my stomach rumbles. I am too busy to sip my coffee and instead gulp it furiously between customers and my tongue swells with every burning dose.

Outside is worse. Outside is the problem. Outside is a camera crew, is a police van and three squad cars. Outside is a pavement taped off from the Spar to the front of the shop and a WPC who is letting people into the shop but not back out again. On the radio I hear the newscaster say that the police are busy staging a re-enactment of the missing boy's last known movements and any potential witnesses should make their way to Moorlands Road.

The WPC squeezes in another three customers, a man and two women, one on each arm, him in suit and shirt, his collar open and his collarbone glinting with chunky gold, them in skirts that hide nothing and tops cut down to their stomachs. One girl turns to whisper in his ear and I see one pink buttock poke from her skirt.

The crowd seems to part as they glide toward the counter. In their wake they leave open mouths and angry girlfriends, sulking wives and small boys flushing red. He reaches the counter and hands over his membership card. I am not surprised the system calls him 007, Moore, Sean.

He has a film reserved. He says, 'Is it ready?'

I nod and say, 'Yes, of course,' and I try to look at him, or the screen or the film I hand over, anything but the girls on each arm.

At the door my bouncer, the WPC, lets them leave, the sailor tries to follow but the officer won't let him. He sulks back to the boobs and jowls woman in Thriller and Horror. The couple in Alphabetical DVDs continue to work hard destroying my display, the octuplet in New Releases is splintering into rival factions, the stag party behind the velvet curtain seems to have found a winner and emerge, triumphant, barging an elderly couple aside as the group blunders toward the counter.

'Here,' slurs one of them, thrusting a membership card and a film at me. The party staggers for the door brandishing *Slippery When Wet* at their head like a bowsprit, scooping up the sailor as they go. At the doorway the bouncer suffers. 'Wayhey! A stripper! Nice one, lads!' She scowls and lets them through.

Through the din floats a voice calling for information, it crackles and buzzes and pleads for people to come forward and the WPC releases her captives. The shop pours out on to the street, blinking and cowering in the sunlight. I feel a breeze and one lonely crisp packet swirls happily around my deserted shop. I sigh and start to reorganise.

Outside the problem begins to wind down. The camera crew packs away and with it go most of the potential witnesses. The tape comes down and disappears, two small boys heading fast for the alley at the end of the road. The police regroup and a new assault begins. Two to the Spar next door, two to the dry cleaners across the road, a couple more off toward the residential streets. Piece by piece I put my store back together again.

It is almost three and I am now starving but Anna is sick again, or dying perhaps, and so I'm stuck here until five when Percy will relieve me. I am almost finished replacing New Releases and am about ready to close and nip next door when two PCs stoop through my doorway, all helmets and body armour and shiny bits of steel.

'Good evening, Sir,' says one, who I recognise as 1765, Bradshaw, Mark. 'How are you this evening?'

1765, Bradshaw, Mark, or Police Constable 8814, Mark Bradshaw as he is this afternoon asks if I would mind helping them with their enquiries. I ask if he can wait here two seconds while I run next door and get a sandwich. He blinks, confused, and I ask again. He nods stiffly and off I go.

My sandwich is awful. Soggy bread and dry chicken. I search in vain for the promised mayonnaise and am forced to admit that the smear of crusty white across one slice is all I'm getting. Police Constable 8814, Mark Bradshaw is showing me a photograph.

'Have you seen this boy before?' he asks. I nod and swallow and cringe and PC Bradshaw's eyes light up and he asks, 'When?' I reach for my coffee, which is now only warm but tastes infinitely better than my sandwich. I brush off my hands and bin the sandwich. I am no longer hungry.

'On the front of the paper a few days ago,' I say. PC Bradshaw doesn't accept this as an accurate answer and frowns at me. His partner, the embryo officerette from the other night, smirks and I find him all too easy to dislike.

PC Bradshaw puts on his best schoolmaster's voice and tries again. 'Apart from in the paper, or on the television, have you seen this boy?' I look again at the snotty little child, at the ice cream stains and sinister grin.

I am pleased to tell Police Constable 8814, Mark Bradshaw that: 'No, I have not.' PC Bradshaw lays the photo on the counter, swivels the child until he faces me and leans back against the fridge. The fridge is my leaning spot and once again I try to get comfortable against the CCTV equipment and once again fail. The recently conceived, the positively post orgasmic officerette leans against the door frame.

Police Constable 8814, Mark Bradshaw isn't looking at me. He is looking at the CCTV screen behind me while he talks to me.

'On Saturday,' he is speaking slowly again so the idiot babe behind can follow. 'On Saturday two weeks ago this boy left home to visit a friend, a friend he was due to stay with until Tuesday. He did not arrive.' He pauses and I look to Officer Infant School behind him to make sure he's still with us. PC Bradshaw is still watching the CCTV screen and continues. 'The friend he was visiting says he received a phone call around seven thirty from the missing boy who was calling to tell him he was going to rent a film.' I glance back to the photograph.

'How old is he?' I ask.

'Nine.' This from boy wonder by the door.

'Friend of yours, is he?' I ask and he frowns, confused. 'Nine,' I say. 'Well he couldn't rent anyway, not without an adult.'

PC Bradshaw is no longer looking at the CCTV screen; instead he is reading the labels on the CCTV tapes.

'Are you absolutely sure you have never seen this boy, Sir?' he asks. I nod. He stands and marches toward me. I shrink back, his armour smells of sweat and smoke, he leans across me and runs his finger across the spines of the tapes. He stops on the one labelled 'twenty-fifth'. He leans back against the counter, his knees are almost touching mine, and proximity makes me uncomfortable. I squirm a little and try to retreat.

'How long do you keep these tapes?' he asks and I tell him a month, we tape over the old ones as we go. He reaches up and rests his arm lightly on the tape labelled 'twenty-fifth'.

'Can I borrow this, Sir?' he asks and I shake my head a little. 'Sir?' he says and the schoolmaster tone is gone. 'Sir, it could be very useful to the investigation. Perhaps he came in when you were busy; maybe it shows what happened to him.'

I shake my head and tell him: 'No, I'm very observant.' I tell him, 'I would have seen him. Not much gets past me.' I add and wink so he knows I'm still after 7451, Algarry, Neville, so he knows we're on the same side.

PC Bradshaw leans down toward me. The buzzer on the door goes and we all look up to see 7451, Algarry, Neville slide through the door. He stops when he sees us. He stares at us. We stare at him, PC Bradshaw leaning toward me, me cowering against the bench, the boy leaning bored against the door frame. I open my mouth and start to point but by the time my finger is angled I'm pointing at empty space. 7451, Algarry, Neville is gone. I sigh.

'Can we take the tape?' PC Bradshaw asks and I almost ask for his membership. Instead I say something like: 'I'll have to check with Head Office.' PC Bradshaw nods.

'See that you do, Sir,' he says and smiles at me. He stands up, steps back and offers his hand into which I drop my damp limp palm. He shakes it, holds it tight for a second and says, 'See that you do Sir, I don't want to return with a warrant.' He smiles again and they are gone and the shop is quiet.

I sigh and get back to work. I sigh and I hoover. I sigh and I sip my coffee and later, as the sun begins to set, I sit and I watch the drunk kids in the front porchway. As always she looks at me, as always I stare back, and once again I watch her mascara dribble down her cheek.

XXVIII

It's Monday and no one answers from Head Office. I pick up the phone and dial. It rings and rings and rings and ...

'Hello, you're through to Total Rental Ltd. I'm sorry there is no one available to take your call.' A machine rattles off options, gives it to me straight: call back or give up. I hang up. I stare at the CCTV tapes. I think hard about the night in question but all I can remember is rain, is a flash of lightning, is a woman skipping through the rain. I pick up the phone and run my finger down the late list. The list is multi-coloured and tells me everything I need to know. 904, Floss, Candy has had *Deep Impact* for four days. 7721, Batt, Amy has *Crabs* and it is a week late. I have no idea why she'd want it that long. I dial the number and I give it to them straight, bring them back or we'll give them up. Out of habit I call Mr Johnson.

'Mr Johnson,' I say.

I hear a cautious, 'Yes?'

'Mr Johnson,' I say. 'It's Total Rental you Total Wanker ...' I hear dial tone. I smile and sip my coffee. I dial Head Office again and the robot tells me where to go. I sigh and sip my coffee and start organising.

Later, as a pale October sun seeps into the clouds, I

stand on the front porchway and watch commuters commute, watch students stude and watch the pensioners pension about. I sip my coffee and stand on the broken tiles and worry about the peeling paint on the window frames. I worry about losing more company property to the police. I worry about the kettle, which makes a strange rattling sound now as it boils. I sweep the front porchway: takeaway cartons, cider bottles, a kebab, a T-shirt and one split condom which oozes and sticks. I gag. I get the mop.

Percy arrives a little before two and I leave before he has the chance to open his mouth. Important business, I say as I breeze out the door. I have hidden the coffee behind the cleaning materials. I am confident it will remain hidden. On the corner I catch the bus into town and head for the train station.

Head Office squats on an industrial estate in Southwood, and so that is where I go. The bus from Tempest Means Station meanders through slums and terraces and shanty towns and I remember how much I hate this pestilent twin to my own home city. At one stop I stare down a side street and search in vain for windows. Each rotting terrace, bleeding red brick and clotting mould, is boarded up. The wood is damp, is dirty, is decorated with alien scrawls, with grinning devils, with throbbing, spraying penises. An old couple cling together for support and safety and climb on the bus. They smile at me as they pass but I shake my head. I'm not getting involved. No help here. An off-licence blazes neon on to the street and a bookies sports an excited crowd but the barbers is whitewashed out, is almost gone. The greengrocers has rotted away, the butchers is a stinking corpse. At another stop an Asian family shuffle on to the bus and look at nothing but each other. They huddle close, backs to the rest of us, and from the back of the bus comes a drunken 'Fuckin' chinks!' The Asian family travel one stop, about a hundred yards, and disembark. I stare out the front window and the road goes on forever. Flashing neon, smouldering shop fronts, damp and dirty boards holding up the streets. I hate this city.

I get off the bus on a crossroads. A pound shop sparkles opposite me, all glitter and show. Another off-licence grins on to the street behind me. Across the road is a pub with yellowed window panes and heavy red curtains pulled tight against the outside world, which seems a perfectly sensible reaction. I cross the road and walk the hundred yards or so to the estate.

I sit on an uncomfortable sofa in the reception area. I sit on an uncomfortable sofa, which I first had to turn the right way up, in the reception area. I sit on an uncomfortable sofa, which I first had to turn the right way up, in a deserted reception area. I look around and can't shake the feeling I've seen this somewhere before, on a smaller screen than this. I think of Danny Boyle and count twenty-eight days backwards.

I sit on an uncomfortable sofa and around me is debris. The floor is covered with papers, invoices, receipts, memos, magazines, newspapers, some crumpled, some flat. All strewn across the reception. Some have footprints. Some have stains. I look down and between my legs is a sheet of paper lying flat. On the top is the company logo and in heavy black lettering is written: Memo

134

to all staff. The memo is blank but across the whole page is a huge sweaty palm print, inky blank at the finger tips, yellowed at the palm.

I sit and wait patiently. The walls are empty but I see fresh-looking paint in neat rectangles at regular intervals across the walls. Behind the receptionist's desk, in big blue letters, is the company logo and beneath it someone has scrawled in red: 'Abandon hope all ye who enter her.' I frown at the poor spelling. From outside I hear a rumble and a flash makes the red scrawl sparkle and I hear the soft metallic scurrying of rain on corrugated iron. Next to the sofa is an upturned table, magazines fanning out toward the door. I pick up the closest and flick idly through *Escapes Abroad* and wait patiently for the receptionist.

I finish the magazine and still no one has arrived. I check my watch and it's almost four. For an awful moment I wonder if it's Sunday, if I've gotten myself confused again, but I remember putting out the New Releases this morning so it must be Monday. I right the table and place the *Escapes Abroad* on top. I fold my hands in my lap and stare again at the walls.

To my right is a door which I assume leads into the main offices. I've never been here before: my interview was conducted in my store by the Undead and a fat balding man who I can't really remember except that he smelled strongly of mint and sweat. I sniff but there is no trace of mint and I wonder if he has retired. He was fairly old, I remember. I shuffle a little on the sofa, trying to get comfortable. I twiddle my thumbs. I get bored. I stare out the small window and watch the rain patter against the streaky glass.

A phone is ringing and I start awake. The room is darker, everything grey and my eyes take a while to adjust so I stare into static and listen to a ringing phone. My back aches, as does my neck. I wonder when I last had a satisfying night's sleep. I wonder why I never feel tired. I listen to the phone ring and the static starts to clear.

The room is darker, everything greys and shadow and inky stains in corners. The receptionist's desk is still without a receptionist. I stand up and move to the desk. The phone is still ringing but the desk is without a phone. I frown. This is a strange sort of reception. I move around the desk to see if the phone is hidden behind but all I find is more scattered paper and more stains. Something dark and sticky drips from a drawer, which is locked. Dark is the colour because the world is black and white. Above me the words Total Rental are now in a dark grey and beneath is just wall, the scrawl no longer there. The phone still rings.

The door to the main offices isn't locked but the door doesn't open easily and I remember coming home from holiday and pushing through a week's worth of post. All of them bills, all of them my father's. I push the door open and it is just more paper. The corridor is long and grey and at the end is an open window. I shuffle through the drift of scrap paper into the corridor proper. The rain still chatters against the roof and the window breathes a cold draught. The papers rustle and the phone still rings.

I call out: 'Hello?' but get no answer. I turn to find a light switch. I'm not stupid. The corridor is long and sinister and if I can avoid it I'm not walking down it dark. I sigh and realise how poor a horror this would make. I'm bored and I'm in it. The lights sputter awake. I wonder if they will flicker to add a bit of atmosphere. They glow pale and but fail to add any colour. Beneath the light switch is a coffee machine. The display smiles blue at me and I press for black without sugar.

I receive black without sugar but doubt very much it is coffee. I sip it anyway. The phone still rings. At the end of the corridor is an open door and the ringing seems to be bouncing forth from somewhere inside. I shuffle onward, through the papers. The other offices are equally empty. I stare through portholes in doors as I pass. Office after office, all empty, all grey. Everywhere is scattered paper, discarded memos, unread newspapers. The black with sugar is awful but hot and I sip it carefully as I go.

The phone rings and the office at the end of the corridor is in colour. I creep around the corner and stand in the doorway. A *Kill Bill* poster is yellow and huge against the side wall. Opposite smiles Ben Stiller and Bobby De Niro. An orange Dustin Hoffman has his arm around Barbra Streisand. They are almost life size and I am a little unsettled by Barbra. The office is neat and tidy. Papers are piled in an outbox. The inbox is empty. On the desk are family photos. Children smile, gardens are a luscious green. A Christmas is red and warm and all wrapped up in scarves and mittens. In one photo is a couple. He stands big and fat and bald and has arm around a tiny skinny woman who grins a huge red-lipped grin and I recognise her as my Area Manager before she died.

The phone is red and I pick it up. 'Hello?' I say. The line is bad, the static is back, but in my ears this time because I can hardly hear. I hear a woman laugh, but it's not funny because she sounds angry and she gets louder. I hear a sharp crack and the laughter stops. A sob. Wet and bubbling and repeated again and again. She cries.

'Hello?' I say. 'Are you alright?' The phone goes dead. I pour my black without sugar into a potted plant on the desk of my deceased Area Manager. I'll try calling again tomorrow. I move out from behind the desk, hold the side of the door ready to swing it shut behind me and stare, wide eyed, at bloody footprints on the dirty carpet and sticky red fingers entwined in mine.

From down the corridor a door slams, papers swirl in the wind and I rush out from the office to see nothing. Paper flutters, the black machine cries blue light into the hallway. And finally I know how my Area Manager died. And I know who did it.

XXIX

The bus from the train station goes past home and continues up the hill. I sit and stare out the window and the cool night and the stone houses which blush orange in the street lights. The streets up here are tree-lined. I think this makes them Avenues. Front gardens with hedges give in to autumn fashion and dress in browns and gold. Home feels small and cramped and I don't want that. The bus is huge and bright and clean, and outside are the terraces, which always feel wide and open and safe. I pass the school and don't get off. At the bus stop an old couple get on. They catch my eye and offer a nervous little half wave. I smile and wave back, polite as always.

I decide not to worry about Head Office. They know what they are doing, they own the company. I decide not to worry too much about 7451, Algarry, Neville either. He is no longer on the late list and seems to be leaving 9987, Santino, Scarlett alone at last. Besides, I suspect seeing me with the police has scared 7451, Algarry, Neville off. Tomorrow I will ring the police station again and find out for definite if they have found any evidence on the DVD yet and direct them to my company offices to check the doors.

As the bus approaches the top of the hill the roads

widen. The houses get bigger but I notice red brick creeping into the terraces. By the time we crest and the road flattens off the houses are semi-detached and huge and red brick and tile. I get off at a set of traffic lights and wait patiently to cross.

The sign above me reads: Welcome to the Royal University Hospital. And underneath is sprayed in thick dribbling red: 'Abandon hope, all ye who enter her.' I wander forward toward the main entrance. The car park is huge with trees dotted here and there and I imagine it to be quite pleasant in the summer. There are plenty of grassy areas and park benches sit beneath trees and street lights. A new glass building sprouts from the grass in front of me and sweeps upward toward the main entrance at the end of the driveway. I glance at the inside as I pass and see rows of empty tables. At the far end of the glass building is a shutter and I assume that by day this is the restaurant.

The doors sigh open as I approach and inside is clean and bright. The floor shines a little, fluorescent lights catching pools not yet recovered from a mopping. The seats are chrome and I can smell bleach and soap and disinfectant, which is what you want from a hospital. On the news I saw a hospital which had bags of rubbish in the corridors and vomit on the seats. This one sparkles under its bright white lights. The reception is unmanned, as receptions tend to be, and so, again, I sit quietly and wait.

I sit and wait and stare. After a while I decide that it's not so much a room I'm in but a space. Corridors lead off to the left and the right. At the far end are some lifts. By the main entrance is another shutter, above it reads:

Friends of the Trust Gift Shop. I wonder what sort of souvenirs they sell. I wonder how many buy them. The reception is a large ring-like desk in the centre. Above it are television screens, turned off, and on the desk are computers and phones. Apart from my tapping feet and the buzzing lights I can't hear anything. My stomach rumbles and it sounds unnaturally loud. I wait.

From one corridor I hear a whirl approach. It swishes and whines and I stare at the corridor and listen to it shuffling ever closer. At the entrance to the corridor one of the lights begins to flicker and I can hear the pop pop pop of the struggling bulb. The swishing is louder and the light flickers and fails to convince anyone it's winning the battle.

From the flicking, popping, whining corridor a fat, round, Indian-looking woman approaches sat atop a swishing, whirling, cleaning sort of machine. I watch, bored, as she looks up, tuts, and hits the light with a mop. The light dies and she tuts again.

'Excuse me,' I say. 'I don't suppose you know where the receptionist is, do you?' She jumps, startled, and waddles over.

'Well, they're not here now, are they?' She is tiny and round and definitely Indian but strangely Welsh. 'They gone home, haven't they?' I sniff and blow air out my cheeks. My hands are together in my lap and I drum my fingers together. The round little Indian woman looks at me. She tries to tilt her head but has no neck so has to lean instead.

'You could try A and E,' she says and points to the corridor still lit. 'Down that way, there is usually someone there all night.' She smiles and rocks upright. I smile back and thank her. The corridor is long and bright and I move quickly past signs that make no sense. Behind me is a swishing and whirling and an occasional tut.

A and E is busy.

I emerge from the corridor to the opening scene of *Saving Private Ryan*. From the sliding double doors leading to the street a bloat of huge women in leotards is steaming toward the front desk. The girl behind the desk has wide eyes and I watch while she tries to sink into the seat. The women vary, some in leopard print, some in zebra stripes. One has a tail. They hold a woman in the middle, keeping her upright: she wears cat's ears and a black leotard. A sash is tight across her chest and reads: Bride to Be. They reach the desk and the Bride to Be crashes heavily against the table edge. She stares blankly toward the receptionist, grins lopsidedly and vomits across the keyboard.

By the door a father sits with his child, who has his finger trapped in a toy car. Behind them a couple in pyjamas sit huddled close. He looks unhappy and I can see she holds a bloody rag to his groin. Across the waiting room are a collection of bleeding limbs, swollen glands, broken bones and misshapen heads. I think quickly of the waiting room from *Beetlejuice* and find an empty seat in a far, dark corner.

A man staggers through the double doors and up to reception. He is clutching his stomach. The receptionist is busy mopping up the Kitten Bride's vomit and watches him wearily. He winces and wraps his arms around across his stomach. The receptionist holds out a bucket but the man shakes his head.

'I am so sorry to bother you all,' he says. He is wearing

a suit, pinstriped and pressed. His shoe heels sparkle but his toes seem dulled, like he'd spilled something that dried crisp and sticky. 'I know you are very busy, but might I trouble someone to have a quick look at this for me?' He takes his hands away from his stomach and even from here I can see his shirt is ruined. He stretches out his arms, his cuffs stained red and brown. The receptionist holds up her bucket and I hear wet slops.

Two nurses appear at either side of the man who collapses gratefully into their arms. His stomach is red and black, the skin white, the shirt pink striped and heavily stained with blood. Something slippery looking and fatty dangles from the wound and a nurse tries to push it back in. The man smiles weakly.

'Bit of a tiff with the missus, is all,' he says and is rushed away.

The child with the car for a finger is suddenly very pale and stares at the blood which congeals slowly on the tiled floor at his feet. His father reads a magazine. The man in pyjamas starts to cry and is held tight by the woman. I notice a coffee machine and weave my way toward it.

I sit and watch and sip my coffee, which I must say isn't too bad. The receptionist types slowly, waiting for the sticky bile to release each key before moving on to the next. Someone brings her a steaming cup and she looks so happy I think she is about to cry. A door opens and a man in a white coat with a clipboard appears. The waiting room is suddenly quiet as he reads out a name. The winner leaps in the air, picks up his finger and dances through the door after the doctor. The losers sit and seethe and the cries of pain and moans get louder.

From time to time a nurse appears to rescue a patient. From time to time the doors spurt forth a horror or a joke, blood and superglue mingle on the floor and a miserable bearded man appears and runs a dirty wet mop over the floor. From time to time I brave the slippery floor and visit the coffee machine. The man in pyjamas is carried away. The child is freed from the car. A man with his tongue trapped in a bottle is wheeled into a room. A woman with a sheet over her face is wheeled out. A nurse smiles at a small boy, a doctor laughs when he sees an old friend with a broken jaw. I sit and sulk and sip my coffee and wait for 9987, Santino, Scarlett, who is yet to make an appearance.

My pockets are empty and so I sit and look as miserable and desperate as the rest. They watch the doctors anxiously; I watch the nurses and scan the floor for loose change. A patient arrives soaking wet and I realise it is raining again. He holds up his hand, which is fused to a screwdriver, the red handle is blackened and a fatty yellow coating is over everything. I hear a distant rumble and the night flashes white not blue.

I sigh and close my eyes and the waiting room goes quiet.

When I finally open them again the place looks brighter, the lights blaze a brilliant clean white, the receptionist is flushed pink, her hair loose and waving. On the floor the blood glistens and sparkles and standing in reception is a nurse in a blue dress, collar and sleeves trimmed with a bright white. I see lips moving, people stagger in slow motion, I see mouths twisted in moans of pain but I hear nothing. Nothing.

Nothing and then the nurse in blue says: 'Mr Arnold?' and I smile at 9987, Santino, Scarlett.

I blink and the scene is gone, blood and sweat and moans and a small girl cries as its mother lies unconscious on a stretcher. 9987, Santino, Scarlett leans down and pats Mr Arnold's knee, flashes a smile and wheels him away. I forget about the coffee and sit and stare and wait.

When she returns she looks angry, which is new and exciting. I've never seen this and stare and smile and love every second. She pouts, her nose crinkles, her eyes wrinkle and she stands with hands on hips talking to the receptionist. When she turns to go I see a bright bloody handprint across her buttock and want to find it funny but instead I'm looking angrily to see if Mr Arnold has returned.

The night wears on. The blood is cleaned and seeps back up through the cracks in the tile. I go without coffee and watch her work. A woman is wheeled in with a blanket over her legs by two laughing paramedics. At the desk they lift the blanket for the receptionist to see, who joins in the joke.

I watch 9987, Santino, Scarlett work, I watch her bloodstained bum wiggle from patient to patient. Sometime around sunrise she appears for the last time and not long after I find myself in bed and I dream of a peach which bleeds when I bite it.

XXX

Head Office are still away on their break and the late list holds no surprises. The police weren't interested. I tried to explain the blood on the door frames, I mentioned by accident the blood on her buttocks, but the woman on the phone kept saying: 'I've been such a bad girl officer, you must, must punish me.'

I sip my coffee and settle into my evening shift. On the desk in front of me is a list of things to accomplish by the end of the night. Asian Cinema will stay, the Horror section needs a revamp, Comedy will be reorganised into The Good, The Bad and The Ugly, the New Releases into The Good, the Bad and the Remakes. The bottom of the list reads: Go to Spar for coffee and Ginger Nuts. I sip my coffee and cross out 'The Good' next to New Releases.

Already the sun is setting and the bats are out, swooping and screaming and dressed in bright green tracksuits. The street is flushed orange and I watch the red butts dance around outside. In the shop is a young woman wearing fishnet stockings and a long black coat. She surprises me by browsing Romantic Comedy. In Horror and Thriller are two small boys who become progressively more excited as they move upward through the age classifications. An old man frowns, confused by the how thin videos are these days, and asks one of the boys, who I assume is a grandchild, whether they will work in his video player at home.

Over by New Releases, in the area soon to be The Remakes, is a skulk of students arguing over whose debt-ridden credit card to use. Outside the cider appears and I look at my watch and see that they are starting a little early tonight. A siren sounds somewhere, a horn blares elsewhere, the kids have gone and could be anywhere and above me, above everyone, everywhere Jessica Alba dances in leather.

I sip my coffee and answer questions, offer judgements. I sip my coffee and smile and hold court and wish only for Ginger Nuts to make my night complete. No, I wish for Ginger Nuts and I wish for her, at home, to hold me when I get there. Above me, above all of us, everywhere Bruce makes an almost fatal error, puts the girl in danger and I feel my chest get heavy. The two boys have chosen *I Spit on Your Grave* and I manage to smile as I tell them to fuck off and come back when their balls drop. The old man is still flummoxed by the skinny cases and the boys run to him for help. He shakes his head, it's all too much for him, and he goes. The boys look longingly at the Horror and Thriller section, sigh and follow.

The woman in stockings and a long black coat is also wearing a black string vest and a pink bra. Her lips are painted blue over pink, her face is painted white but her neck is tanned and golden. She stands and sulks and hands over *You've Got Mail*. I change it over and she hands over a five pound note with a bored sweep of her wrist and a yawn. I wish her a good night and get a raised finger in return. Then she's gone.

Outside the night is almost too much for the street lighting and it hangs close to the bulbs. The kids are back, red pinpricks of light glowing hot, flaring up into lungs, prowling the dark space outside the shop. Next door I hear the shutters clatter down and the Spar closes. I check the time and I'm right: an early night tonight for the Spar. In the shop is a dog which sniffs the carpet in the centre aisle. Its owner passes through the Good Comedy, ignores the Bad, which I think is sensible, and carefully browses the Ugly. Outside the kids who come on my porchway are arguing. For once she is not crying, instead she bares teeth and spits and he steps back into the darkness. From the opposite side of the road, squatting by the dry cleaners, two red eyes raise smoky eyebrows which drift through an inconspicuously open car window.

The list in front of me catalogues my successes but the bottom still reads: coffee and Ginger Nuts. I sigh because the Spar is now closed and pull out a new sheet of paper on which I write tomorrow's adventures. The top of the list is: coffee and Ginger Nuts. The buzzer on the door goes and the dog leaves. Its owner looks up, opens the door and scurries after it. I boil the kettle and spoon the last of the coffee into my mug. I'm pouring when the buzzer goes again.

'I'll be two seconds,' I call up.

A familiar face appears around the corner saying, 'Don't worry, mate. It's only me.' I nod but don't smile and make a big show of throwing the coffee jar into the bin. Percy is still smiling,

'I don't suppose anyone has in been in looking for me?' I shake my head. 'Only they only had until today see, I was hoping they'd turn up.' I shrug and shake my head again. 'Oh well. I fancy a good Action film,' he says moving back on to the shop floor. 'Any recommendations?' he asks and I slump up the stairs to the counter.

Percy wanders from section to section running his finger across titles as he goes and I see the streaks appearing on the covers where his dirty fingers have been. I search for my duster but can't find it. He swings a plastic bag and reads the back of *Once Upon a Time in Mexico*, which is actually really good but I'm not telling him that. He is talking and I hold my head in my hands and breathe deep from the coffee before me. My stomach rumbles and I wonder when I last ate.

A case is slapped on to the counter and Percy grins.

'I'll have this one.' He says. 'I like a bit of Salma Hayek.' I change over the film and Percy taps against the desk. He is still smiling when I come back. He is always smiling. I hate him.

'Oh,' he says, and grins, which makes a nice change, 'I nearly forgot.' He reaches into his bag and pulls out a jar of coffee. 'Columbian,' he says. 'I've drank quite a bit of yours so I thought it only fair.' I eye up the jar and he rummages in the bag again. 'I got these too.' Ginger Nuts appear on the counter. I smile accidentally but Percy notices.

'Is that a smile?' he says. 'Wow, you must have had a good night.'

'What?' I say. 'What are you talking about?' but he doesn't get the chance to answer because at that moment the night explodes.

The buzzer on the door goes and a blazing light appears in the doorway, white light streaming from her dress. I blink and there is 9987, Santino, Scarlett, in her thin white dress. She smiles and waves and clutches her heavy pink sports bag. She pads quietly toward Romance. She is barefoot and damp little toe prints follow behind her. Percy has his mouth open but he isn't talking, he is staring, the same as me. He closes his mouth.

'Hi,' he says and I can't believe how brazen he is. He walks up to her, smiles and says, 'Hi.'

She smiles back. 'Hi,' she says. 'Can you help me? I'm in a bit of a hurry, I've got to be at work soon, and I'm looking for a Cary Grant film.' Her voice is soft and warm and melts in the air.

Percy's mockney cawing cuts straight through me. 'Yes, of course,' he says, 'Right this way, madam.' She laughs and follows and he starts taking films off the shelf and explaining the plot, the history, his clumsy attempts to give them contemporary meaning. I hate Percy. I try to look busy, try to get my mind off him. I reach under the counter for my duster and my fingers find a bag.

Cary Grant is contemporary only because his films are ripped off so often and his history is flawed because most of Grant's films were ripped off from the French. I hate him because he makes her laugh and she touches his arm and says: 'Thank you, you're so helpful.' The bag is slim and light, a Spar bag folded around something. I unwrap it.

At the counter she smiles at me and hands me the film, *An Affair to Remember*. I smile back and say, 'You know, the original is so much better.' She frowns a little and her top lip pokes out a little.

'The original?' she says and I nod and smile.

'Yeah, it's a French film – *Love Affair*, it's called. It's got ... oh, what's his name?' I click my fingers while I think and she blinks in time 'Boyer, Charles Boyer. He is so much better than Cary Grant,' I smile. 'I'll get that one for you instead,' I say and move away.

'Hold on,' she says and her nose is crinkled. 'Hold on, no, I want this one. I don't mind a recommendation but at least let me refuse.' She is pouting, being playful again. Teasing me.

I mutter something like: 'Oh don't be so silly ...' but she brushes it off and starts saying, 'You know, just because something is a remake, just because the original is French and remake is Hollywood, doesn't mean you can look down on it.' I try to say something clever, something to fix it, but it comes out like, 'But ... I ... I'm sorry ... I just ... Percy said ...' She folds her arms and Percy appears next to me and smiles.

'It's OK,' he says and takes the case from me.

I just stand stammering things like, 'I ... erm ... It's just that ... I thought ...'

'I'll sort this out for you,' Percy says and they smile at each other and she mouths 'Thank you' and I watch her lips and feel my eyes fill up. I look away, stare into the bag. She touches Percy's arm as she pays, smiles at him, ignores me completely and she leaves.

'Wow,' says Percy his mouth full of Ginger Nut. 'She's really pretty, eh?' and he nudges me. I am so angry I shake. I feel my nails digging into old scars and my fists are clenched tight. I take deep breaths but I feel my face get hot.

Percy looks at me and says, 'Are you OK?' and I shake my head and I feel tears on my cheeks. He spots the bag. 'Oh, hey, hey that's mine. Just leave it, OK?'

'Get out,' I say.

Percy looks confused. 'What?'

I tell him again to get out. 'Leave the biscuits,' I say, 'and fuck off.' Percy is stupid and says he doesn't understand. I say it louder: 'I said "Fuck off" Percy, now do it!'

'Now look,' he says, moving toward me. 'Don't over react, just give me the bag and I'll sort it, it's really not what you think.'

I yell, 'Sort it? Sort it? It's too late for that.'

Percy raises his hands and smiles and I want to kill him. I feel the sweat on my back, feel blood on my fingertips and Percy just smiles and keeps coming closer and says, 'Alright mate, you don't want to get involved in this, believe me. Just give me the bag and I'll go.' I can hardly see through tears and hardly speak because my chest is heaving.

'Just fuck off, Percy. You're fired, you're fucking fired.' Percy leaps forward, his fingers digging into my wrist, he tugs at the bag and I swing toward him. He claws at my fingers, desperate to release my fingers, and I want to punch him for what he did to her. He pulls again and this time I trip, my foot knocks against his and I fall. I hear a thud and a crack. Feel something hot and sticky on my face. The buzzer goes on the door and I collapse to the carpet, hardly able to breathe, the bag torn from my grasp.

I lie and sob and heave on the floor and I can't breathe my chest is so tight. I feel tears run across my cheeks, run off my chin and on to the carpet. My chest heaves again and I weep and cry out loud. Above me, above everyone, everywhere, a bloody splatter congeals on the corner of the fridge.

I hear the buzzer go and I sob and scream 'Fuck off,

Percy' and the buzzer goes again. I am alone and I cry
and I pull my knees to my chest and hold tight and rock
and sob and stain the carpet with tears and blood.

When I stand the CCTV monitor says it is almost twelve.
My face is swollen and red, my back and chest ache. My
jeans are bloodstained, smeared red where my bleeding
palms are held tight to my knees, where the blood drips
from my forehead. I don't care. I turn off the computer
and watch the drunk kids on the porchway. She cries and
won't look at me, his neck is crossed with swollen red
stripes and she presses a hand to the glass to reveal
broken nails.

XXXI

At first it doesn't register. I see the glass fly; I see the sparks and smell the smoke. I am vaguely aware of an ache in my fist and I can hear my footsteps crunch instead of shuffle but it doesn't really make any sense. I ignore it and it is only later as I drink coffee using my unfamiliar left hand that things start to come together.

I fear the television is beyond repair and it sits malignantly in its corner smouldering. The screen is cracked and broken, the middle missing and is showered across my living space floor. I sip my coffee and listen to my blood drip from my right fist on to my kitchenette floor. I inhale coffee and the plastic-tasting smoke. I cry into my mug.

My knuckles sting and I'm glad because I deserve it. I stare at the blood pooling on my tattered lino floor and I cry. I run through the conversation again. I remember Percy offering his recommendations. I remember watching him hand her titles and I remember hearing her laugh although I didn't hear what he said. I did nothing different; I don't understand how it went so badly. I offered recommendations, I explained why. It's not my fault

Percy was wrong. It's not my fault she made the wrong choice. Why get angry with me?

I sip my coffee and my right hand fumbles with the packet of Ginger Nuts. I try to squeeze a biscuit to the top of the packet but my fingers won't work properly, won't close properly, the blood makes the plastic packet slippery. The packet slithers out of my grasp and it falls with a crunch on to the bloodstained floor. I put down my coffee and have more success with my left hand. I chew a soggy, iron-tasting Ginger Nut and I notice they aren't McVitie's but store brand. I push another to the surface to examine the colour and it appears red and shiny, rust-coloured creases gleam in the moonlight.

I don't understand the difference. I did exactly the same as him. I check my watch and it is almost two. On top of the hill I know she will be working and wearing her blue dress with the white trim and looking forward to her film, which is wrong, because her choice was rubbish. I smile and imagine us arguing over which film to rent, over her slowly learning to appreciate fine art and us laughing over the time she thought Cary Grant was good. I smile and my knuckles ache.

I rest my coffee on the bench and move through the bedroom to my tiny bathroom. I turn on the light and stare at my fist. It's strange because it doesn't really hurt that much and it looks like it really should. I turn my hand palm down and try to stretch out my fingers. I can't; instead a shooting, stab wound of a shock runs down my whole arm and I feel my jaw tensing with the pain. I can see glass in the cuts and try to pick it out. My left hand is stupid and shakes and can't get a proper grip on anything. My fingers slide clumsily over the juicy mess of my knuckles. I need coffee.

I sip my coffee and I stare at the TV and I fear it is beyond repair. I fear that 9987, Santino, Scarlett will never be safe until she is in my arms. Percy won her over far too easily, she has no chance for happiness when someone like Percy can make her smile, can turn her against people like me. I hate Percy and the thought of him sends that same stabbing pain up my arm. The rhythmic drip drip drip beats faster and when I look down I realise my fist is clenched again. The pain becomes an ache becomes a reminder and I sip my coffee and brood and wonder if she knows how lucky she is that I intervened when I did. I wonder if she knows how close she was to being caught up in Percy. I try to sip my coffee but the cup rattles against my teeth.

I feel faint and so head to my tiny kitchenette in search of food. The cupboards are bare. Tomato sauce and mayonnaise in the fridge. I close my eyes and lean against the bench. My head is spinning, the room moves in opposite directions to my head and my chest feels tight. I rest my hands against the wall and the pain forces my eyes open, my mouth open, but there is no air in my lungs with which to scream. I stare at my mangled claw, at the fresh blood on the wall and smiling, sparkling glass nestled deep in muscle. I think I need an ambulance.

I laugh and am appalled at the sound but unable to stop and I'm thinking: *Yes, of course, an ambulance.* I grasp the phone with bloody fingers and grin and dial. Nine. I giggle a little. Nine. I can't believe I never thought of this. Nine. My hand shakes as I put the phone to my mouth.

'How my I direct your call?' comes a voice and I tell it I

have hurt my hand and need an ambulance.

'Can you walk?' it asks and I say yes. From somewhere behind the voice I hear a giggling laugh, a high-pitched 'Oooh, doctor, no' and the voice on the line says, 'Then walk to Minor Injuries.' And the line goes dead. I throw the phone at the TV and now the TV is certainly beyond repair because the phone is snug and warm and comfortable in the TV's plastic bowels. I am no longer laughing.

I slump against the wall. I reach for my coffee but my right hand is dying and instead of coffee in my hand I have coffee on my floor, which steams slightly and mingles with the blood in spirals. The mug handle lies, abandoned, but I retrieve the mug. I stare and sigh, wonder how long this will take to clean.

From below comes a banging and a faint, low 'What the fuck is going on up there?' From above comes a banging and a faint, low moan. I listen to my upstairs neighbours and I start to cry again.

I remember her in her dress, I remember her smiling at her patients, I remember her touching Mr Arnold on the knee as he is wheeled into another room. I remember her flashing him a smile. I remember the lingering touch she gave her patient. I remember her patient in a wheelchair. I figure it out. Epiphany. The loose ends fall into place. I get geared up, ready for the final scene. The hero saves the girl. I open drawers, throwing cutlery around my tiny kitchenette.

I am deeply embarrassed that all I have is a breadknife. The drawers are empty, my downstairs neighbour is threatening to call the police, and the best I can do for my Scarlett is a breadknife. My right hand is numb and stiff and my head feels light. I slump down into my chair, my head spinning, my chin against my chest.

I'm surprised at the pain. Before now I had thought nothing could be worse that the pain that ripped up my arm from my slashed knuckle, I thought nothing could be worse than Percy's smile and my Scarlett touching his arm. I am wrong. The knife is reasonably new but unfortunately rather blunt and my first attempt does very little. I scowl angrily at my slightly scuffed jeans and the bruise I can feel brewing beneath my as yet untouched skin. The jeans are too thick, designed as industrial wear. I slide them off, throw them into my bedroom and stand in my living space in pants and socks. I raise the knife higher and bring it down harder and a little blood spurts and the pain tenses my muscles and my shoulders arch upward and I shudder. A tiny slash in my skin and blood bubbles from a less than impressive nick. I aim carefully for the nick with my left hand but miss and a new bruise swells. My leg is numb and I squint through tears of pain. The blood refuses to come. I can still stand.

My left hand is stupid and cannot manage this simple task and I search my flat, desperate. I glance to the tiny kitchenette, to the door to my tiny bedroom, I run through the contents of my bathroom. I curse the electric razor my Mam bought me last Christmas. I stare at the wall and rub my painful thigh. I stare at the wall.

The knife tip fits neatly into the tiny hole in my thigh. I push, slowly, firmly and the serrated blade slips and catches against the slowly widening wound. The blood starts to flow and I hear myself whimper. I stagger sideways a little and watch the blood trickle from the split in my leg. I count the three steps between me and the wall.

My left thigh throbs where the knife sits and I feel the serrated edge pull against the skin as I shuffle around to face the wall, a shudder of pain runs up to the base of my spine. Three steps to the wall, lead with the left leg. I force my swollen and twisted right fist around the handle and I hold tight. I run at the wall.

The handle hits the wall first and my weight comes in behind it. The knife judders into my leg and I feel the blade, like teeth, rip into my flesh. I hear screaming, which I think is me, and I realise as I hit the floor that I can't reach the phone.

XXXII

I hear voices and a wail that could be sirens but I can't move. I feel weak and fragile and I think I'm strapped down. I feel something tight across my chest and ankles and it's comforting. The pain in my leg is almost gone or is everywhere and feels gone. I can't tell. Something is over my face and smells weird, taped against my forehead. I picture John Hurt in *Alien*. I try to feel my stomach but my arms are stupid and won't move properly. I feel a hand wrap around my own failing fingers and a voice tells me to relax. I do.

For a horrible second I am on my back staring up at a bright, white light. My body is numb and my head feels light and I float in silence and wonder if I went too far. Something hot and wet slaps across my face and I hear a yell: 'Shit, we've got a bleeder.' My bubble bursts and I hear a scream and a sob and sirens. Heads and shoulders run past me and I tilt my head to see blood sprayed up the wall next to me.

A smiling face appears in front of the light, and I recognise the receptionist and smile back. She takes down my details and says someone will be along soon. I lie, peacefully numb and quite happy, and listen as those around me cry and moan and whimper. For some reason something has been taped to my head but my leg feels fine so I don't worry too much. I lie and wait for my Scarlett.

A doctor appears and frowns and says, 'What on earth have you done to yourself?' He picks up my limp right wrist and I see my hand and bloody knuckles strapped to an ice pack. I try to shrug but my shoulders are still strapped to the bed. Instead I smile and laugh and relax back into my bed.

'Well,' I hear him say, 'let's get these pants off you. Nurse? Can you get him cleaned up?' He pokes at my forehead and my head spins. I see the ugly grinning gash in my thigh, watch it spitting blood at me, listen to it giggle and gurgle. I whimper and close my eyes.

I wake up sat upright in a bed. I am disappointed to find I'm not attached to anything that beeps. No tubes, no electric pads, just a strange little peg thing on my finger. I can't hear screams. No one cries. All is quiet and peaceful and I look around at the long, boring room. The other beds are full and I hear a soft snore from a distant corner. Opposite is a man with a big, round, bald head and huge beard. He meets my stare and nods. I smile a little and nod back and settle into my bed.

My right hand is wrapped in bandages and aches when I try to curl my fingers. I can't feel my left thigh at all and when I reach down it is strange that I only experience my fingers' sense of touch and not my thigh being touched. It feels like it's not my leg. I smile and look around to find my Scarlett.

A nurse approaches, moving from bed to bed with a clipboard. She ticks boxes and smiles and checks the pegs on people's fingers. She doesn't smile when she reaches me, instead she says, 'Good, you're awake. Breakfast?'

'No.'

'You don't have a choice of yes or no. It's cereal, porridge or toast,' she says. I choose toast.

'Is Scarlett here?' I say and she frowns. 'She works here.' I say, 'Scarlett Santino? She's from Carlisle, number 9987.'

The nurse says, 'Oh. Are you a friend?' I nod and smile She smiles back. She pushes my head back into the pillow, pulls my eyelids toward the ceiling. Something is still attached to my head and she checks the tape that holds it there. 'She'll be on tonight. I'll send her to see you.' I thank her and she smiles again, scribbles something on to her clipboard and goes.

Later I eat my toast and drink my juice and watch the bearded man have a tube inserted between his legs. He squirms and complains but the nurses are very quick and they give him ice cream after. He smiles and raises his spoon to me. I smile back and offer a salute with my cup. I settle back into my bed and close my eyes.

I wake up for lunch. Chicken casserole and steamed vegetables. I sit up and eat and watch the bearded man opposite who glances around nervously and a little plastic bag next to his bed fills up with yellow and pink. A nurse walks past and frowns at the bag. He flushes red and looks away when I raise my chicken to him.

In the bed next to me is a woman with huge breasts and only one leg. Occasionally she reaches down to scratch her non-existent leg and she thumps the bed and cries.

I ask to use the toilet and a nurse hands me this strange cardboard tube thing and closes my curtains. For a while I lie there holding the tube between my legs and I feel my cheeks flush red. I decide I don't need the toilet after all and return the tube. The nurse says she will leave it by the bed for me and leaves. The curtains stay closed and so I stop drinking my juice and stare, bored, at the floral curtains.

I stare at my curtains and listen to the nurses. One of them has a boyfriend who makes her leave her uniform on. Another says she wishes her husband would pay her any sort of attention at all. A doctor walks past and asks her if she is free for drinks later.

The woman next to me starts crying again and I hear a nurse rush to her side and hear soothing murmurs and soft weeping.

Finally my curtain is opened and the nurse is angry because my tube is still empty.

'Well, fine,' she says. 'If you change your mind just push your button.' I try to tell her I don't have a button but she has already gone. Opposite the bald man with the beard is being fussed over by doctors who seem fascinated by his pink plastic bag.

The woman next to me is gone and instead a skinny black man stares at me with huge eyes, his neck wrapped in bandages. I look away and examine the slightly bloody wrapping around my hand.

The scary black man goes and so does the round, bearded man. The lights are dimmed and I discover I have a reading light. Dinner is pasta in a sauce which I don't really like but the nurse that delivers it says I don't have a choice so I chew carefully and avoid the big lumps of tomato.

One by one around the ward reading lights flicker out and die. Nurses close curtains and lower headrests. The bed next to me is empty for a good twenty minutes before an old man arrives with a huge plaster across his chest. He coughs and wheezes and occasionally spits thick, juicy-sounding phlegm into a cardboard bowl.

For a long time I stare at my floral curtain and listen to the sounds of sleep across the ward. The old man snores and splutters as he sleeps. I hear him roll over and smell him fart. From the far end of the ward I hear a gentle sobbing. The nurses are huddled in an office by the main door and whisper and giggle but they are too faint for me to hear anything but static.

When I open my eyes I guess that it must be around six because the shift seems to be changing. I hear nurses passing on information and moving quietly up the centre aisle in pairs. The door opens again and I hear a soft voice trying to find out who called her here. I tense because I know the voice. I brush my hair away from my face and suck in my stomach. My dressings are clean and I look like I'm recovering.

I try very hard not to whimper. I'm the hero and the girl doesn't want a crying hero but it's difficult and I bang my hand against the metal bed frame, rub my knuckles against the corner and I feel hot, fresh blood. With my stupid left hand I punch my thigh hard and my mouth opens in a silent scream and I smile, breathless, at the red which seeps through the dressing. I wipe my eyes as footsteps approach my curtain.

The ward is dark and my Scarlett creeps beneath my

curtain. In the low light I can see the blue dress and the white trimming glows a little. She has her hair tied up and I smell flowers. I turn on the reading light and she jumps a little.

'Oh!' she says. 'You scared me.' She stares at me for a moment. She crinkles her nose and pouts. 'I know you from somewhere, don't I?' she asks, 'Is that why you asked to see me? Wanted a familiar face?' She smiles but my eyes are wide and my blood runs hot in my cheeks and I'll admit I'm a little annoyed she doesn't recognise me. After all those nights together, nothing.

She picks up my limp wrist and examines the dressing. She tuts and shakes her head.

'Hang on,' she says, 'I'll be right back.' she slides between the curtains and I hear her pad softly toward the office. When she returns she has a clear plastic box full of dressings and tape and she smiles and I smile back.

'Let's sort this dressing out,' she says, and starts to unravel the bandage around my knuckles.

She holds my hand as she cleans the mess that is my hand and she feels so soft, so warm. I smile so much I show my teeth and I try not to laugh. She bites her lip as she works and I bite mine too and feel the blood run hot in my cheeks, in my neck. I feel my heart beating, feel my breathing quicken.

'Right, one down, one to go' she says and looks at me and smiles. A strand of hair has fallen over her face and she puckers her lips to blow it out the way. I feel the blood run hot in my chest.

She uncovers my thigh and I see for the first time how high up the wound is. She grimaces and looks up at me.

'Oh!' she says and bites her lip. 'That looks painful.' I

nod, quick tiny neck movements. 'Let's get this dressing off and have a proper look, shall we?' she says and her fingers trace the dressing around the inside of my leg. I feel the blood run hot in my legs. My knees tense up.

Her touch is light and soft as she removes the dressing. Delicate fingers make sure my dignity is maintained and she takes out a wet cloth thing and strokes the wound on my leg. I stare up at the ceiling and cling tight to the sheets.

When I look down she is drying the wound with cotton pads and I can see the curves of her breasts down the collar of her shirt. The blood runs hot in my groin and my buttocks clench. My Scarlett smiles at me as she takes fresh dressing from the box. 'It'll be over soon.' I nod and feel the strain in my neck.

The dressing is cool and I realise I'm holding my breath. I exhale and my breath shivers past my lips. Her fingers press the padding over the wound and place a strip of tape across the middle. I feel her press gently to secure the tape, then her fingers slide sideways, following the tape around the inside of my leg. I stare at the ceiling and feel the blood run hot in my cheeks, my neck, my chest – everywhere. My toes curl and my back aches and I panic and feel my stomach tense and I inhale. My fingers are stupid and are meant to protect her but they don't work and instead they knock the gown from my crotch and I tense again, my muscles spasm and I breathe. My shoulders drop and my neck relaxes and for a second I float, ecstatic and dreamlike. My Scarlett whimpers.

I stare at her and her eyes are wide and she is shaking. A desperate breath escapes her lips and she raises a hand toward her cheek. I feel sick. I feel dirty. She puts a finger to her face and feels my love, hot and sticky against her red cheek. She whimpers again and the curtains open wide as a nurse runs in. She looks at me, at my crotch which my stupid bandaged hand tries desperately to cover, she looks at my Scarlett, at my love which dries on her cheek and she screams and drags my Scarlett away.

I blink and roll out of the bed and crash to the ground as my legs gives way beneath me. I panic and my fingers claw at the bedclothes as I pull myself up and throw myself on to my good left leg.

A nurse is screaming at me and the rest take up the cry as I blunder through the floral curtain, dragging my useless leg behind me. No one tries to stop me as I hop and stagger and pull myself toward the ward's main door. I hear someone say something about security and I fall face-first through the heavy double doors.

Behind me the doors swing open and shut and I hear cries and sobs from the nurses, which ebb and flow as the doors swing back and forth. I crawl forward and drag myself upright again, leaning against the wall, and I slide down the corridor. The corridor is long and bright and I see a lift at the end which I aim for. Somewhere behind me I hear footsteps and yells and my head is moving in circles again, the weight of whatever they stuck to my forehead unbalancing me. I try to focus on the lift but my eyes fill with water and I slip on something wet and land heavily on my knees.

The footsteps are running now and the yelling is louder. I hear an angry male voice yell, 'Hey, hey stop right there.' I'm on my feet and hopping toward the lift, my crocked fingers stretched out ahead and my wasted leg trailing limp behind.

I can't see for tears and the pain makes my head swim and I flail desperate and horrified and dirty and crying and something cold and metal hits me in the face. I press my hands against a metal plate and try to work out if I've fallen over again. The footsteps are running and the yelling is louder and I hear: 'Here, Jimmy, I'm over here, he's at the lifts, hurry up.'

The metal slides sideways across my face and now I know I'm falling and the floor I hit is tiled and cool and painful against my chin.

The footsteps yell: 'Hey, hold that lift!'

A rasping voice near my ear whispers, 'Going down, son?' I look up into wide, dark eyes.

I make a sound that is meant to sound like 'Yes, please' and I hear the doors slide shut.

I wheel the wide-eyed black man through reception and try to look respectable despite my puffy eyes and the dribbling trail of blood I leave in my wake. I hop quickly behind his wheelchair, using it as support and I aim for the taxi rank outside. My bare feet slap against the tile as we move, a breeze cuts through my gown. My mangled claw seeps blood through its dressing and a receptionist stares at us but we smile politely and the scary black man wheezes out a 'Good evening, dear' as we pass.

'I once got a nurse like that too you know,' he tells me as I crawl into a taxi. I stare back through the window and he smiles at me. 'Only I got her in the eye.'

He winks and spins his chair around. We pull away and I watch him glide back inside and out of the rain.

XXXIII

The taxi driver wants to charge me double because I bleed on the seats but I am still wearing a hospital gown and so have no money. He mutters things I choose not to hear as we meander down the hill into Elmfield Park.

'This your place?' he says and nods toward the door. I tell him it is. 'Right then,' he says and climbs out. 'Let's get you up there and I'll find some way for you to pay this fare.'

The driver lets me lean on him and I stumble from the cab, falling against a bruised-looking car parked opposite my flat. I glance at the door I have dented and a disappointed window is wound up tight, a red eye glaring down at me. I shrug and the taxi driver and I clamber up the stairs, me resting heavily against the damp walls as we go. My door leans against the frame. My landlord has attached a note which reads: 'You owe me one door and one new lock. Hope you're feeling better. Xx.' I frown at the kiss-kiss and the driver helps me inside. He leaves with my toaster and a handful of DVDs and I sit in my chair and sip my coffee.

My TV is beyond repair. It sits silent in its corner, a phone nested deep inside. The floor is a mess of coffee and blood and dirty big footprints criss-crossing my living space. The carpet around my chair is no longer grey but brown from where I lay and bled. My coffee mug handle lies where I dropped it but the mug is held tight in one good hand.

My fist still bleeds, weeping pathetically into a tea towel which has had to replace 9987, Santino, Scarlett's handiwork. She is no longer my Scarlett I think. I wonder if she can ever forgive me. I can almost tighten my right hand into a fist and almost straighten my fingers and almost believe she might. It aches and I feel the draught from the lean-to door in the joints of my fingers. I stare at the green striped gown and the Property of Royal University Hospital label and the bloodstains and the crotch stains, which are now dry and crusty.

The clock on the wall is speckled with rusty red and reads six in the morning. In two hours I am due at work. I sigh and sip my coffee but can see no alternative. I retrieve the phone and plug it back into the wall. I limp back to my seat and place the phone on my lap. For a long time I just look at it and shake my head and sip my coffee and wish I could think of another way. I run through my projected list of adventures I had planned for the day. Nearly all of them require me to be able to grip and manipulate and carefully position. My fingers need to type. My heart needs to pump the blood that will power my legs which will run down the four steps to the store room. I try to move my fingers in an approximation of typing and find that they won't. My middle finger doesn't move at all and just points straight ahead until I try to curl my hand into a fist again. I try to stand to run the four steps to the store room but my left leg is sluggish and sore and doesn't bend right.

I blow through puffed cheeks and pick up the phone and try to remember Percy's number. Twice I get it wrong and twice I receive abuse down the phone. My second attempt disturbs an old lady who tells me to go fuck myself and when I start to cry she says: 'Oh, I'm sorry duck, I'm just grumpy.' I wipe my eyes and place a cushion over my crotch lest it go off again. I dial a third number.

The phone rings and rings and rings and rings and I sip my coffee with my good hand and it rings and someone picks up and coughs into the phone.

I hear spit and retching and a wheeze and smoke curls from the earpiece as I say, 'Percy? Did I wake you?' I look at the clock and it reads six fifteen. Percy is still coughing. I hear a tap run and a gulp and the smoke from the earpiece is extinguished.

'Percy?' I say. 'Percy, come on, hurry up, this is important.'

Another wheeze and finally I hear Percy say, 'What time is it? Are you alright? I'm really sorry mate, I didn't mean to ...'

I sigh again and take a deep breath and just come out and say it, 'I'm not coming in today. I'm not well.' There is a pause. For the first time in the three years I have employed him Percy is silent. I almost smile.

'Shit, it's serious isn't it? Are you OK? They didn't do anything to you did they?' He is speaking too quickly for my still-mourning brain. I say something that could be 'flu' and Percy says, 'Fuck you too, mate. I had no choice. I've said I'm sorry.' I shake my head but of course he doesn't know this. I hear the click of a lighter and he inhales loudly. I smell smoke.

'Anyway, didn't you fire me last night?' I tell him it was a joke and he laughs and says, 'Well you got me mate, I had my CV ready and everything.'

My tongue feels sluggish and my mouth is dry. My head is floating away again and I can feel sleep behind my eyes so I sip my coffee. I can't keep this up for long and so I try to bring the conversation to a close.

'So can you open?' I slur and he sucks and a cigarette and blows smoke down the phone

'Yeah, no problem, mate,' he says, 'I could definitely do with the money.' He pauses and inhales. 'Do I get over-time?'

My bed is soft and warm and I curl up best I can beneath the covers. My dead leg hangs useless off one end and I cradle my damaged hand and dream of her eyes wide and scared and of black men on wheels chasing nurses. I sleep and I dream and I cry quietly on to my pillow.

XXXIV

'What the fuck happened here, then?'

I wake with a jump to find Percy perched on the edge of my bed. He grins and I watch smoke drift through the gaps between his teeth. In one hand he has a steaming mug of coffee. In the other a smouldering cigarette is held loosely between two yellow fingers. He brings the cigarette to his lips and sucks. I watch the tip glow red through gummy eyes and blink and cough while he blows smoke sideways out his mouth toward the window. He sips his coffee and looks down at where I lie. I am suddenly aware of my naked, broken leg lying next to him and I can't help but feel vulnerable. He smiles again, smoke curls upward from his nostrils and he nods toward the coffee.

'Want one?' he says.

Percy pours me my own coffee while I stare into my open wardrobe. I still wear last night's hospital gown, blood splattered and dirty. It itches and I deserve it. My clothes hang limp in front of me and my limbs dangle dead, arms flopped in my lap. Percy brings me coffee but I just stare into my wardrobe. He puts it on the floor beside me. It may as well be in Wales because I'm never going to reach it. I inhale the coffee and watch Percy's smoke spiral across my ceiling. I sigh.

Percy is speaking but I just blink. I watch him as he talks and I think about the Navigator thingy in *Dune* and its beak-like mouth and the smoky spice that billows out as it breathes. I watch him talk and I blink and wonder if I will ever move again. I doubt very much I will ever want to. I sit and blink and smell coffee and cigarettes and wonder what Percy is saying. It looks serious; he looks agitated.

He moves his arms a lot and conducts the smoke which swirls and dances and I feel my cheeks getting heavy and imagine them sinking to the floor. The smoke is shapes now and I am hardly even aware of Percy anymore. I watch the smoke: a languid, stick figure man dances with a curvaceous woman. I watch the smoke: the figures mingle, entwine, roll over each other and bulge outwards across the ceiling. I watch the smoke: a feathery grey hand caresses a soft white cheek. I watch the smoke: wide ghostly eyes stare back at me and the hand is on her cheek.

Percy stops talking. I look at him as he swims toward me. A sharp intake of breath, my heart like wet sand in my chest and I am crying again. Percy hovers and I know that if he touches me I may never recover. He reaches out an arm. I sob. I want to move away but my broken frame slumps, still, perched on the side of my bed. Percy blows smoke out the corner of his mouth and his outstretched hand flaps the smoke from my face.

'Let's get you a proper drink' he says and he rummages in my wardrobe.

I don't remember getting dressed. I very much hope Percy

did not do it for me. I wear the jumper my Mam bought me for my birthday and my ridiculous jeans, still rumpled from a night on the floor of my bedroom. I lean heavily on Percy as I limp off the bus. Percy smells of coffee and cigarettes and sweat and something herbal that I don't recognise. My shoulders hang low and my cheeks dangle heavily beneath my chin. I feel them swing slowly from side to side as we go.

Percy is talking and his free hand waves another cigarette. I watch the smoke and the trail it leaves behind us and I blink and think about nothing but breathing. I inhale and taste ash. I exhale and feel my body deflate. I sigh and Percy sits me down.

There is a drink in front of me and my head flops against my shoulder and I watch bubbles rise and I watch condensation dribble. I am aware of noise and can smell smoke and crisps and alcohol. From nearby I hear a belch and can smell rotting meat. My eyes are heavy and my limbs are suffering in a higher gravity than I am used to. My arm makes a pathetic attempt to reach the edge of the table but succeeds in nothing but a couple of raised fingers.

My thigh throbs, my knuckles ache, my head throbs and I stare at Percy, who folds the smoke into patterns and stories. He is speaking and grinning and squeezing smoke through his teeth. I sniff and blink and abandon my body to retreat somewhere dark and cool. I try to sleep.

I sit and I dream and I dream of horrible things. I dream of my Scarlett, the Scarlett who was once mine, and of her cheek, singed forever. Branded by my love. I dream of the Scarlett who was once mine and I worry she will never be safe until she has me to come home to. My lips are moist and I taste salt. I am aware of noises around me, of shouting and laughing and breaking glass, but it doesn't concern me. I exist only in this bubble and this bubble is all I deserve.

A pressure on my arm, brief and flat, and a hot tingling feeling remains. Again, that swift, hard touch against my arm. I hear a clap and I recognise the hot tingling as pain. A third hard clap against my shoulder moves my whole body sideways and my decaying limbs stiffen in response. I find that I have no need to open my eyes as I never closed them. I bring the world back into focus. I blink and breathe and somewhere behind my eyes I feel my bubble stinging my retinas. Percy is frowning and says something. He points at the yellow, bubbling drink before me and I drag one grey arm to the table. I drink and see Percy smile. The taste is evil but Percy mimes me to taste more. I drink and see Percy smile. I burp and smile a little too. Somewhere behind my eyes I feel my bubble burst and the noise rolls over me and for a second I drown under the weight of my senses.

I feel my thigh aching and throbbing and my knuckles scratching against the stained and sweaty dressing. I feel my back stiff against an uncomfortable wooden chair. Around me is noise and I flinch at the wet laughter from behind me and hide behind my hands at the prickle of angry young men in the corner. I watch them and they dance together as a wave. They rise and sway and fall and crash to their seats in frustration and rage and I hear a commentator say: 'Oh! What a miss!'

I smell smoke and Percy is saying, 'I thought that might help.' Predictably he is grinning; unusually his drink is also smoking, sitting low, a glass smothered by a grey haze.

'So, come on then,' he says and points at me with a cigarette held loose between two fingers. 'Are you mad at me?' he nods toward my hand and raises his eyebrows. Ash rises from his bushy brows and I see his yellow teeth revealed.

I drink and breathe and say, 'I fell.' He laughs and I smile a little.

'Fair enough.' He grins and sips his witches' brew, smoke falling across his chest from the glass.

Percy buys me another drink and I feel a little warmer. My thigh stops throbbing and my knuckles look vaguely ridiculous in their mummy's wrapping. My head still swims, but the water is warmer now. More surprisingly, I think, Percy bothers me less today. I lean forward into the mist he creates and rest my elbows on the table. I tuck my hair behind my ears, my fingers tracing the padding across my forehead and I inhale my lager and sigh. Percy smiles. He always smiles and I push a burp past my cheeks and wonder what he has to be so cheerful about.

'What has he got to be so cheerful about?' I hear myself say. Percy checks over both shoulders and follows my gaze. He prods his chest with one, yellowed cigarette holder and we both realise I am talking to him. He holds up his hands.

'I have a drink,' he says, which is true: he does. 'I have a cigarette,' he says, which I see is also true and it grows from between two fingers. 'And', he says, clicking my glass with his own, 'I have someone to share them with.' He offers me a cigarette and my lips panic and hide inside my mouth. My chin wrinkles. I politely refuse and he shrugs. 'Maybe later then,' he says and winks at me.

I am wrong about Percy. I have ... one, two, three, four empty glasses in front of me and I rest my head against the back of my chair and blow smoke toward the ceiling. I feel warm and a little dizzy and my stomach bubbles happily. Percy is talking and I drag him forcibly into focus.

I drink the last of my drink and I burp and grin and Percy says, 'So where to next?' His glass steams slightly and I breathe deep and hold it and blow smoke across the table. When Percy reappears through the fog he is standing.

'Come on,' he says, and I stare through wide eyes as he helps me up. 'Let's get you some air.' My stomach bubbles loudly. 'And maybe some food, eh, mate?' He is smiling and I think, *Yeah, I'm wrong about Percy. He's alright.*

'You're alright,' I say and drape an arm across his shoulders.

Percy says 'I know' and he places a cigarette between my lips. I grin and feel my lips get hot and blow smoke toward the ceiling and we go out the door.

It's dark outside and cool and I slip a little but it's alright because Percy catches me. A yoke of massive women is carrying a woman in a kitten suit and I wave because I know them from hospital. There is a breeze which is lovely against my cheeks and me and Percy head up the hill and I watch the paving stones go by.

Blue neon winks at me from a huge, curved window and I wink back. The sign above the door reads The Round House, and I look and it is round, sweeping across the corner of the street in a massive curve. I drag Percy inside. The bar is huge and wooden and feels smooth and I spread my fingers out. A fat frowning barman comes over and I say, 'Drinks, please, fat frowning barman.' And I grin and blow smoke toward the ceiling. I discover my pocket is full of crumpled bank notes and I hold one out to the angry-looking barman.

'Here you go angry-looking barman,' I say, and two tiny little glasses appear on the bar.

I lie my head next to it and frown because it's really, really tiny. I stretch out a finger and poke it and it wobbles and a clear gold coloured liquid splashes on to the bar. I watch Percy drink his in one go. I stand up and my leg is healed completely now, which is good, because I need my leg. I need it to power my heart so it can run up and down the four steps that lead to the store room. My fingers are stupid and can't pick up the glass. It falls over on to the bar and my Egyptian mummy's hand is all wet and sticky. I grin and blow smoke to the ceiling and Percy grins too and we both grin at the barman who frowns and I say, dead serious like, 'Why the frown, barman?'

Me and Percy are somewhere new. It's square. Not round or triangle or rectangle. No, it's in a square with a tree in it. My fingers can't work the tiny, tiny drinks so I have a pint and so does Percy. Percy's new friends are drinking vodka and coke and are women.

My head won't stay still. It's wiggling around on my shoulders and is really, really annoying. I blink and stare with wide eyes at the women. I drink my drink and it dribbles down my chin a little bit but I don't mind too much and grin.

Percy is talking and looks at me and nods and the

women look at me and smile and I swallow and burp at the same time which hurts my throat. My stomach is bubbling again but not happily this time. I burp again and cringe a little because I can taste bile.

One of the women, who says she is called Tara but it's pronounced Terra, shuffles next to me. She smiles at me and she has blonde hair and huge breasts and a fat pink mouth which wobbles as she speaks.

Her lips flap up and down and she says something like: 'You want to get some air, hon?' I feel my face get hot and my stomach boils. My head falls against Tara the Terra's shoulder and I am staring at her massive breasts. She rests her head against mine and she smells of vinegar and says quietly, 'You can have some of these too.' She pushes her arms together and her breasts ooze up out of her bra and seep across her top. I feel her hand on mine and it's not soft like my Scarlett's, but cold and clammy and clumsy. Her fingers are thicker than mine and she rubs a circle into the top of my hand. I feel my chest burning and my stomach hisses and my throat feels acidy and sore.

I burp and I feel her hand on my leg. My stomach lurches and I gag a little but she is stupid and gets things wrong.

She says something like, 'That's right, all yours' and her fingers walk up my leg toward my crotch. I shake my head and try to say no. I shake my head and shuffle sideways and look up at her flabby pink mouth. She is blonde and evil and I feel guilty and I look to see if Scarlett is here.

The pub is busy and loud and I feel my pulse quicken because I see a dark-haired woman storm out the door.

I yell, 'Stop, Scarlett, please ...' Tara or Terra or something else I hate thrusts her hand against my groin and leans forward and pours her breasts over my chest and I feel her lips against mine. My stomach lurches and I feel fire in my throat. I taste bile.

Tara or Terra or something else I don't care about whimpers and cries and gags and I watch her dribble my burning bile down her chin. Her breasts are shining and slimy and steam slightly and her eyes are wide and wet. I think of my Scarlett and I think: Yeah, that's what you get.

'Yeah,' I slur. 'That'sh wha y git.' I try to stand but I bang my leg against the table and I see Percy's drink fall into his lap. I feel big, heavy hands on my shoulders and I wave to Percy and I feel a breeze, I feel weightless, I feel cold stone against my cheek. I taste old coffee and cobble and I sleep and I dream of nothing.

XXXV

A distorted and disconnected voice wakes me with depressing news: local boy feared dead, rugby team in drugs scandal, local business under investigation by HM Customs and Revenue.

My mouth feels dry and has a hot, bitter taste. A sticky, sickly grumble shivers up from my stomach and I belch. I roll over under the quilt and an evil smell seeps through the covers. I groan and lick my dry lips. My eyes are sticky and the room is too bright and for a wonderful moment I don't know where I am.

From somewhere below me I hear a door slam and raised voices. Outside I hear birds and no traffic and I can see the sky through a big leaded window. From below I can smell coffee. Another burst of violence from downstairs and the front door slams. A moment later a gate rattles shut and there is quiet again but for the chirp of birds and my gurgling stomach. I lie on soft pillows and stare out at the sky, white with cloud and bright with winter sun. The room is cold but the bed is warm and I wrap myself tight in the quilt.

Footsteps on the landing mean I have to open my eyes again and I reply weakly to the tapping at the door. I smell coffee and toast and perfume and my Mam smiles a good morning. She puts a tray of toast and butter on the bed and a cup of coffee on the bedside table. She opens a window.

'Well,' she says and I smile weakly and try to keep my eyes open. 'You must have had an interesting few days.' She looks at my injured hand. The dressing is clean and fresh, no trace of dirt or drink or blood or vomit. 'I changed it for you last night, I don't know what you had managed to spill on the old one but it was in a disgusting state.' I stare at the toast and my stomach growls a warning. The coffee smells good and I reach across for the mug. As I move the quilt slips down away from my chest and I realise I am naked. I blush and so does my Mam.

'Did you ...?' I ask and she shakes her head quickly,

'Oh, no,' she says. 'You did that yourself once I'd cleaned up your dressings.' She lowers her eyes and threads her fingers together.

She moves to the side of the bed, sits down next me. She frowns a little, strokes my hair away from my face, strokes my forehead. 'So what happened?' I shrug and sip my coffee.

'I fell,' I say. She raises her eyes to meet mine and for a moment we just watch each other. She watches me lie and I watch her wring her hands together, I watch her finger her wedding ring. She looks away and sighs and I hear her breath catch as she exhales. She wipes her eyes and smiles at me.

'Eat some breakfast,' she says and closes the door as she leaves.

I limp downstairs in my father's dressing gown, which has appeared on the landing during my coffee. The toast lies on the tray uneaten and I am unable to carry it and use the banister, so it remains on my bed. I hold the empty coffee cup and boil the kettle and hobble into the dining room to find my Mam.

Eventually I find her in the garden, her elegant fingers wrapped around a delicate china teacup. I smell honeysuckle and witch hazel and the slightly soapy Earl Grey in Mam's teacup. She is sat on a bench beneath the kitchen window and I lower myself down next to her. I sip my coffee and admire the pale whites and blues of Mam's winter garden and stare at the trees at the far end, which still cling desperately to their foliage, reluctant to brave the cold completely naked and alone. My Mam gently pats my injured thigh and her touch is warm and comforting. I sip my coffee and she sips her tea and we sit in silence.

A breeze forces me inside. My knuckles ache and the cold cuts deep into my joints. My head still throbs. I shower and dress in a shirt I borrow from my father. It is white with red pinstripes and fits me almost perfectly. My own clothes, still damp from Mam's washing machine, are in a bag ready for me to take home. My jeans have survived so I shuffle back downstairs, swinging my sore leg out wide to avoid bending it and dropping it on to each painful step. I wear my ridiculous half-mast trousers.

Mam is in the kitchen, stood motionless in front of the sink. She has her hands in the hot water and she stares at the garden through leaded windows and heavy eyelashes. I place my hand on her shoulder and she tenses. I frown and move in behind her to hold her properly. She turns into my arms and I feel her wet hands on my back. I feel her head on my shoulder.

I stroke her hair with my undamaged fingers and she

collapses into my chest. She shudders and her fingers press tight into my back. She cries and I feel my father's shirt slowly soak up tears and it hangs, wet, where my Mam weeps.

I don't know how long we stand in each other's arms but by the time we part the warmth from Mam's face has dried her early flurry of tears. Her eyes are red and swollen, her cheeks grey and thin, but she smiles and sniffs and says: 'Look at me, I'm so silly.' I try to stroke her shoulder but she flinches away and holds her arm across her chest. 'No,' she says, 'I'm alright. Really.' She rubs her arm and I step back.

I move to fill the kettle again but Mam shakes her head and says, 'No, you'd best be off dear.' She smiles and sniffs and raises a hand to wipe at her eyes. 'Your father will be home soon and I should really get the lunch on.' I nod and move to embrace her again. I move fast and at first she tenses, raises her shoulders and crosses her arms but I am warm and comfortable and she relaxes into me for a moment before gently pushing me away.

'Go on,' she smiles. 'And don't forget your things this time,' she says, and I pull on vomit-flecked shoes.

By the front door someone, I assume it is my father, has thrown my boxes into a black bin liner. I open the bag and rummage carefully until I find an envelope, aged and sellotaped, and a pink heart on the front. I select one particular photograph and drop the envelope back into the bag.

Lucky for me today is bin day and as I pass a neighbour's gate I drop the bag into their bin. The bright white sky is fused with grey and brooding navy blue. I

tense my shoulders up around my neck and limp to the
bus stop.

XXXVI

The sun shines and I stand on the front porchway and sip my coffee. I inhale the steam and smile because the Spar had a special on and I treated myself to an Irish Cream blend. It smells hot and comfortable and soft, with a hint of vanilla. I stand on the front porchway and sip at my Irish Cream blended coffee and I try to relax.

Inside the shop is no one, only Ben fumbling to introduce his parents to Bobby up on the big screen. Above the counter, above everything, everywhere, Bobby is looking tense and uncomfortable. I forget for a second and shift my weight from my stiff right leg to my torn left and the pain leaps up my spine and into my shoulders. I almost drop my coffee. A small child passes in huge sunglasses and dungarees. It grins at me and my face crunches into a painful mess as I shift my weight back again. I breathe deep. My left hand closes the fingers of my right hand tighter around my coffee. I try to sip but instead dribble down my shirt. I sigh. My two days off have almost destroyed the shop.

The carpet is pitted with chewing gum and muddy footprints are caked across the aisles. Alphabetical DVD is no more, instead is just a mess of titles and stars. Comedy and Horror have combined and for a moment I wonder if that could be a nice little subsection – horrors so bad they are funny – but think no, too confusing for the average customer. New Releases is a mess, Blockbusters mix with Indie mix with Foreign mix with my Asian Cinema section. In the Disney section by the door someone has placed Adult movies behind *Aladdin* and *Beauty and the Beast*. I remove *Slippery When Wet* and *Buttman in Asstown* and take them back behind the curtain.

I keep my coffee close by and I organise and alphabetise and make a difference to the store which no one will choose to see. Above me, above all of this, everywhere, Ben is drugged and on stage and telling everything to all. I sip my coffee and remove *School Girl Sleepover* from behind *The Lion King* and hobble back to the heavy velvet curtain.

The pale sun trickles down the window of the dry cleaners opposite and I run my finger down the late list. It is a virgin list; neither Percy nor Anna has bothered to highlight those in need of a reminder. I take out the pens.

The list is multi-coloured. Yellow for one day, pink for two, green for three or more, left white if they're not coming back. I pick up the phone and dial those in green. The buttons are either greasy or sticky, alternating number to number, and my fingers slide and stick across the keypad.

'Miss Spencer,' I say into the phone, but it isn't Miss Spencer, it's someone growling, deep and throaty and wet, and in the background a whack and an 'Aahhh, Hmmm, Yeahhh' which drags on forever. I hang up the phone and search beneath the counter for a cloth.

On the radio the news mumbles misery: Iraqi diplomat killed by car bomb; Bush says global warming is down to Communism; local boy still missing, parents in plea for information. Outside, opposite the shop, a bullied-looking car sits, blind, its windows firmly shut against the setting sun.

I work down the list, reminding, prodding, negotiating and being generally persuasive. Some names are still white and I decide to call them on the off chance.

'Mr Johnson,' I say and smile into the receiver. 'How're things, you thieving wanker?' A small high voice lisps back, 'My Daddy thays you can fuck right off.' And the lines goes dead. I smile and sigh and put the kettle on.

Through the steam, up the steps toward the counter, two shadows linger, huge and billowing, flapping past the steaming kettle. My heart pumps the blood which powers my legs up the four steps. One shadow really is huge. It blocks out the street lights, masks the kids on the bikes, relegates them purely to sound. The second is slimmer, taller. It wears a suit.

Shadow number one places hairy knuckles on the counter, taps fat wet fingers against the coated plastic surface. Shadow number two is in suit and tie and leans, casual-like, against the counter, its weight comfortably balanced against the edge. This one is no puppet; this one is not yet dead.

Shadow number two speaks, well-considered words, well-formed syllables. 'We've been having a word with your ...' he glances quickly around the empty shop: 'supplier.' I nod, wondering if I'm being offered a discount. That would please the Undead. Shadow two continues. 'He is short on some of his deliveries.' I nod, despite the

189

fact that they arrive every Saturday, on time, just before lunch. 'He claims this is your fault.'

I am about to shrug when Shadow number one rumbles, 'We very much like your ...' and shadow one glances quickly around the empty store 'supplier. He has been with us a number of years now, always prompt, always profitable.' The shadow leans forward, a round bald head, a fat pear of a nose, all burst capillaries and pot holes. I smell smoke. Wet lips spit at me. 'Until you.'

Shadow two leans forward, a double act, which is making it difficult for me to think. This is getting weird. 'We know that your ...' – he glances quickly around the empty shop – 'supplier had to get a little rough with you.' A thin yellow finger wafts from shadow number two, strokes at my forehead, curls around my hair, which has slipped across my eyes. Cracked lips whisper at me. 'Evidently not rough enough.' Both shadows lean back, fat fingers drop from the counter, angular elbows fold away. Shadow number two continues. 'As we said, we like your supplier. We want to help him pay us what he owed.' Shadow two has eyes that seem to suck in the light and I feel the whites drain from my eyes, see his glowing softly white. 'That means you pay him what you owe. Or we help you find the cash.' I breathe, suddenly aware that my lungs hold a burning ball of gas, a singular sun in my chest, which had been ready to explode.

I say something like: 'Oh, thanks, that's very kind of you, but ...'

Shadow number one is rubbing hairy knuckles into sweaty palms. He holds up one finger to stop me and rumbles, 'No. Believe me when I say that the last thing you want is our help.' And they turn away, march into the sunset. I am frowning but breathing, my fingers already flitting toward a stack of the shop's unpaid bills. From by the door a shadow growls, 'Two days. I suggest you get those takings up.'

Opposite the shop, in front of the dry cleaners, two red eyes awaken, a window slides casually downward and a tormented car wheezes away toward the city proper.

Outside shadows die. They dissolve into tarmac and seep between the cracks in the paving stones. Children on bikes inhale deeply on cigarettes too big for little lips, they swig with glee from a battered Diet Coke bottle.

Inside is a woman, huge and floral; her hair stands up, supported by scaffolding and dangerous-looking pins. She is talking to me and I suspect she has been for some time; she is red in the face and smiling and pauses to take long, deep breaths before each new wave of enthusiasm. I have been nodding and wondering if I have misplaced a bill. I have been nodding and sipping my coffee and thinking about 9987, Santino, Scarlett and wondering if I've ruined my chances with her.

The wallpaper-wearing woman before me is waving a dirty brown DVD case, one of ours, and pointing to it. For a moment I wonder if there is some sort of problem with the disc, skipping and sticking or something, but no, she smiles and breathes and pours hot air back into the world.

I sip my coffee and nod and wonder vaguely what she might be so excited about. I try to see the label on the DVD case. *An Affair to Remember*. For some reason it sounds familiar. Massive Miss Floral Print is still speaking and finally I listen.

'Cary Grant?' I ask.

She pauses, confused, mouth still open. I hear static. She closes her mouth. 'Well, yes, of course.' She frowns at me. 'That's what I've been saying to you.' She smiles, shakes her head. Her jowls jangle. 'Surely, there will never be a man as sexy and sophisticated as Cary Grant.'

I put down my coffee. Force my claw into my good hand, wrap fingers over scar tissue. I stare at the woman, at her pig eyes, her snout, her jowls gently swaying in the breeze.

I ask, 'Why?'

'Why what?' She looks confused. Uncomfortable almost, her free hand raises toward her slippery cheeks, self-conscious now that I am actually paying attention.

'What was so wonderful about Cary Grant?'

The woman has left, intimidated by intense questioning, and now I stare at the sewerage-brown DVD case, Total Rental crusted in dirty, rusted red across the front. Inside squats Cary Grant and I wonder if I have been too hard on him. I wonder whether he deserves a second chance.

I sip my coffee and watch the kids outside. The girl with the extra smile has someone new and is pressed up against the window so hard that his hands can't get between her hips and the glass. He pulls away, annoyed. With nothing to grope behind he lunges instead at her chest. She laughs, lifts her top and a cheer squeaks into the night from a dozen glowing tracksuits, a dozen dancing cigarettes. A pink bra clasp clatters against the window pane.

I tap my fingers against the DVD case. On the computer screen flashes 'Press enter to return selection.' I hover my useless hand over the enter button. Above me, above everyone, everywhere, an epiphany moment for Tom, who holds Christianity hostage. I make a decision. I press escape, cancelling the return, and drop the DVD case out of sight next to my jacket.

XXXVII

I have borrowed a TV/DVD player from the shop. This is awkward because I had to take it out of the packaging to plug it in. The walk home was wet, the alley slippery with mud, decorated with condoms hung from fences and filled with rain. They glowed blue and pink and red, fairy lanterns leading home the wicked. The box is damp, falling apart at the edges.

Worse, I did not return Wallpaper Sample Book Woman's DVD. I have it in my hand and watch the clock. Slowly it ticks past twelve; the DVD is now a late return. Tomorrow it will appear on the late list. My fault. I sip my coffee with my good hand and stare at the borrowed TV.

In the corner, under the window, my old TV glowers at me. It sits against the damp patch, shattered shards of screen glistening with sweaty beads of moisture. Rain is scattered across the window, grime dribbling down the pane. From below comes another TV, gunshots and sirens. From above a door slams, and another. I hear footsteps in the stairwell, hurrying past my newly fitted door.

Way past midnight, I decide it's too late to change my mind. I put the stolen DVD into the borrowed TV/DVD player. I sip my coffee. I watch.

An Affair to Remember. My coffee is cold, I am frowning. I just don't get it. Grant starts the film engaged to one woman, yet attempting to seduce others. He succeeds in breaking up the relationship of a woman who, up until now, had been perfectly happy.

The credits roll and I listen to the rain. Above me I hear movement, floorboards murmur as light feet shuffle above. I have not heard any footsteps returning, climbing the stairs.

He is a womaniser. He is arrogant. He treats the women in the film as if they were there only to amuse him. He is no better than 7451, Algarry, Neville. Grant's rental history would read: *Lesbian Nurses, Lesbian Nurses, Lesbian Nurses*. He smiles with Percy's rubber-cheeked smile.

But he got his copout Hollywood ending.

I want mine.

I pull myself from the bloodstained chair and shuffle toward the bathroom, filling the kettle on the way.

My eyes are red, ugly bags hanging like rainclouds beneath. I look pale, tired. Swollen pockets of pus are crawling across my nose, red and throbbing. I turn off the light, brush my hair into a side parting and stare at the cut-out in the mirror before me. I put on my best trans-Atlantic drawl.

'Hey baby.' Hair slides from behind my ear

I flatten my errant hair again.

'Hey baby.' Hair slips back against my cheeks. I stare at my greasy hair. At my greasy face. At my greasy mirror. She wants Cary Grant. I can do Cary Grant. I head into my kitchenette.

The knife is slightly bent and still caked in blood. I rinse it under the tap in the sink. I stare at my lank, limp, dangling locks of hair. I run my finger along the wet, cold blade, shudder as my finger creeps through its teeth. I wrap a lock of dying hair around my claw and raise the knife, measure about an inch from my scalp. I start to saw.

It hurts, feels like the skin is being pulled away from my scalp. I feel air against my skull. I saw and pull and my eyes water and my spine shudders as the knife rips and chews at my hair. I can hear the strands tearing, feel my scalp stretching and can almost hear a squelching, bubbling as the blood fills the space between bone and skin. More than once I slip, the knife slithering from my sweaty palm and slicing into the skin. Blood dribbles through my eyebrows, creeps down my cheeks, mingling with tears. It drips from my chin.

When I am finished mangled clumps of hair fill the sink, splattered with thick ruby splashes, and I stare at the new me, panting, crying in the mirror. My scalp is oozing blood, tiny, silky droplets seeping from the follicles from where hair has been ripped out. The knife clatters into the sink. I slide my blood-smeared hair into a side parting and hold it there while the blood clots and dries and settles into position.

The phone wakes me. My heart beats quick and loud, I can feel it in my chest, bursting through my rib cage. It takes me a moment to realise where I am. My good hand scrabbles across the carpet; my claw lies under a pillow, dried blood clinging to the cover. I'm lying on the bed, fully clothed in half-mast jeans and a jumper I stole from my father. I move my claw across its faded red stripes to scratch my stomach. I run one shaking hand through my scalped and slashed hair. The phone still rings.

I sit up and my head feels light, disconnected somehow from the rest of my body, which is running on some primal instinct toward the ringing phone. I am aware of some fear, some desperate desire to not answer the phone. I feel stretched, my body heavy and sluggish, weighing down my brain which floats somewhere above me, bouncing gently off the ceiling.

My good hand picks up the phone; my claw rests lightly over my eyes.

'Hello?' I don't expect a response, and I'm not disappointed. Through casual static I hear, far away, a contented sigh.

'Who is this?' Again, the satisfaction is audible. Peace made sound. The static builds and I wait.

'Please ...' My brain is sinking, my feet squash the sticky carpet, I can feel the individual threads in the carpet wrapping around my toes.

'Who are you?' My calves swing loosely beneath the floorboards, my feet dangle, weightless, and now it is my brain that drags me down, screaming something I choose not to hear.

'Scarlett?' the static ceases and for a second there is silence, just me quietly, softly falling through my floor, my brain spiralling down beneath me. Down the line, a giggle, girly and innocent. I smile.

'How are you?' I say and feel my waist edging past the carpet. A moan. This time, all pleasure, and louder. I smile. Again a moan, long, breathy, fading into a whisper and the sound of smiling. My claw wades through the carpet, past the floorboards. A hint of static, white noise, and another long groan of bliss. My claw fumbles with the button crotch of my half-mast jeans, my body floats somewhere between my flat and another one way, way below me.

'Scarlett ...' I breathe and down the line is a scream, a yelp of pain and a hard wet smack, like a hammer into meat. My eyes open. The phone goes dead and I am lying on my floor, my claw crushed beneath my hips.

From below comes a banging, my neighbour screams 'Stop that fucking noise, you little wanker!' I listen to the phone, to the dial tone.

I picture Cary Grant, smooth, sophisticated, arrogant and witty. I drag my carved and shocked hair into a side parting. I grab my jacket.

XXXVIII

Mould creeps across my little platform, the edges warped and twisted by the ever-present rain. The trees shiver in the breeze, shaking loose dying leaves and captive water. Somewhere above the flaming glow of the city the stars are out, somewhere high up above the brooding clouds I can make out the pinprick flashes of an airplane. I wonder what it would be like, sat up there, above the weather, with peanuts and vacuum-packed chicken.

9987, Santino, Scarlett is late. My watch says it is well after three, she should be here by now. I swing the camera from room to room, waiting.

It has been too long since I was last here, I've been selfish. 7451, Algarry, Neville is still on the loose and I've spent my time drinking with Percy and cleaning the shop. Anything could have happened. I stare up at the darkened windows on the third floor, watch the street lights reflected in the liquid surface of the glass, crying orange tears as the rain falls.

I hear a door open on the ground floor, distant cursing, and a meow. A dark shape appears for a moment, perched atop the fence in front of me. It stretches, arches its back and raises whiskers to the night air. It stands, silhouetted against the crumbling facade of the street, sniffs the air and leaps into the undergrowth. The terrace is silent and for a long time I sit and watch and sip at tepid coffee.

Sometime around four the second floor erupts into life. Lights flood the night air for a moment, shadows stretch out behind me, branches snatch at the sky and I stare at the blinding glare coming from the windows before it dies, leaving only one. A hallway, long and dimly lit but visible enough against the darkness, slithers into the bowels of the building. I see a woman, still bruised, still crying, still staring out at the sky. She clings to the shoulders of a wet-nosed boy, her fingers stroking his hair. She looks in vain for the stars, her eyes wet, silver ribbons rolling softly down swollen cheeks. She turns, drags the boy from the light and disappears, melts into the darkness.

The cat brushes past my legs, demanding food. Tonight I have Sheba. I open the can and lower it on to the platform.

It is getting close to five when I raise my head. My neck feels fossilised, solid. It aches as I move. It is still dark, no traffic, no breeze, just the cat softly purring on my lap.

Something woke me: my heart is racing, like earlier with the phone. I listen to the pounding in my chest and wonder how the cat can sleep through it. I flick on my camera and sweep the third floor. Nothing.

I wonder if I missed her. I scan the living room for any sign of her, a jacket hung, a mug on the windowsill, bloody prints on the walls. Nothing. The cat stretches, yawns, and leaps down toward its can of Sheba. I scan the building and listen to the cat lapping up sauce from the can.

On the ground floor a window is open and I hear

snoring and the soft chatter of late-night radio. The top floor remains lifeless and deserted. From the second floor comes a scream.

I glance toward the second-floor windows and sip at my cold, slimy coffee. A light is on toward the back of the house and I can dimly make out two shadows projected on to a wall in the hallway. Arms wave, voices are raised, a door slams and another scream. At the hallway window a dark-haired man appears and draws the curtains.

The cat moans and continues to lap up sauce. The can is tiny. I don't remember sauce.

On the third floor, a light, and at the window appears 9987, Santino, Scarlett. She is dressed in white, a loose-fitting dress and a pink knitted cardigan, far too big for her, slung across her shoulders. She moves windows toward her kitchen, I slide my hair into a side parting and the camera follows her.

Back in the living room she cradles the phone against her neck and pours a glass of white wine. She smiles into the phone and sips at her wine.

I smile, even through the pain in my neck. I feel lighter, relieved: she's safe. The wind picks up again, dying branches rattle and sway in the darkness, a dance for winter, a dance for death, and I suddenly remember that somewhere out there 7451, Algarry, Neville is still dangerous, is still stalking his victims. I've been lucky so far, we both have, 9987, Santino, Scarlett and me. I've abandoned her once, I failed her once. I won't do it again.

On the ground floor the snoring continues, the second floor is quiet, darkness behind the curtains. On the third floor she laughs into the phone and paces. The cat moans, shudders and continues to lap up some liquid in the can.

It looks up at me, its slitted yellow eyes open wide, its whiskers dripping. It moans again and I see something bubbling from its mouth, its tongue dark and shiny. I lean closer.

The cat laps at blood, which dribbles from its jaws back into the can. I sweep the cat from the floor and hold it close. It protests, claws digging in to my thighs, but I force its mouth open and see the blood, see the long fresh wound across its tongue. I glance at the can on the floor, at the sharp edges and the pool of blood.

I stroke the cat, smooth its fur, calm the claws from my thighs and together we watch her pace the room. She giggles, bites her lip, runs her hand through her hair.

With my good hand I adjust the camera, zoom in close so the window frame is no longer visible and we sit, nice and cosy, in her living room. Another night in together. I stroke the cat and watch my Scarlett and I wonder if maybe she is on the phone to the vet. 'Our cat is hurt,' she says. 'Cut her tongue on a can. She's bleeding. What? No, I'm OK, I've got my boyfriend here, he'll look after us both. He's amazing.'

I watch her smiling, see how grateful she is that I'm here for her. She runs a hand down her dress, stretches an arm up against the living room wall. She bites her lip and runs her hand back up, across her breast.

The cat is calmer, breathing deeply and I watch as she readjusts the phone, and a mischievous little smile flickers across her face.

She stretches her arm out again, arches her back against the wall and, with the phone still tucked into her neck she slides one hand up the inside of her thigh and into her dress.

I'm still stroking the cat but I feel my jaw clenching, my leg twitches slightly, causing the cat to whine. The top floor is dormant, the second lifeless, the ground floor asleep, but on the third floor my Scarlett moves her hand beneath her dress, small, circular movements across the top of her thighs.

I stop the recording and zoom in as far as I can, framing her face on the little screen, and I stare at her lips, a whorish red, her cheeks flushed cherry with shame. Her lips part and I see a slither of wet tongue, she mutters into the phone and closes her eyes. The cat is whimpering now and so I stroke harder, feel the fur between my fingers, my fingernails seeking out the skin.

On the screen, at the window, everywhere, she arches again, mouth open wide, and I feel clawing at my thighs, at my hips, teeth bite into my fingers. I watch her eyes screw tight shut, her mouth opening and smiling and moaning all at the same time. Her cheeks are red and I squeeze my good hand closed.

I stagger through the undergrowth, camera slung under my arm as branches claw at my face and brambles whip at my legs. I think I'm crying again because I can't see, nothing stays in focus and my face is hot and wet. I taste salt and blood and my jacket tears on a branch and I fall hard into a ditch.

For a moment or two I just lie there, I want to curl up against the cold and the wet and the betrayal. I want to stay here until she comes looking for me. Until she comes and begs me for forgiveness.

The tripod lies bent beneath my ribs and soon the pain is too much for me and so I open my eyes.

My legs feel weak, my left leg is stiff and cold and won't walk but shuffles instead. I wipe my eyes. The tripod is ruined, twisted and broken and covered in mud. My clothes smell of damp and sewerage.

I have run more or less in a straight line from my little platform, across the backs of the terrace toward the road. Not far off I hear the hissing wheeze of a bus, a blaring horn, and see the rusty glow of early morning street lights. I glance to a distant third-floor window and wonder whether I should go up there. Demand an explanation.

From the darkness behind me I hear a crack, a branch snapping, and I turn, ready to shoo the cat. Over the hill the sun is rising but here, beneath the trees, is a liquid dark, drowning the pale morning. I search the undergrowth for yellow eyes but I'm surprised by muddy boots.

A dark haired man stumbles from the darkness, his rubbish slung over his shoulder. He falls to his knees, the huge bin bag thumping hard into the wet ground. We stare at each other. I take in jeans, a food-stained jumper, pasta sauce maybe, tomato. He glances at my mud-splattered clothes. He opens his mouth to speak but I don't want this. I don't have time. I run.

The sky is streaked with grey, the pavement painted with oily rain. I stare up at the third-storey windows, at closed curtains and darkness. From this side, from the street side, it looks like another world. Sandstone, black railings, brass fixtures. I stare up at the third-storey window. There is something dark and hot and sticky between my fingers, dribbling to the paved street. My breathing is quick, my heart hurts, beating hard against my ribcage. I am furious. The flat is labelled 'Santino'. I slide my hair into a side parting. I ring a buzzer.

XXXIX

I'm waiting for 7451, Algarry, Neville. I think it's about time we had words. His records don't show any patterns for rentals and returns, no set film night, no particular times, so I'm going to work every day, all day. I'm already tired. *Lesbian Nurses* has been away for well over a month now. The police count you as missing after forty-eight hours so I try them again. The guy on the switchboard is telling me, 'No, it's still away being tested,' but in the background I swear I hear a woman say 'Can I have a sponge bath, nurse?' And I hang up.

I drink my coffee on the front porchway where the kids will be but it's daylight now so I'm alone. One by one I go down the list: yellow for one day, pink for two, green for three or more. Left white if we've given up.

'Mr Johnson, its Total Rental here, give us back the film you thieving twat' I say to a bored and tinny sounding robot. It cuts me off.

It's dark by five and already the kids are out, wearing tracksuit tops that glow in the dark. One of them, all in white except for luminous green stripes down his arms and legs, has thrown an empty beer bottle high into the air toward a street light and now it flashes on and off, a flickering orange glow, like fire.

Through the posters on the window one kid is little more than a neon yellow flare, a walking highlighter. The kid is nuclear and I drink my coffee and watch as he pisses on the corner of the front porchway. If she turns up, the girl with the stitched-on grin will have wet feet tonight.

Behind me, above me, above everyone, everywhere, a dead child is being cloned but Bobby doesn't look too worried. In the Chart section two men hold hands and wonder about renting *Football Factory*; in Alphabetical VHS a woman flicks slowly through the films stopping at every romantic comedy, stopping at every romantic drama, skipping quickly past every tragic romance.

I wonder if I should call her. See if we can work things out. The radio spews bile into the night sky: unconfirmed suspect in missing boy case; local businessman abandons employees and flees country. This reminds me I still need to speak to Head Office.

I pick up the phone and I swear there's no dial tone, just a woman giggling: 'That'll never fit in there ...' she says and then a scratched tape player answers. I don't bother to leave a message and instead I dial the number for 9987, Santino, Scarlett but there is nothing there, only silence, no answer machine, nothing, like the number no longer exists.

From nowhere the shop is busy, the rain spits and slithers but fails to make any lasting impression. In Alphabetical DVD an animated teenager and a bored-looking twentysomething browse the Hs. She complains loudly and pointedly that *Harry Potter* is missing. I sip my coffee and smile because I know that *Harry Potter* is where he belongs, the Children's section.

In New Releases three Asian teens listen while a heavy-set, bespectacled student-type tries to explain why American gross-out comedies are cultural touchstones. The three Asian teens nod in unison.

Past ambling heads the rain squirts down the window, pools on the front porch and washes away urine, coke and ketchup. The kids swoop and call into the thickening darkness, behind the counter the radio hosts a call-in show and crackling locals covet their neighbours and abuse the ethnic community.

Headlights sweep past outside, shadows flicker across the faces in the shop and the bell chimes as a damp but tidy figure strolls past New Releases.

Another Hitchcock moment, zoom in and back away as the shop floor distends, my stomach is sucked out toward the desperate night. Soggy but neat, new suit, with an umbrella swinging languidly from his right hand. Bright blue tie, crisp white shirt, boots caked in mud and he smears as he walks. I am holding my breath.

7451, Algarry, Neville stops at the counter. I drop my coffee. My mug shatters and for a second the noise of the store stops, all eyes on me. He smiles at me and takes a mobile phone from his suit jacket's inside pocket.

'One moment,' he says. The silence lasts long enough for a rumble of thunder to seep around the flaking door frame before shattering into a dozen conversations. I stand still, barely daring to breathe, my heart pumps the blood that demands my body to run. But I can't. My teeth grind and I feel my tongue flicking furiously inside my mouth. I scratch my uselessly short hair, try to hide my blushing cheeks. I try to inhale.

Pigtails arrive at the counter, on tippy toes, and shyly push *Shrek* toward me. A pair of wide brown eyes stares hopefully at me from behind the counter, long eyelashes flutter. In Children's DVD the sulky teen discovers *Harry Potter*; in Alphabetical DVD two men clutch handbags and discuss which *Die Hard* they prefer. Across the aisle two women giggle and mutter and plot a girly night in and in New Releases 7451, Algarry, Neville runs his fingers across the covers holding the phone to his ear. He shouts into the phone, angry words, accusatory words. He sighs dramatically, hangs up the phone and heads for the door, his hands dragging across the display as he goes. The door closes and streaks of blood snake across the latest blockbusters.

On the radio a special report interrupts Xenophobes Anonymous, a woman gone missing, foul play suspected, blood found in her flat. In New Releases an elderly woman complains about the dirty cases. Pigtails coughs and raises her eyebrows, tiny wrinkles frowning.

She leaves in tears, a lump already forming under her blonde hair. It starts to rain and the flickering street light begins to buzz. The shop empties, the lights dim and above me Greg suspects everything is not as it seems. In New Releases I stand in front of Tom and wipe blood from his cheek. Four long, straight trails of blood run the length of the wall, occasional pauses where someone has rented. By the door a man and his son stand and I catch his eye, hold up my bloodstained hand. My mouth is open, it moves, but something in my throat won't work. The man holds his son, backs away and I stumble forward, pale and wide eyed, one bloody hand outstretched, and finally my throat returns. I moan and limp toward the door, desperate for him to see this. Desperate for him to help.

Outside the rain splatters against my face and I watch man and boy retreat to a parked car. Above, the street light flashes and the stars sulk behind sodden clouds. On the porchway I shuffle past the girl, her fingers pressed tight into the boy's back. I mutter an excuse me and make my way toward the kettle.

I drink my coffee and watch the kids on the porchway through the posters on the window. I wonder if she's wearing heels tonight.

Outside the rain is light and spins carelessly in the wind and for a second the street light comes on fully, a bright white light in which the rain seems to be floating upwards. The kids stop to watch, glowing through the window like dirty angels and then, with a bang, the bulb finally goes and all the light that is left outside is what is left over from in here. It spills past the posters and the kids go back to fumbling in the front porchway. I listen to the bulb as it tinkles to the ground.

The girl with the extra grin has her skirt raised, her buttocks squeak against the window panes. Outside a police car sweeps through a puddle and stops by the Spar. The kids in the porchway run and I wonder they bother.

7451, Algarry, Neville smears blood across my New Releases selection and no one cares, kids messing about in my porchway will go unnoticed, but shoplifters, they get attention.

The coffee isn't really doing it for me today, maybe I've had too much, I'm immune, desensitised, and my eyes are starting to close when I hear footsteps in the shop. It takes me a full five seconds to realise that 1765, Bradshaw, Mark is drumming his fingers impatiently on the desk.

'Evening, Sir' he says and behind him the kindergarten cop nods, a light grey fuzz slapped across his chin.

'Is that a beard?' I ask, but I'm just being polite. I don't really care. I'm all talk, all coffee. 1765, Bradshaw, Mark is in uniform and looks serious so tonight he must be PC Bradshaw of the local police force. He leans forward.

'We've been watching your tape.' I look to the right at the empty space where the tape should be. I didn't do that. I would have remembered; I wouldn't have done it at all without Head Office approval. I open my mouth but PC Bradshaw is psychic and says:

'Anna Hathaway.'

I nod. Anna. Typical, the one day she turns up and she hands out company property to anyone who asks. PC Bradshaw smiles but doesn't look happy.

'Would you mind coming with us, Sir?'

XXXX

The coffee is incredible. I can taste each individual instant granule. They swim and swirl in the hot water in my plastic mug, strangely separate from the water, aloof, noble. I sip at the hot water, sucking up another ground, which I let melt on my tongue. I feel sick.

The room is oddly high budget, genuinely weathered and tatty. I remember watching a British crime thing on TV a while ago, the suspect sat in the interview room waiting, tapping fingers on the desk, pacing, your basic nervous criminal type. The room was nothing like this one: it looked brand new, well lit, slightly cardboard. This one has an American cop drama feel: dimly lit, stained seat, dark patches on the floor, paint carved off the walls. On the table in front of me is carved 'Abandon hope, all ye who enter her'. I suck on my coffee grounds.

PC Bradshaw and the boy sidekick were very quiet on the way here. I asked about *Lesbian Nurses* but couldn't hear their reply as the radio exploded into the night, a woman demanding 'Get off her this instant, and get on me instead, doctor.' I assumed they need more information on 7451, Algarry, Neville so I sat content as the boys in blue drove me through the heavy night into the city proper.

I drum my fingers on the table, stretch out my aching

leg. My claw rests on my lap and I feel the tendons scrape past scar tissue as I try to itch my throbbing thigh. In one corner a camera blinks at me, red light winks at me and I play the nervous criminal. I drum my fingers on the desk and wish I smoked, just for effect.

I'm sucking on the last of the coffee when the door finally opens and PC Bradshaw comes in. I expect PC Foetal but am pleased to see an older, plainclothes officer instead. PC Bradshaw moves behind me and leans against the wall while the plainclothes officer shuffles to the seat opposite me.

He moves like my former Area Manager, like he is already dead but no one told him: slow, clumsy steps. His hand misses the back of the chair twice before he pulls it away from the table and drops into it. His eyes are closed and for a moment I wonder if he really is dead until they flicker open, red and burning with grey irises and pupils too big to be real.

His skin is grey, like his eyes. The bags beneath his burning retinas are bruise coloured and stubble clings to skin pulled tight across his jaw. I can smell sweat and mint.

He drags his eyes to mine then past me to PC Bradshaw. His shaking hands make a tiny gesture, a tipping with one hand and a look which pleads, which wraps his eyebrows together. I hear the door close. We are alone.

He does not speak, his eyelids hang heavy and I wonder how he died. No obvious wounds, my eyes flick across his suit looking for blood. Nothing. The suit hangs well though, no creasing, well tailored but shabby now, unloved. A breast pocket is hanging loose, threads poke out from the buttons, a shoulder is stained darker across the length of the seam. The door opens and water appears before Officer Zombie.

He rattles a pharmacy bottle across his palm until two red pills nestle in his palm. He drinks and swallows and I can only assume this is what keeps him at least nominally alive. He breathes deep and raises his eyes back to mine.

'Could you confirm your name for me please, Sir?' his voice grates through his chest, a painful growl which seems to hang in the air as he clears his throat. He sounds northern. I nod and confirm my name.

'Thank you, Sir.' He rasps and swallows. He blinks, runs his shaking hand across a clammy forehead.

'Do you know why you are here, Sir?' I nod and he reminds me vaguely of my father, similar accent but softer, lighter.

'*Lesbian Nurses*,' I say and I hear PC Bradshaw spitting a laugh toward us. I turn, frowning, but the limbo officer speaks again.

'*Lesbian Nurses?*'

'Yes,' I say. 'You took it, you tested it, you found the blood.'

The grey eyes are on mine, the pupils huge, and the face twisted by confusion.

'My name is DS Delphin,' his voice scrapes across the table, 'I am one of the officers investigating the disappearance of a young boy from Elmfield Park. He has been missing for almost three weeks now. You have heard about it assume?'

I nod, but I'm confused. I don't understand where this is going, unless 7451, Algarry, Neville is involved in that too. Kidnapper, murderer. PC Bradshaw must have noticed the blood stains he left tonight too. The child's blood smeared across my DVDs.

The door opens and a WPC arrives carrying a file, she places it in front of DS Delphin, but he isn't paying attention. I am running my fingers across the carved graffiti on the table and he is watching my fingers tracing the A, the B. The WPC leaves and as the door closes I hear, 'Oh, my nightstick, oh god, oh ...'

DS Delphin opens the file and pushes a photograph across the table; he slides it beneath my wandering fingers.

'Do you recognise this boy?' he asks. I look, it is the same picture I have seen in the paper, the same photograph PC Bradshaw showed me. I tell him this.

'Have you ever seen this boy, in the flesh?' In the flesh. I frown and feel my cheeks burning, bile in my throat, I don't want to see anyone in the flesh. I shake my head.

'Are you sure?'

I nod. DS Delphin returns to the file and retrieves a selection of black and white photographs. He lays them out on the table in front of me, one at a time, deliberately pausing between each photograph to make sure I am paying attention. I recognise long dark hair, too-tight jeans.

'Sir? Is this you in these photographs?' I nod.

'And this figure here,' he continues. 'Do you recognise it?' I nod. It's the boy.

'You just told me you have never seen this boy before in the flesh, you told PC Bradshaw you had never seen him in the flesh.' In the flesh, in the flesh, I don't want to see anyone in the flesh. 'You have lied to us Sir, and we want to know why.'

I examine the photographs. Me and the boy by the ice cream freezer, me touching the boy's back, me pushing the boy toward the top of the frame, me pushing the boy toward the door. I don't understand.

'I don't understand,' I say. 'I don't remember this at all. These are fake, they must be.' DS Delphin is shaking his head.

'What happened when you got him outside?' he asks. I shake my head.

'What happened when you got him outside?' he asks again. His skin seems to tighten, to stretch across his skull, his eyes are wider now, the lids hidden away but still red, still raw. I shake my head. My mouth is open but my head is still shaking.

'What happened when you got him outside?' DS Delphin is shouting now, the words shredding through the air, he swallows, he swallows, he gags and looks toward PC Bradshaw. 'Mark ...' he whispers and the door closes as PC Bradshaw exits.

He stares at me, still trying to swallow, his eyes no longer grey, just red, pupils which drain the light from the room, and so he sits in shadow, gagging and retching. My hand is shaking. I try to trace the graffiti but it's gone. My thigh hurts, my claw feels cold.

PC Bradshaw arrives with more water and DS Delphin drinks, swallows, sighs.

'You had an accomplice,' he whispers. 'Who?'

I am still shaking my head. My claw is slowly shrivelling in the cold, the light dims and DS Delphin stands up.

I hear his knees cracking and his spine seems to unfold as he stands. He stretches his arms above his head and his shoulders spread like wings. He paces the room, the shuffle gone, huge and dark, his skin no longer grey but sprinkled pink. He breathes deep.

'You were admitted to hospital recently, yes?' The voice has lost its snake-like edge, coming out wetter, like distant thunder. My head is still shaking. I can't stop it.

'Stop lying to me, you were admitted to the RUH last week with a head wound and lacerated knuckles. You still wear the bandages.' My claw is a tight fist of pain. I manage to nod; I taste hot, salty sweat.

'Did he put up a struggle?'

My lip quivers and the table swims as my eyes moisten.

'Did he fight back?'

I feel tears running down my chin, they land on my claw and I am shaking. I sniff and blink and my cheeks are flooded.

DS Delphin leans forward, his eyes black, his face burning, he speaks again, his voice filling the air and I am drowning in it. I choke and he speaks.

'Did he not like you putting your filthy hands on him?'

I gag and splutter and vomit splats across the floor, I heave and cry, tears bubbling from under my skin.

'I ...' the acid smell of bile and stomach fills the room,

'I ... I want ...'

DS Delphin braves the scent and hovers, inches from my face.

'I ... I need a solicitor ...' I say between breaths, between sobs.

DS Delphin sits, his shoulders hunch forward, his body curls up. I hardly hear him as he whispers.

'Get him out of here.'

XXXXI

I swim uphill, salmon-like. Toward the school, toward 9987, Santino, Scarlett. My Scarlett. The streets are wet and slippery, streams trickle downhill from drains and manholes and the rain escapes.

Twice I collide with clumsy locals, twice they slip to the ground, twice I shuffle onward, dragging my aching leg to the sound of swearing and crying. The streets stretch out forever, corridors of sandstone, cheap film sets with plywood supports. My eyes feel wide, feel alien, my cheeks still hot. I can taste my tears still but I have no idea whether or not I am still crying. I just walk.

Eventually I see the bus stop and sit for a moment, sheltered and alone. A young woman pauses as she passes, undecided on the bus. She looks to the sky, glances at me, huddled and shaking, my red eyes and quivering lips. I realise I am singing, muttering words I barely remember, rain rain, go away, leave me here alone again. She walks on. I haul myself over the wall using elbows and my one good hand and drop, panting, into the undergrowth.

Two buses come and go while I sit with my back to the stone wall. The light is borrowed, street light through the trees, darkness beneath the falling canopy. Only a few trees still live, the rest creak, dead through the drizzling night, street light slithering across branches and sagging leaves. I creep through the darkness beneath and the leaves shiver as I pass.

Soon I see the terrace ahead; it leans from the shadows, illuminated by the same borrowed light which glides across the building's plastic surfaces, flickering like fire in the rain. The wind returns, whistling under the trees and from ahead a flapping and fluttering which makes me think of the sea.

The undergrowth is gone, cut back to the fences and trodden down, a crop circle, the middle of which is my little platform. The flapping again and I notice at last the plastic fence constructed across the whole area. Police Line, it reads: Do Not Cross.

From the fence comes torchlight, two winking eyes which bob as they move, casting great sweeping glances across the night. I look to the third floor but there is only darkness. As best I can with one rotting leg, I run.

The bus rattles when it stops, shaking itself apart, shedding its skin as we wait for elderly passengers and drunken youths and miserable students. Occasionally a police car screams past and we flash blue and I cower into my seat.

The driver has his radio on. Suspect in missing boy case. I shudder as I breathe, my claw won't open, the scar tissue is swollen and red and fresh blood stains the bandages.

Eventually the bus shudders away from the city, shrugs off the drunken teens, up into Odd Down. Beneath I watch the endless streets winding down toward the river, orange and yellow and flashes of blue. The bus trembles by the cemetery and I stumble out into the rain.

Somewhere up here is Percy's flat. I wander the red brick, looking for a familiar street name. I have been here before, but only once. A party invite from Percy not long after he got the job. I remember standing outside listening to the music falling from his second-floor living room, watching a disco ball spin, watching the smoke seeping from the open window and me turning around. I have not been back since.

Percy's flat is in a converted semi in a cul-de-sac. The street is tree-lined, expensive cars in driveways, neatly trimmed bushes, roses. Only the flats in the corner with weed-infested gravel and a rusting fridge bring home any sense of the real. I crunch across the gravel. One buzzer reads Ground floor: Wazzer, another reads First floor: Potter, D and lastly is Percy, second floor.

My finger is on the buzzer but I'm not pressing. I watch the smoke curl from the speaker by the door, I listen to a baseline throb from somewhere above me. I wonder if I could get to Mam's, but no, they're probably waiting for me there already.

I buzz.

Smoke pours from the speaker and a crackling, 'Alright? Who's this?'

'It's me' I say, and there is a pause. The smoke drifts toward the sky, the rain punching holes its dense cloud.

'You'd best come up then, mate, eh?'

I drift through thick tobacco smoke, it swirls behind me, little hurricanes as the air moves. The corridor moves with the smoke, the walls bending as I limp toward the music. The baseline continues and the mist throbs to the beat, is amplified in the atmosphere. I stagger down the corridor and hours later the smoke engulfs me wholly.

A space opens up to my left, a darkness the smoke seems to avoid, an emptiness from which I feel a chill breeze. I hear a stifled laugh, a tapping and cracking, something rustles and the smoke drifts across the door frame. From somewhere up ahead Percy calls and I shuffle on leaving the void behind me to be swallowed by the fog.

I walk for days, the smell changes, the smoke is thicker, earthier, blue almost. The baseline pounds and the fog bounces in time, my heart beats in time, skipping with every missed beat, pumping a rhythm through my body. I'm getting tired and I hear Percy again ahead of me. He tells me to sit and I do.

The couch is warm and red and I sink into it, I curl my leg beneath me and fall into the cushions. Above me the blue smoke swirls and spirals across the ceiling. For the first time in ages I can see the floor, a broken sea of takeaway boxes and beer cans stretch out into the distance, something glows and flickers in the mist, a box of light which flashes and twinkles.

I breathe deep and feel safe and wish I had come sooner. From the gloom comes Percy's face, long and angular. He grins, of course, the edges of his mouth stretching past his cheeks, impossibly wide.

'What's up, mate?' he says, barely audible above the baseline. My heart speeds up as the beat powers forward at double time. Percy drifts back into the darkness, a tight red glow at his lips.

'Percy?' I say and watch the tiny red eye wink at me through the haze. 'Percy? Where are you?' Two red dots, angry eyes glaring at me, bobbing toward me, two torches beneath the trees.

'Percy, I need help, I don't know what's happening.' My heart pounds irregular and insistent with the beat, a swift one two and a pause during which my heart does not beat.

A yellow smile seeps into view and a hand holds a rolled up cigarette, it is held out to me and I take it without thinking.

'Calm down man, have a quick one of that and tell me what you need.' It tastes odd, not like it smells. My throat is hot and dry, it burns past my windpipe but sits warm and cosy in my lungs.

'He did it,' I say. 'I wasn't there when she needed me and he did it.'

A frowning clown floats just behind the smoke which seeps from my nostrils. 'Who? Who did what?' he says.

I can hardly hear it myself but I know my lips are moving '7451, Algarry, Neville.' I say. '7451, Algarry, Neville.' Through the daze comes Percy, his face longer than it should be, his chin dripping on to the floor. 'He killed her,' I say, 'and framed me for that boy.'

Percy's head twists to one side, his grin is back and smoke drifts from between his teeth, curls from his nostrils. He opens his mouth and the music stops. The beat is gone; my heart is no longer pumping.

'The music,' I scream, 'put the music back on!' Percy looks confused, canyons crack the skin across his forehead, he smiles. 'Percy, you fucker, put the music back on.' Percy isn't moving, I drift in darkness and silence, my heart is still and Percy just fucking smiles.

'My heart, you fucker, you've stopped my fucking

heart.' Laughter explodes from somewhere nearby, Percy turns toward it, his eyes red and angry, a sneer and I feel his hand on my shoulder.

I can't breathe and spring from the couch, the flickering light ahead drifts into focus, the smoke clears and I see a news reporter standing in front of my Scarlett's flat.

'Police have confirmed that a woman has gone missing from her home in Elmfield Park. Police were alerted by neighbours who heard screaming.' A thump in my chest, I inhale smoke. 'So far details are sketchy but police have confirmed they have found what appear to be bloodstains in this flat behind me.' A thump in my chest, I exhale. I laugh, I shouldn't be here. I know exactly where I should be. The music starts again and my heart beats with a frantic pace.

Percy drifts into view again. 'Are you OK?' he says and I nod and am already dragging my leg behind me past the darkness in Percy's flat and out into the night, out to find 7451, Algarry, Neville.

XXXXII

For a while the smoke follows me, trailing behind me as I stagger through the streets. My leg is stiff but pain free, my claw flexes as I go, smoke twisted around its talons. The rain has stopped and as I escape the music my heart beats regularly once again.

The street shines with broken glass and lying water but I look down the hill toward the school where the night flashes blue. I wonder how much time we have left. My watch says it is sometime after two and the city is dead. Dark windows, locked doors. Only the flaming street lights still burn. The night is cold.

It is another half an hour before I reach the shop and I am shivering with cold. My eyes hurt, my shoulders are heavy and the key rattles against the lock, too big for the opening. I spit and thrust it in but I have to wiggle it more before finally I hear the locks click and the door opens with a sigh.

The carpet near the door squelches as I walk, the alarm beeps and from the storeroom a disturbed scurrying. Behind the counter I flick on a light and enter 1138 into the pad by the CCTV monitor. The beeping stops, I no longer squelch, the rats have scampered. I sit in silence while the computer whirs into life.

I need to find 7451, Algarry, Neville. My Scarlett needs my help, that's why he is trying to get me out of the way. That is why he doctored those tapes. It's not a difficult thing to do, any idiot with an Apple Mac can replace poor-quality CCTV footage.

The screen flashes black and red, a tiny red box flashes in one corner: Purge. I type 'No' as I do every day, and like any other day I wonder what sort of company encourages its records to be deleted at the beginning and end of every shift.

Although dated and slow, once the system is up and running, and once you learn some of the shortcuts, it runs quite smoothly. More importantly it stores a lot of information. By pulling up the records for 7451, Algarry, Neville I can find not only his address but also copies of the documents he used to register, a complete list of films rented, times in and out, total fines paid, total spends, even a list of extras: popcorn, ice cream, nachos.

At present he has *Love Object* out on hire, which I grudgingly admit is a good choice. Anna hired it out yesterday whilst I was at the station. According to the time code he rented only minutes after I was driven away.

I move through into Member's Details to find the address. At the top of the screen I see Anna's name as she entered his details initially way back in 2001. I sigh. Anna gets fired tomorrow. Under address it reads 'Customer forgot details, will fill in next time, sorry, Anna.'

The kettle boils and I find slightly soggy Ginger Nuts in the cupboard. Unmounted shelves lie scattered across a corner, the handle of the hammer poking from beneath a completed and fully stocked unit. I pick it up and place it with the box of nails by the sink. I pour the kettle and return to the counter.

For a long time I stare at the screen, at the note by my ex-employee. She has no idea what she has done. I sip my coffee and chew on damp biscuits. Down the back the rats get braver, I hear them gnawing on the unmounted shelves. A little before four I turn off the lights and shut down the computer.

I amble toward the front door, straightening as I go, blood still streaks most of the New Releases. I'll have to sort that in the morning. When I reach the door I check everything is as it should be and twist the lock.

I blink and a face from the darkness presses at the glass, a sideways grin, glazed eyes. Through the glass I hear, 'Got *Lesbian Nurses*, mate? 'Zit back yet?'

I feel cold, calm and smile politely at the drunk. My hand shakes a little as I open the door but my voice is clear, my breathing even.

'Certainly,' I say. 'Right this way.' The face smiles through stubble, suit damp and smelling of smoke, shirt creased, tie bright blue. He fumbles in his suit and falls through the door.

"V got me memb'ship card somewhere,' he mumbles.

'No need,' I say. '7451 isn't it?'

XXXXIII

The clouds are bleeding outside, stained red by the rising sun, and birds trill and cackle on the rooftops. Someone else's coffee cup rattles against the counter as I pick it up. My heart pounds, my stomach has sunk into my knees. I feel sick.

The hammer lies where I dropped it last night, splattered with a sticky red, drying brown in the damp backroom. I can't move it. Making coffee was tough enough. Being down there was tough enough.

I stand in the porchway, breathing deeply the crisp air, watching as early-morning shoppers float by. I hold the key in my claw, dangling loosely from a talon and a sign on the shop door reads: Back in five minutes.

A family stand expectant by the door, looking from the sign to me to my coffee to each other. I shake my head and the father frowns.

'Rats,' I say.

I have already rung Anna. She cried, which was odd, I thought she'd be happy to no longer have to get out of bed to tell me she wasn't coming in. She can sleep straight through now. She can finally let go. Percy was confused. He wanted to know why he couldn't work today, which was even weirder. I have had to give him paid holiday for the day to keep him away. I hung up when he started asking what happened to me last night.

The family lope down the street, the father suggests the bookshop. They laugh. I sip my coffee and breathe through pursed lips, my breath shakes as it leaves.

On the radio I hear a crackling news reporter: 'The search has now widened to the fields behind the missing woman's flat. As the sun rose police began sweeping the area. A source has told us that a dead animal has been found but could not comment on whether it had any bearing on the case.'

Bastard. The cat. I glance down the back, into the wet shadows, and my pulse quickens. I feel my teeth grinding.

The shop is open, the takings must be raised and I try to calm down by reading yesterday's mail. I select the unpaid bills and push them into an envelope addressed to Head Office. Shadows one and two said it had to be today. Literature on New Releases has arrived and I glance at it, uninspired.

At the bottom of the pile is a white envelope; in green across the top is 'HM Revenue and Customs'. I very nearly push it straight into the envelope for Head Office but it's the last letter and I'm not ready. I need more time. I open it.

Employees of Total Rental

Due to financial irregularities and suspect account keeping we have begun a criminal investigation into your parent company, A. A. Leach Holdings Inc ...

I pick up the phone and read on.

Investigators will soon be requesting that you hand over all accounts and stock lists. We are aware that due to the nature of your business your stock lists do not always match that which you have in store and so we ask that you suspend all rentals forthwith and concentrate on retrieving stock from your customers ...

The phone rings and rings and I stare outside at the sun rising pink behind the dry cleaners. I sip my coffee and stare at the passing shoppers and the phone rings and rings and, nothing. The line goes silent. Not even a dial tone.

Above me, above everyone, everywhere, Snow White sings to squirrels. Today is a Sunday and the early morning traffic files politely by. The shop is mostly empty, just a young family in the Chart section playfully fighting over what to watch today. In Alphabetical DVD a kid is nervously flicking through everything checking the back of each case to see if they contain any nudity. My claw tightens and I feel a dull ache in my thigh. I glance eagerly down the back.

By the time I hear 7451, Algarry, Neville stirring down the back there is a row of young children sat cross legged in front of the counter, watching the dwarves decide what should be done with the woman they just found wandering in the woods.

From the back room comes grunting and something is knocked over but only one little girl in a fairy costume notices anything. I smile at her, turn up the big screen and head down the back.

Between me and the outside world lie two doors. One solid wooden door and beyond that is a space about a metre square then a heavy steel plated door with a heavy iron gate, all of which have to be opened before I put the bins out.

I have no bins today but I open the wooden door anyway and smile. 7451, Algarry, Neville blinks at me, eyelids slightly drooping, stare slightly glazed, but he obviously recognises me because he starts to moan behind the thick layer of duct tape wrapped around his head to keep his mouth shut. Using the same duct tape he is secured to an old stool, the tape wound carefully around his ankles and around his waist. He holds his bound hands up in front of me and whimpers. In one hand I hold the hammer, in the other a pair of scissors and I watch while his eyes slowly focus.

From above comes a curious 'Hello? Is anyone serving?' I pause, put down the hammer. She calls again and I move back up the stairs closing the door behind me. A woman, obviously harassed, smiles politely and asks, 'I'm really sorry, but I'm obviously quite harassed, and I noticed all the kids in here watching the film. Would you mind me leaving mine for two minutes while I nip to the chemist?' She leans forward, fingers her collar, pops open the top button. She squeezes her arms together. 'I'd be ever so grateful.' She purrs. Behind her her child has already sat down and is staring up at the big screen with one arm around the little girl in the fairy costume.

'Course you can,' I say. 'No problem.' She smiles gratefully and hurries off.

'Alright guys,' I say. 'I've got some stuff to do down the back so if anyone comes give me a nice loud yell, OK?' They nod in unison and turn their attention back to the screen.

Down the back 7451, Algarry, Neville is struggling. The hammer and scissors are where I left them on the shelf and I've brought the box of nails from next to the sink.

He's getting louder now; the sweat on his face must be loosening the tape around his mouth. I put my good hand on his chin and force his head round so I can see the pulp that was his ear, turned almost inside out by the blow, it's barely recognisable anymore. It looks torn where the lobe should be and I remember about the rats.

He struggles harder and I can see the tape coming away round his mouth. My claw can just about manage to grip the hammer and I hit his mashed ear hard with a backhand swipe and his eyes glaze over again.

After re-taping his mouth I work quickly and above me, above everyone, everywhere, the dwarves set to work too. From the line of children sitting cross legged on the floor in front of the counter comes the soundtrack because they're singing along: 'Whistle while you work.' And I do. 7451, Algarry, Neville is dazed and I slice through the tape holding his hands together. One hand I tape to the back of the stool, twisting his arm behind him, the other I lift up over his head and place it palm up against the thick wooden wall. I purse my lips and whistle.

I rest the letter against his palm, the green government heading facing toward me, then put a nail between my teeth. I hum along with the kids on the shop floor, just humming a merry tune, and his arm begins to stiffen and struggle. His eyes are opening again and I push the nail hard into the palm of his hand.

He's louder now, much louder. His eyes open and focus on the nail I'm holding against his hand. Above us, above everyone, the children sing 'Hi-ho, hi-ho' and he struggles so much I almost drop the nail.

My claw jams the side of the hammer into his face and his nose bursts, I bring the hammer down hard on the nail and he screams behind the duct tape. Quickly I bring the hammer down again and again and finally I'm through the skin. He's really screaming now and I'm glad the kids are singing because otherwise they'd probably hear him.

My stomach is gurgling, my breathing stumbles, but this must be done. I read the letter as I raise the hammer and bring it down hard but this is taking a lot longer than I planned. The nail is wedged between two bones because I'm hammering it in too close to his wrist. I should have aimed for the knuckles. I read the letter and close my eyes and think of my Scarlett and bring the hammer down full force. I can hear the nail scraping on bone.

He thrashes around so much that I miss the nail altogether, so his hand turns purple and yellow, lymph oozing from broken skin. I swipe at the nail with another backhand across my body and something snaps in his hand and the nail finally plunges into the wood.

Two more quick blows and it's in tight, so I hammer the nail down, bending it toward his bruised skin to make sure he can't pull his hand away.

The kids are yelling so I swing shut the heavy wooden door and head up to the counter. The shop is busy again; the parents of my audience come in to collect and I manage to smile though my whole body is shaking.

'Anytime,' I say, 'it's always quiet on a Sunday and they're no trouble.'

There is blood on my jeans and in my hair. I claw it

into a side parting. I leave the big screen singing and head down the back with the battered yellow radio. It mumbles under my arm: another bomb in Iraq, local child last seen outside local shops, shamed rugby team win a cup, woman missing. I place it on the shelf with the hammer and nails.

I'm too tired to nail his other hand; it's bound tight to the stool and really makes no difference. He knows I'm serious.

I drink my coffee and watch 7451, Algarry, Neville as he slowly regains consciousness. His suit is ruined, heavily bloodstained like the floor around him, but his shoes still sparkle. His hair is flattened and wet with sweat, his umbrella swings forward and backward between my fingers. The shop is empty and Snow White sings alone. I scratch at the scabs under my hair, one breaks and I wince. Blood trickles through my hair.

His arm, limp and hanging, tenses and struggles again. His eyes open wide in shock and pain. He stares at me, green eyes red rimmed, and his pupils are dots, pinpricks against the dirty green. He looks fragile so I move slowly, gently putting down his umbrella and pulling up a stool so I sit opposite him.

Still moving slowly I reach up for the hammer.

Blood dribbles down my forehead.

He tenses and I can see him edging away, sinking into himself. I dangle the hammer between thumb and fore finger, the claw end toward the floor. Leaning forward, elbows on my knees, I can smell him, sweat and urine and stale deodorant. His nose is already swollen a painful purple, like the hand nailed to the wall, like someone was inflating him, like a giant blow-up doll.

I breathe deep. Swallow down the sickness; concentrate on the coffee smell rather than the mess on the floor.

'You ever play twenty questions?' I ask. His eyes widen a little, fresh sweat on his forehead.

'Come on,' I say. 'Nod for yes, shake for no, you know how to play.' He nods nervously.

'Alright then. Let's begin,' I say and manage to smile. 'Your name is 7451, Algarry, Neville, yes?' He nods slowly, bunches his shoulders a little in a shrug.

'No,' I say, 'no shrugs, no maybes, just yes or no. Shall we continue?' He nods, still staring at me with those knife-point eyes.

'Do you know a 9987, Santino, Scarlett?'

A slow shake of the head. The head of the hammer is level with his knee. I swing it a little, letting the claw head tap against his knee caps. More sweat on his face running down the duct tape like tears, mixing with blood, sparkling in the flickering fluorescents.

Again. 'Do you know 9987, Santino, Scarlett?' Another shake, this time eager, more desperate and I swing the hammer a little harder and his eyes close. The sickness fades and I breathe long, shaking breaths through my tense jaw. He whimpers behind the duct tape.

'Do you know 9987, Santino, Scarlett? Do you know my Scarlett?' He nods, and I win. his eyes open, pleading. He nods and nods and whimpers.

'Good,' I say. 'Do you know where she is?' He shakes his head, small quick movements. I turn up the radio so he can hear the news broadcast: assassination in Iraq, local rugby team stripped of title. Missing woman still not found.

'You hear that?' I ask and he nods. 'That's 9987, Santino, Scarlett. She's missing. And you know where she is.'

He looks at me, his green eyes red rimmed and full of tears and shakes his head and moans behind the tape. Blood curls across my lip. I swing the hammer a little harder and his shoulders start to shake and the tears stream down his face.

'Yes you do,' I say, though the words can only crawl past my tight lips. He shakes his head and his shoulders and his whole body is quivering, tears drop on to his lap. I swing the hammer harder and he cries behind the tape.

I swing the hammer harder and he whimpers; I smell fresh urine.

I swing the hammer harder and he is crying and pleading behind the tape but lying with every breath. I taste blood.

I swing the hammer harder.

I swing the hammer harder.

And harder.

And harder.

XXXXIV

I dribble snot into hot soapy water and scald my hand, scald my claw, but still it is not enough. My breath judders across my chest and I watch myself as though underwater, silken threads glittering across my cheeks.

I scrub beneath the nails, rub my talons raw and my body heaves and my lungs explode with each breath. With my forearm I wipe my eyes, spread snot across my hairy arm. In the mirror is me, pale skin, pink eyes, hair plastered thick against my scalp, rivulets shimmering toward my chin. Tears cleaning my cheeks of blood. My stomach heaves above my half-mast jeans, clumps of hair around my nipples, around my bellybutton, and I shine with sweat. Tears drop loudly into the sink and are lost. My stomach quivers and my breathing shakes.

Slowly, the water turns pink.

Behind me, in a bag, my T-shirt, once blue, now black, drying sticky and rusting. My watch too is stained a guilty red, it ticks loudly beneath the blood, counting out my thumping heartbeats.

I take off my jeans, the legs speckled red and black and damp with sweat, with urine. I wrap them into a tight little ball and thrust them deep into the bag. My underwear too is ruined and I peel it from my clammy white skin and drop them into the bag.

My options are limited. All I have is the suit I wore to my interview at the shop. I lay it carefully across the bed, brush tears from the material, drip blood on to the lapel and return to the bathroom. The shower spews steam and I stand in the bath as tears circle the drain. The soap is nearby so I wash.

The suit still fits, in fact it's even a little loose. I turn side on to the bathroom mirror. I've lost weight. I smile and sniff and wipe my eyes. I pat my stomach and smile, my eyes drooping to meet the corners of my lips.

I look at my wrist but the watch is gone and so glance up to the clock in the kitchenette. Almost five and outside darkness creeps through the city, drinking in shadows, lying heavy against the sandstone and cardboard. I sip at my coffee and the mug rattles against my teeth. I breathe deep, sucking in the steam, the smell, the familiar. In the bathroom the radio still crackles, a soft south-western drawl floats through the flat. I close my eyes and breathe out, my lips a pouting O. From the stalking darkness outside a siren screams and my body spasms. A shatter. My sockless feet are hot. The last mug lies broken beneath me.

The phone rings and the rain patters softly on the window. I glance outside at the street weaving upward, the houses squat against the hill, empty, burning red as the street lights warm to the night. I pick up the phone and hear breathing. I smile.

'Scarlett?' I ask and feel a weight slip from my shoulders and my heart seems to swim in my chest, I feel it flutter against my lungs.

'I ... I thought you'd gone.' From the end of the line comes a sigh, relief and joy, and I sigh back.

From the radio comes the news jingle, angular notes and discords, and a BBC voice announces: 'Police have just confirmed that the body of a woman has been found in the school field adjacent to the flat from which the missing woman disappeared.'

My claw tightens, I feel cold.

'Scarlett?' I ask but the line is silent.

'A source close to the investigation has informed us that the body is that of a young woman and was found hidden in the undergrowth, not far from the perimeter wall.'

My hand is shaking again, I feel my heart beating in my ears, feel a pressure building behind my eyes and from down the line comes a soft, rolling cry and she weeps down the phone.

'Indeed we can also inform you that the body has been found alongside another body, that of a young boy. The police believe that surveillance equipment found earlier today may be connected. Investigators will not confirm whether they believe the boy's body to that of the missing boy, Frankie Delch.'

From somewhere at the end of the line the weeping grows and she wails.

'What has been confirmed, however, is that the police now believe the disappearance of the young boy may be in some way connected to the murder of this young woman.'

A thump, a hard wet slap from the phone and a whimper.

'Scarlett?' I yell, 'Scarlett?' but the line is dead. I rush to the radio but the smug southern rambler has returned.

I twist through the stations: jazz, hip-hop, something in French, someone loud and cheerful and laughing. The radio hits the wall and splinters, plastic spinning to the lino, the soft tinkling of metal on porcelain. The phone rings.

'Scarlett?'

'You what? No, mate, it's me.'

I smell smoke, watch grey tendrils crawl from the mouthpiece, stroke my cheek.

'Percy?' Always fucking Percy, he just can't leave me alone. 'Fuck off Percy,' I yell, 'I'm expecting a call, I ...'

'This is important, listen ...'

'I'm waiting for a call, Percy. You're tying up the line, now go.'

I try hard to stop yelling, to sound calm, to sound reasonable. I hear my breath quivering as I speak.

'But listen ...'

'No, Percy!' I'm screaming now, I feel the tendons in my neck straining, talons dig into in my palm and draw blood and I listen to the drip drip drip on to the floor. 'Get off the fucking phone.'

'Just fucking listen, you arrogant little shit.' My blood drops to the floor and I count the silence by the splashes. Percy is breathing hard down the phone and my eyes are wide. My mouth is open but nothing is happening. I hear static. 'Look,' he says, 'I'm sorry but this is important.'

'What is it Percy?' It is only as my chest deflates that I realise I was holding my breath. I feel the energy seeping away, hear it pooling on the floor by my feet. Cooling coffee and steaming blood.

'The police have just been round. They wanted the keys to the shop.' I'm nearly out of time, the blood trickles softly over talons, warm and soothing. Percy is still talking: 'I don't know how they know but you need to move it, they'll find it. Hello?'

XXXXV

The alleyway is flooded, the mud sticks to my shins as I wade behind the old brickworks. Above me dark clouds hover and spit as I slide, dropping my bag. The condoms glow in the dark and I follow, deeper and deeper into the darkness where street lights cannot follow.

From beyond the alleyway I hear the rumble of traffic, horns demanding attention, a squeal of brakes. I wear a hat, a beanie bought by my Mam. I am incognito. Head down I swim onward, dragging the bag of soiled clothing behind me. The condoms stretch on forever, floating in the air, glow sticks guiding me, taking me somewhere, but I don't yet know where.

Overhead a razor slices the air, cuts into my breathing, pounding, heavy ear-splitting thumps into my head. A light, like God, glances across the brickwork chimneys, runs a silky white stain down the shaft. I hear the blades whumping above the city; I see the shadow against the clouds. It banks away, the eye blinks and is gone. I stand between thighs that tower over me and stare at the swollen red within.

I drop the bag and it lands with a hard wet slap in the mud. My suit is ruined, splashed with filth, one shoulder has darker stains running in a cross across the seams, my shirt hangs loose behind me. I stare at the thighs, stare into the darkness between. I tuck in my shirt and above me the words are sprayed in dribbling scarlet paint: 'Abandon hope', it reads, 'all ye who enter her.'

I slither between the thighs, the condoms thin out, the street lights die in the gloom and I wait, breathless, in the darkness.

The night is blue, the street flashes a lazy strobe, crackles with urgent radio. I poke my head around the corner and stare up Moorlands Road. Three police cars are parked opposite the shop, an ambulance idles, standing proud in the middle of the street, while an angry taxi blares its horn. From the tarmac before the dry cleaners a red eye winks at me.

Radio static crackles and drifts across the road. A WPC is guarding my door again, the stag party nowhere in sight. By the police cars the kids on bikes wave fist-sized cigarettes and pass around a bottle of yellow-looking coke. The Spar is open and customers spill across the pavement, drip against the shoulders of two more PCs who string white tape in a barrier between the drainpipes and the lampposts. The WPC shuffles backward, holds open the door, and the paramedics emerge.

Like on TV the stretcher is on wheels, like on TV a white sheet is bloodstained and lies across a swollen lump, like on TV a camera crew skids to a halt and leaps from the van, spotlights making the blood glow, the sheet has rubies for eyes. The radio screams against the intrusion and I hear through the static a voice saying: 'Well, you have been naughty haven't you?' I flinch and the static breathes: 'We must find a way to punish you.'

The camera crew jostle with the customers, dance with the PCs, and I'm sure I hear a very BBC voice ask: 'Can you tell us what happened to you?'

Above me, above all of us, everywhere the bright white eye burns into the street, blinds the camera and the strangely slow whump whump whump consumes my heart. It pumps the blood which powers my legs which make me run and I force my useless limb into action. It screams as it moves, pain lancing across my ribs with each painful landing. I aim for Lower Bristle Road, I aim for the buses.

We glide over smooth tarmac, the road laid out ahead like calm waters and we sail away. Outside the city glows like fire, it flashes blue as they fight the flames but they continue to burn and the showers of blue dribble away as we head out toward the Boatsman and beyond to the wilds outside the city.

Drunken students splutter, swearing, filling the front section of the bus. They sway with the bus, they fall into each other and surface with a different face. The moving platform of the bending bus is drenched with a babble of giggling children who leap from platform to platform as the bus drifts around corners. Here, in the back, a blind man sits, his dog at his feet. He strokes his beard, he wipes dusty sunglasses, his back straight, shoulders back.

A flashing white car screams past us, heading toward Elmfield Park, but I do not flinch. I am safe. I close my eyes and sink into the seat. The dog growls and I hear a dry, whispering voice: 'Don't do it, son.'

The blind man sits, unmoved. The bus rolls as the traffic gets choppy but he stays as he is, a gyroscope as all around him we fall with the rocking waves. His dog is looking at me, bright brown eyes and golden fur. Its green jacket makes it look military. I salute and stare at the blind man.

Outside a posse of elderly tourists decide not to enter the bus, the students cheer, the babble falls as the bus casts off. The blind man turns his head, his glasses on me. 'Ring the bell, lad,' he says, and so I do.

The bus drifts onward through the night and I look back to the street where the blind man stands in the rain. Back straight, shoulders back. Soon, I know, the bus will dock. I still don't know what I'm doing; I just know I need to see her. On a hill past the university is a warm yellow glow and I feel for the wind, I hope for calm seas.

XXXXVI

I smell honeysuckle and nearly cry. 7451, Algarry, Neville has won. He has framed me for the boy. He was found in my shop. I can't believe I was so stupid, I fell into his trap. The houses are ivy-covered, sheltered front doors of heavy wood and neat gloss paint. Hedges and creepers embrace garden fences, winter has not yet reached here; purples and blues and reds bloom under yellow street lights. The clouds weep, a despondent drizzle clings to my face, to my ruined suit.

Somewhere behind me the body of Scarlett lies in a morgue, a phone call to Carlisle and tears down the phone. I can't be there to console her mother, I hope she understands.

Mam's front door is closed tight against the weather. The frosted glass is dark, the house beyond in silence. I touch the door knob, feel the cold metal, stare at the tarnished gold finish. It does not move. I feel something heavy in my chest, feel my lungs contract. I can't see and taste salt. I need my Mam.

Ivy climbs the walls to the side of the house and I edge past the bins, a fence surrounds the house and drips with honeysuckle, the smell sweet and sickly. I wipe my nose with my mud-stained sleeve and tear open my trousers on a blackberry bush. I sit on the back step, my hand wrapped around my bleeding shin, my claw nestled in greasy hair. A fine mist floats in the air around me, drifts across the garden, scatters across the city in the valley below. Moisture sticks to my skin, tears slide across my cheeks, splash on to my knees and blood oozes between my fingers.

A distant heartbeat, a wink from the brooding sky behind, a tiny, dark shape moves beneath the clouds. I am short on time. I sniff, pull myself to my feet and finger the handle of the kitchen door.

The kitchen hides. Surfaces cower beneath the shadows, the night lies like a cloak across the house, heavy and soft and warm. I smell disinfectant, the wire rack by the sink glints with stolen luminescence, winks at me, encourages me. The cloak lies too weighty to move and so I slink through shadows, past a stack of drying dishes, round the stools, which scuttle backward as I approach.

The house is silent but for the drip drip drip of a tap in the kitchen and the low growl from the central heating. I sit in the front room, straight backed on the edge of the couch. My father's pit by the fire is engulfed by the night, my Mam's cushions bathe in the street light. The curtains are open and outside I watch the beaten sky cry softly. Despite the warmth I shiver, my chest flutters and something deep in my stomach, something clinging to my ribs, is falling toward the floor.

I sniff and breathe deep, I don't have time to cry, mine is not to wonder why. My talons cut into my punctured palm and I wish, more than anything, that 7451, Algarry, Neville had just left us alone. I stare out at the night. At the purple clouds.

Upstairs I hear a snap and my eyes water

instinctively. Upstairs I hear a snap and I raise my hand, raise my claw and bury my face. Upstairs I hear a snap, the slap of my father's belt.

I pause at the foot of the staircase; they slide sideways as cold, clammy tears swell across my vision. I crouch in the shadows and look up. A bronze bar of light leans against the wall at the top of the stairs. A perfect sliver of warmth, of life, and I shake below, my pale skin wet with sweat and fear. In my good hand I notice silver sparkling, the cold comfortable in my palm.

The stairs creak. I ascend slowly, reluctantly, shaking. The banister slips past my claw, my talons scrape the paint and I climb.

Above me, above everyone, everywhere a snap of leather and a whimper and the bronzed shaft of light shrinks as an arched back grows from the shadows.

My boots leave a muddy trail behind me, the carpet devours my filthy stains, sucks the moisture from the grunge and sighs. My claw shakes, talons rattling against the banister, its peeled skin spirals through the air to rest in the desperate pile beneath. Mam's bedroom door is open, a slice of light to my left. Next to me the arched back straightens, bends backward, a shadow flashes across the wall, a snap of leather, the whack as it hits the skin and a moan, deep and sodden.

My breathing flaps through my ribcage, my heart a bird, desperate and trapped and I edge toward the door. The snaps and slaps and smacks come faster now, my fingers close tight on the cool metal and I hold it fast to my chest to still my fraught heart. My claw extends before me, my talons twist around the door frame, the light making my bloody nails shine. I leave a bloody palm print

247

on the door frame as I enter.

I blink in the light and shudder at the snapping of leather, at the slap of the skin. The walls glow red, the heavy velvet curtains are new and hang low and crimson over black skirting. Outside the air begins to move in rhythm, a distant thudding, and on the bed is my father, face down, arms out to his sides and he lies crucified on the bed.

Across his hips a woman sits, a hooded red satin cloak and long naked thighs. Her toes curl and she slaps the belt diagonally across his back. Thick red welts criss-cross his back and he moans and sighs through gritted teeth. The woman in red leans forward to bite his ear. She whispers and he laughs softly, whispers back.

She tenses her thighs, raises her cloak and I watch her pink buttocks clench and my father rolls beneath her, grinning and red faced, emerging on to his back. The belt rests against his chest and his eyes, wide and dark, meet mine, red and wet.

The woman is pushed to the bed and my father rears up, a roar in his chest, the blood rushing to his face. He shakes and clenches his fists, his penis erect and pointing to the knife in my one good hand. The woman screams as he approaches, his left hand is raised across his chest, his knuckles sweaty and shiny, his face red and tense.

The woman on the bed is scrabbling to escape the duvet, wrapped up in panic as she flees the bed, and my father steals the light from the room, roaring forward, beast like, teeth bared. His knuckles tense and I know exactly how they will feel when they dig into my cheek.

He screams, the woman screams, I scream, his arm drops toward me and a streak of light, of chilled air, of comforting steel arches upward, through my father and glistens red and silver above me.

The blood sprinkles the ceiling.

My father staggers, his arms hang limp. He stares at me, his blue eyes on mine, his pupils swimming through tears. A soft red mist falls quietly, warm against my cheek. From the bed is another scream and a cry and I stare into eyes the same as mine as my Mam shrugs off her hood and crawls from the bed. I still hold the knife, it wavers by the ceiling, blood oozing down the blade, dripping on to my boots. I feel cold, wet fingers on my arm, and my father reaches out, curls his hand around my claw.

He slumps to the ground, his back to the wall and drags me down with him. The knife falls into the carpet and I sink to my knees opposite fading eyes that are watercolour blue. His chest is soaked with blood, dark hairs clumping into clots as blood trickles down, over his stomach, pools beneath his navel. His throat a grinning gash of red and puckered skin.

He breathes short, quick breaths and blood froths in the wound, bubbles and bursts as the blue fades from his eyes.

Fingers grip my shoulders and I fall sideways, land by his twitching toes and my Mam is forcing her hands to his gurgling throat. He tries to speak, his mouth opens and hangs, blood spits from the wound, bursts from beneath my Mam's fingers. Mam is crying, weeping, her whole body shudders with each breath. She kisses him, their lips meet, their tears mingle. My father raises a shaking hand to her face. He strokes her cheek and grins. His eyes close, his breathing slows and I hear a drumming in the air, feel the pounding pressure behind my eyes as my heart beats a heavy whump whump whump.

I wrap my arm around my Mam and pull her away from him. She screams and claws at the floor as I drag her backward. As we reach the door I slip my claw beneath her cloak and hold her tight to my chest. Her skin is warm and soft, smooth like silk. I slip both hands inside the cloak and circle her hips.

She screams still, but it splashes across her lips, wet with tears, drowning in sadness, and so I cling to her tight.

'It's alright,' I say, 'I'm OK. I'm OK.' She weeps, her head against my shoulder.

'I'm OK,' I tell her, and raise my good hand to brush her hair from her face. 'I'm OK.'

Her arms are around my shoulders, my claw around her waist. I stroke her cheek and feel her heart beating against mine. A talon creeps below her waistline, beneath the cloak she is naked. I can feel her chest heaving against mine. She breathes fast, like my father, but deep, trembling inhalations. She stutters as she exhales and I feel her chest hard against mine. Slowly my talon slides across her liquid skin, the fingers of my good hand trace her cheek. I kiss her forehead.

'I'm OK' I soothe and my claw is across her buttock. I kiss her cheek.

'I'm OK.' My good hand drops to her shoulder, brushes hair from her neck. Her eyes are closed, tears clinging to her lashes. I kiss her neck.

'I'm OK,' I murmur and I taste the tears on her lips. I feel her arms tense. I kiss her lips. I feel her heart beating with mine and I don't even notice as my tongue enters her mouth. She bites.

I scream and spray scarlet spit across her wet cheeks. I taste hot, coppery blood. 'But I'm OK,' I drool, and my mother slaps me hard across the face, blood dribbles from between my lips.

'You're OK? *You're OK*?' She is crying and yelling and I watch the muscles in her stomach spasm as she retches. 'You killed him! You killed your Dad!'

She drops to the ground, crumbles before my eyes, dissolves into the carpet. She drags her withered skin to where he lies, curls up inside his arms. She spreads the cloak across them and doesn't even look at me as she whispers: 'Get out.'

I stagger blind down the street behind their home, tripping over bins, sinking into puddles. My eyes burn, hot blood in my face and steaming tears scalding my skin. At the end of the road I see a light, it spills across the potholes, puddles of gold in the street. From the open door way of the garage I hear music, soft and static laden, a white noise I can lose myself in, and I crawl on hands and knees across broken glass toward it.

Breathing hard I rest my back against a wheelie bin, out of sight of the garage door but close enough for me to soak up the light. I close my eyes.

Through the crackling static I hear the music stop.

'Following a busy night for the local police force, sources have claimed that the police are now searching for a missing shop clerk. The shop clerk, who is as yet unnamed, is wanted for questioning for not only the kidnapping of young Frankie Delch but also for both the alleged torturing of a local man earlier today, and the woman found late yesterday in the grounds of a local school.'

I beat my head slowly against the bin, fresh, hot tears spilling across my already-drenched cheeks.

'Police have recently confirmed the identity of the body found yesterday as local woman Rachael Deckard, age twenty-eight.'

Rachael Deckard. I'm thinking of a number in my head: 82. 82, Deckard, Rachael, recently started renting kids' films.

'Miss Deckard was planning to marry later this year, speaking earlier today, friends told reporters that she had been looking forward to starting a family.'

My eyes open, I slither on to the road and drag my long dead body toward the bus stop.

XXXXVII

I arrive at my Scarlett's baptised. The rain has rinsed me of my father's sin and I stand at the corner with a second chance. My Scarlett is alive. I can feel it.

A police car is parked outside her building, its engine hums quietly. I check my hands for blood, wipe at my face with my sleeve. My suit is dark, no stains will show, not under the street lights, and I stride as best I can toward the slumbering police car. I stand by the window, straighten my tie in the reflection and wait for some attention.

In the police car are McDonald's wrappers, is a half-drunk cup of takeaway coffee, is a cigarette slowly burning between twitching fingers which rest on a well-pressed knee. The officer snores softly, his mouth open. I breathe deep. I need a name. I should never have come this far without one. I need a name, a good copper name. I close my eyes and flick through Alphabetical DVD but nothing appeals. In the car the officer drops his head against the window pane, his fingers slide inward toward his thigh. 'Marlow,' I whisper and bang against the window.

'Hey,' I yell, banging against the window. 'Wake up, you're supposed to be on duty.' I keep hitting the window, even after the officer springs awake, burns his thigh; I keep tapping at the window because otherwise my hand will shake. I pull off the beanie, smooth my hair into a side parting. I am thankful it is dark. The officer brushes ash from his trousers, blinks and focuses weary eyes on mine.

'What the fuck do you want?' he sighs, rubbing his eyes. My mouth feels dry and rustles as I speak.

'Marlow, CID. I need the keys.' I'm talking too fast, breathing too much. He looks confused, lifts one giant hand to rub the back of his neck. 'The keys!' I say and jerk my head toward the building.

'Sir?' He really is stupid. I take a long, relaxing breath.

'The keys, please.' Police dramas play in my head. I snatch at the magic word. 'Son.'

'I'm sorry Sir, they'll be at the station.' I deflate, cling to the roof of the car to stop my legs from giving in. 'I could call someone to bring them over.' He twists his head toward his radio, his shoulder shines 7902. I slide down the side of the car.

'No.' I yell. 'No, don't do that.' He looks at me, my tatty suit, my stained tie. I am unshaven, pale, tired. I must look the part.

From his shoulder a woman mumbles, her mouth full. 'Oh baby,' she says. 'This tastes sooo good.' But I'm busy, I'm on duty, I try to look stern.

'Well,' he says, 'the landlord will have some keys, Sir.' I stare at him, feel my nostrils shudder as I exhale. My claw is a tight ball against my thigh, my shoulders droop. 'He lives on the ground floor.'

I smile, genuinely smile. I think I'm grinning. My claw falls open, a rush of air into the lungs, my stomach un-clenches.

'Well done, son,' I say and limp toward the front door.

The landlord wasn't home, but his wife was easily convinced. She was weeping, blowing snot into an already soggy tissue.

'My cat ...' she explained. 'I know it sounds ridiculous, what with poor Rachael and all. But still ...' I nodded, raised my good hand to rub her arm but stopped halfway. Scratched my head. I understand about the cat, I wanted to tell her I got him for her, but I'm Marlow, CID, so I couldn't.

'Is this the key?' I asked, expecting a big ring, full of varying keys. I held a single key, black plastic base, square, silvery end.

'It's a master key,' she sobbed. 'It'll open anything you need.'

The police are incompetent. On the second floor is a web of police tape, luminescent white ribbon criss-crossing the corridor. In the centre lurks an officer, squatting in the shadows, nestled in the web. I nod and stagger upward.

The police are incompetent, it is on the third floor where the crime has been committed, but they are too lazy to tread the extra stairs. Not like me. I do what needs to be done: I do what she needs me to do. I spit on the key before plunging it into the lock, the lock is moist and I turn easily inside.

Her flat smells of strawberries, a hint of sweetness in the darkness, and I drift through the hallway toward the living room. For a little while I stand at the window, stare down into the trees where more police tape glows softly through the shadow. I close the curtains.

The police will never find her. They don't know her like I do; they don't share the same connection as us. I move to the kitchen and her mug sits on the bench next to the kettle. I smile, turn the kettle on. The cupboards are full of pastas, pulses and spices. Tinned fruit and rice pudding in one; crackers, biscuits and sharing-sized bags of crisps in another. My mug hangs from a stand by the microwave, the coffee in a pot nearby. I spoon in coffee for two and wait for the kettle to boil.

Sweetener lies next to the coffee and so I add one for her. The fridge is fairly empty, nothing perishable, some cheeses in Tupperware, some margarine, mayonnaise. No milk, no vegetables. On the fridge door is a shopping list, held down by a fridge magnet. The magnet has a cartoon donkey falling from the sky and below it reads: 'Beware the donkey of death / that falls from the sky. You can choose the way you live my friend / but not the way you die.' I laugh. Typical Scarlett. I add milk and fresh veg to the list.

I've spent quite a few nights in the living room and so I pass straight through into our bedroom. The lilac glows softly, the bed made carefully complete with a tartan bedspread which covers the lower half of the bed. On her side of the bed is a bedside table, cluttered with hair bands and scrunchies, a silken sleep mask hangs from the bedpost by the pillow. My side is tidier, only a book. I glance at the cover, *Don Quixote*, and some watermarks where my coffee mug rests.

I take off my jacket, find a hanger in the wardrobe and hang it carefully on the back of the door as I don't want to get her clothes dirty and damp. My shirt is stained a murky yellow colour under the armpits, caffeine seeps through my pores and stains the once-white shirt with nicotine-like sludge. I slip off my muddy boots and push them carefully under the bed.

I wake up curled on her side of the bed. Her pillow smells of shampoo and coconut and I breathe deep. I wonder where she is. I roll on to my back and stare at the ceiling. 7451, Algarry, Neville is no longer a danger, but she has been missing for a while. He could still have got to her, I could have missed it. My heart beats, slow and sick against my ribs. I feel cold and stretch out my claw, talons cracking as they move. I roll over, face my side of the bed. The book is marked around a third of the way through and I flick through a few pages. I'm not up for this; I can't remember what happened earlier. I'll have to start it again. I sigh and roll back and face the ceiling. My eyes flick across the wardrobe, sweep over the wooden moulding, rest on the corner of a box, on a small pink heart.

The box rests on the coffee table next to my coffee, string tied tight to keep it secure. The sides are beaten, bent and rounded, the lid is stippled with tiny splashes which have stained the cardboard. I hold scissors in my good hand. I feel a little guilty about this, it is obviously private. But then again, I remember: she's a member now, no secrets. I cut the ties.

The box is full of litter. An old cinema stub for *Domestic Disturbance*. But I have no idea why she'd want to remember that. I pull out bus tickets, a rail ticket for a return to London. I check the dates and find it is now invalid. Just more rubbish. A photograph of her and a friend, her blonde, Scarlett dark, and both smiling. They are on a boat, on a river, towering buildings behind and the sun beating down on tanned skin. I don't know the friend, she's not a member.

I pile things neatly on the table, I sip my coffee, I organise. Rubbish in one pile, photographs in another. The friend appears in another dozen or so pictures, always with her arm around my Scarlett. I decide I'll ask Scarlett when I see her, see if she wants to have her round for dinner one night.

The bottom of the box is full of shredded pink tissue paper but is way too heavy for there just to be that. I push my fingers through the pink and feel hard plastic corners. I pull out a video. I laugh. Typical Scarlett, no one watches video anymore, the quality just isn't there after repeated watching. I glance at the label. 'Me and Candy.'

In front of me is a video player, it hides beneath the DVD player, it gathers dust. I push in the tape.

From the doorway comes jingling keys.

XXXXVIII

On the screen my Scarlett smiles into the camera, laughs and I can hear some murmured joke from behind the camera. The production values are low but the acting seems genuine enough. She wears a dress, light and white, and I recognise it from the night of the storm. She wears make-up, but not a lot: a hint of eye shadow, blush on the cheeks and her mouth glistens pink. She licks her lips. The camera rolls and rocks and is eventually still. My Scarlett moves to one side and behind her is a bed. Our bed.

Behind me keys drop to the side table by the door. Something heavy rolls on to the laminate floor and I hear it scraping the wood as it comes. I frown and sip my coffee.

The screen goes dark for a moment, the edges blurred pink and someone steps in front of the camera. A woman whispers, 'Are you ready?' and I hear my Scarlett: 'Oh yeah.' From the hallway I hear heeled shoes clip and clop and flop to the floor, kicked off feet. On the screen is the friend, still blonde but dressed in black, tight and revealing. She stands next to my Scarlett facing the camera. They both smile.

Bare feet pad down the hallway, I hear the bathroom door close, hear a tap trickling. On the screen the friend pouts to the camera, squeezes her breasts together and my Scarlett giggles, copies. I sip my coffee, the mug rattling off my teeth. From the bathroom I hear a flush, I hear humming, the bathroom door creaks open and on the screen the friend kisses my Scarlett.

Footsteps behind me, a sharp intake of breath and an urgent, 'Who are you?' I don't turn around. I watch the friend as she kisses my Scarlett, I watch her hands cupping her buttocks. I watch the tongues slither.

'Who the fuck are you? What are you doing here?' Her voice shakes, I hear her panicked breathing, but mine is level, is calm. I am dimly aware of the steady beat of my heart and imagine I can hear hers beating a drum roll against her chest.

'Are you with the police? Shouldn't you be downstairs?' On the screen, in my head, etched into my heart, the friend slips the dress from my Scarlett's shoulders and kisses her neck. Behind me is a shocked little breath, she sucks in the air and her larynx quivers but on the screen she moans and smiles and gently pushes the friend's lips toward her chest.

I slide my hair into a side parting.

'What is this?' I ask, my voice steady but quiet, a whisper drifting through the flat. I can hear her heart, the drum roll rising, a heavier beat amongst the lighter tapping behind her breast.

'What the fuck do you think you're doing?' she moves toward the screen, the padding of sweating feet in surround sound, right to left as she passes. 'This has nothing to do with what happened downstairs. I want you to leave.' She stands in front of me, blue and white checked dress, tights. She is tanned, tired.

'What is this?' I ask and nod toward the screen, my coffee held tight in my good hand, my fingers turning white.

'I want to see some ID,' she says. Her voice trembles, she is shaking, 'Then I want you to leave.' Behind her comes giggling and I hear bedsprings creak.

I am almost quiet. 'How could you?' I close my eyes, breathe deep and taste her sweat in the air. 'How could you?' Her eyes are wide and wet and she screams.

'Get out, get out, get out!'

I stand up and she whimpers. Behind her, before me, everywhere, comes moaning and the friend has her arse in the air, her mouth on my Scarlett, and I say again: 'How could you?' The mug shakes in my hand, my sweaty fingers are white, my knuckles red. 'In our bed!' I step forward. 'In our fucking bed!' I yell and my Scarlett moves slowly away from the screen, puts the couch between us.

'Who ... Who are you?' she says quietly and I hear the drum roll, insistent, dramatic under her dress and my own whump whump pounds against my ears. 'You're not police, so who ... Wait. Aren't you ...?'

I laugh. 'This is so typical. I give you everything, I give up my nights to protect you, I spend every free moment with you in this flat.' She is staring, wide-eyed, edging toward the hallway. I shuffle past the couch and we stand, feet apart, the corridor between us.

'I take care of him for you, and you ...' I step forward, she glances to the hallway and I move sideways to cut her off. I've seen this film, I know what happens.

'You choose another over me.' I step forward again. 'Well it's not going to happen again.'

She runs, pattering feet scamper into the kitchen, on

the screen the friend holds something long and purple up to the camera, grins and turns back to the bed. I limp to the front door, turn the locks and pocket the keys. As I pass the table by the door I kick at her suitcase and the wheels squeal and slip as it tips. As I limp down the corridor I pull the out the phone cord. We are staying here, together.

In the kitchen she holds the trembling phone to her ear but all we hear is 'Oh, god that's good, do it again' from the front room. She is crying, her cheeks sparkle, shiny globs of snot hang from her nose and she wipes with a tanned arm. She holds a knife in a shaking hand and the light bounces across the room, skips over the surfaces, the fluorescents buzz.

'You would not believe what I have done for you,' I say, and lean heavily against the door frame. I feel fresh tears build behind my dry, red eyes. My lips quiver as I speak.

'I ... I don't even ...' she speaks in waves, the words spilling out between sobs. 'I don't ... even ... I don't know who you are ...' I drop a hand to my belt, slide it from the fraying loops. 'Oh god, no ...' she says but from the big screen comes 'Oh god, yes, yes ...' I let my trousers fall and touch the dank bandage, stained red and licked with yellow. She raises a tremulous hand to her cheek.

'Please,' she says, the knife waving, slicing at the air between us. 'Please, just leave me alone.' And from the big screen we hear her pant: 'Oh, god, I hope this never ends ...'

I step out of my trousers, the belt still tight in my good hand. She retreats into the corner, eyes flicking between me, the belt, the knife and the window.

'It's OK,' I tell her, my voice soft, my heart steady and

calm against the rolling drums I see pounding at her chest. 'No one is watching.'

She looks at me, glances at the table by the window and throws the knife.

The handle pings against my leg and I fall on to my knees, fresh blood bubbling beneath the bandage. I drop the belt and wrap my hands around my thigh.

My Scarlett is on the table, wet hands scrabbling furiously at the window handles. She weeps, her face reflected by the dark glass, and I watch her mouth open and close, her face twinkling into the night outside. Her long hair hangs limp with sweat, curls down her back, her tanned arms flash across the surface of the window. She bangs desperate fists against the window, she unlocks the handles.

'No,' I whisper. 'No.' We need this time together, we need to sort this out. We can still be together but not if you scream from that window, not if the police come here for us, not when they find out what we did to him.

I pull my aching frame to its feet. 'Scarlett, no, please.' She turns to me, her eyes red, her face swollen, her lips spitting her breath into the air. I hear her heart, the drum roll as it reaches its peak. I move forward, dragging my leg across the floor and I move fast. She screams, spins on the table and kicks a chair at me. It slithers into my good knee and I fall.

I hear the drum roll. It fills my head, it makes my ears bleed and my eyes want to burst. I can feel it in my temples, feel the pressure throbbing. She is at the window again, scrabbling furiously at the handles, screaming into the night. I fall toward her but my hip connects with the table, slams against the sharp corner. My heart pounds my love which pumps my muscles which power my arms which shoot out and forward, my clumsy fingers reaching for her, to hold her, to protect her. I slip, my treacherous thigh buckling, and I feel my palm hit her shoulder. My talons wrap around soft hair. A scream and glass breaks. The drums stop. A slow, fading whump whump behind my ears. The soft tinkling of falling glass. My sharp, quick breath. I stare at my guilty palm.

I lie against the table, my stomach pressed to the tablecloth, my legs buckling beneath me. A few strands of black hair linger in my talon. I press it against my cheek and I drag myself to the window.

From the big screen comes heavy, happy panting, from the hallway fists beat against the door. I hear muffled yelling from the corridor outside. From the big screen comes a whispered 'I love you' and below me, below everyone, everywhere, my Scarlett lies, broken, in the mud-covered garden.

Acknowledgements

Thanks to Sarah Duncan for making me work harder when I thought a short story would be enough. Also to the tutors at Bath Spa University School of English and Creative Studies for the early support.

Thanks as well to Ted for the timely confidence boost when the rejections were rolling in, and to friends and family too numerous to mention for humouring me when all I could do was talk about the novel.

Finally, those hard-working bods at Tonto Books. Without them I wouldn't have had this chance and I don't think I could have asked for anything more from them.

About the author

Nik Jones is a teacher and occasional barman from Consett, County Durham. He attempted to live in Canada, but, having been asked politely to leave, he had little option but to attend Bath Spa University and study Creative Writing and Media Communications. It was here he started this, his first novel. He is currently working on his second novel, and plotting an escape to Peru.

READE MORE FROM TONTO BOOKS:

The Road to Hell
A novel by Sheila Quigley
Hardback, £18.99, 9781907183034

Dirty Leeds
A novel by Robert Endeacott
Paperback, £7.99, 9781907183003

Make It Back
A novel by Sarah Shaw
Paperback, £7.99, 9780955632679

Being Normal
Short stories by Stephen Shieber
Paperback, £7.99, 9780955632624

Everything You Ever Wanted
A novel by Rosalind Wyllie
Paperback, £7.99, 9780955632631

Tonto Short Stories
Paperback, £9.99, 9780955218309

More Tonto Short Stories
Paperback, £9.99, 9780955218354

Even More Tonto Short Stories
Paperback, £5.99, 9781907183041